What readers are saying:

'Wow! What a journey this is... a complex weaving of space, engineering, Luna, and most of all, humanity.'
(Top 500 reviewer)

'Edge of the seat stuff pretty well for the whole book.'

'The best scfi book I've read in ages!'

'Amazing. Really enjoyed reading this book as much as I have all of Kilby's books'

'...kicks into overdrive to the point where it is nearly impossible to put down'

'Very well written, fantastically created, and quite believable. Very hard to put down. Can't wait for the next book in the series.'

'This is a clever and fascinating take on Moon survival after a massive solar storm hits Earth. Good solid characters, and fast moving pace........it's a ripper of a yarn.'

'One of those books you can't put down.'

BY GERALD M. KILBY

MOON BASE DELTA
Solar Storm
Resource Control
Power Vacuum

THE BELT
Entanglement
Entropy
Evolution
Enigma
Exodus
Emergence

COLONY MARS
Colony One Mars
Colony Two Mars
Colony Three Mars
Jezero City
Surface Tension
Plains of Utopia

TECHNOTHRILLERS
Chain Reaction
Brain Gain

SHORT STORIES
Gizmo Origin
Winds of Mars

SOLAR STORM

MOON BASE DELTA
BOOK 1

GERALD M. KILBY

OUTER PLANET
MEDIA

For notifications on upcoming books and access to my FREE starter library please join my Readers Group at geraldmkilby.com.

CONTENTS

CHAPTER 1
LUNAR GATEWAY

When word came to the crew of the maintenance ship Aurora that they had less than four hours before the next burst of solar radiation hit them, there was a collective groan of protest. It was bad enough that they were embarking on a very delicate survey operation of the old Lunar Gateway, a very unsound hunk of space history, but having to do so during yet another bout of high intensity solar activity just added to the stress that the crew were already feeling.

And nobody was feeling this stress more than Renton Hicks, the youngest and latest addition to the engineering crew —just fresh out of training and his first time in space. He had departed from Earth only five weeks earlier and had been assigned to this ship as a junior engineer. Now his excitement at finally being able to fulfill his dream of working in space was being severely tested, as the harsh and dangerous realities were becoming clearer with each new solar flare alert.

Captain Mackenzie Arnold, a brash no-nonsense Aussie, had sensed the young man's building anxiety and had been at pains to assure him that this level of solar activity was rare.

"It's not always like this," she counseled. "You just picked a bad time to join the team, right slap bang at the peak of solar activity."

She was referring to an eleven-year cycle where the sun's magnetic field completely reverses its poles, and midway through this cycle is a time of increased solar activity—the solar maximum.

"Granted, this one's a tad rougher that any of the others I've ridden through," she added. Though, she then went on to assure him that they were in no real danger—they always got plenty of warning, and even if you did get zapped by solar radiation, it was never as bad as people kept making it out to be.

This went someway to allaying Renton's fears. The captain was a veteran after all. Someone who had come up at the tail-end of the third wave of lunar colonization, some twenty-five years earlier, around the time he himself was born. She had pretty much seen and done it all since then—and lived to tell the tale.

Yet, since departing their lunar orbital base less than a week ago, the crew of the maintenance ship had had to hunker down inside the most protected section of their vessel on nine different occasions. Each time for longer and longer durations. Renton was no expert on astronomical events, unlike their Systems Analyst, Alice Tyler, the second-youngest member of the crew, who was utterly fascinated by each solar flare and subsequent coronal mass ejection. To Renton, it seemed like these events were becoming more frequent and intense, not less so. Still, no one else seemed quite as rattled as he was by the constant flaring, so he'd best get a handle on his anxiety and move on with the job.

"Coming up on the space station. Four minutes to intercept." The voice of the flight officer, Yuna Djinn, reverberated through the operations bay of the ship, kicking Renton out of his worrying, back into the here and now. He glanced up at the primary monitor and watched for a moment as the maintenance ship drew in closer to the ancient Lunar Gateway space station. He considered the term, *space station,* to be a rather grandiose moniker for what was just a few tiny cylindrical modules connected together via rudimentary docking ports, all of which was completely dwarfed by their own ship.

"I can't believe people actually lived and worked in that thing." He threw this observation out for the general consumption of the other crew.

"You gotta remember that *thing*, as you call it, is over ninety-eight years old," Alice replied, while still concentrating on a data readout, her hands gesturing over the surface of the interface.

"We're talking the real early days, Renton," Matteo Cristoforetti, the second-most senior engineer on board piped in. "The very first space station in lunar orbit, where it all started. Nostalgia is the only reason they still have it up here." Matteo relaxed in his seat. Like Renton, he had nothing to do until they actually started the drone survey. "It's a piece of history that they've spent an absolute fortune on maintaining."

"It's a lost cause, if you ask me," said Becker De Havilland, the crew's Chief Engineer. "It's been stripped bare of all useful tech, so it's got zero function other than being a symbol for the old space agencies. When it goes, it will be the end of an era."

Renton, being so young, had no great attachment to this artifact of human space history and struggled to understand why it had attained such a mythic position in space history. True, it's where it all started, where the first wave of colonization began, but the time and resources needed to keep it from crashing onto the lunar surface hardly seemed worth it to him.

Yet he was reminded of an old power station cooling tower that had dominated the skyline back in his small hometown. The story went that when it was being built, most townspeople objected to this ugly industrial blight being foisted on their pretty little town. Public protests grew and several of the leaders were elected to the town council on this single issue alone. But it was all to no avail, if the townspeople wanted a stable and reliable electricity supply then this was it. Eventually pragmatism won out. But as a compromise, it was agreed to give the tower a candy-stripe paint job in an effort to mitigate the sheer brutal ugliness of it.

And so, over time, it became part of the landscape, this candy-striped tower, and the new generation that grew up with it couldn't imagine the town without it watching over them. When the power station eventually became too old and too inefficient to operate, it was decommissioned and the great plumes of water vapor that had poured forth from its gaping maw ceased forever. Yet the structure remained, and since it was a municipal facility, public discussions had to be conducted on how best to utilize the land that would now become available. Needless to say, this lasted for decades and the town council found itself in the unenviable position of having to maintain the crumbling tower, patching up the masonry, and giving it a new paint job every so often, since by now it had embedded itself in the cultural fabric of the town.

It had even become a favorite vista for local artists whose work adorned the walls of local cafes and bars, some of whom adopted it as a logo or theme. Its image also became part of the town's public relations efforts, being introduced into most of the promotional paraphernalia that was pumped out every year for the annual orchard festival. Peak love was reached when townspeople started wearing the t-shirt.

But time and entropy finally caught up with the aging structure and moves were gaining momentum to have it demolished. News of the impending destruction of the town's beloved tower invoked a furious reaction, and for the second time in its life, public protests were called. In an ironic twist, the children and grandchildren of the very people who had wanted it demolished all those years ago, now protested for its salvation. It had become a totemic symbol for the people and its loss would rip the very soul from the town.

In the end, it survived. It was now the centerpiece of a recreational park. Its lower flanks were a climbing wall, its upper levels a cafe and observation deck that afforded people spectacular views across the valley. People flocked from miles around to experience it. It was where Renton himself had spent many a happy day with his friends.

As he readied the survey drones for deployment and instigated the initial visual scan of the old station, he could see the parallels between this aging piece of space history and the beloved town tower. This artifact had also become totemic in the minds of many who lived and worked on the Moon's surface and orbital platforms. It had been faithfully orbiting the Moon for over ninety-eight years, even though its functional life ended more than sixty years ago. Since then, it was kept in orbit by continual maintenance, most of which consisted of patching up the aging hulk. The Federation of International Space Agencies—FISA—had hoped to keep it going until the centenary celebrations, but the truth was that they simply couldn't afford it anymore—and things had moved on. As FISA's dominance in lunar colonization had faded so too did the symbolism of the Lunar Gateway. Their budget was stretched to the limit and something had to give, so it was agreed that the old Lunar Gateway would be decommissioned. The question now was—how this should be done?

They had a number of options. The first, and technically the easiest, was to let it crash-land on the lunar surface. But it had an unusual orbit, a near-rectilinear halo orbit, bringing it around 3,000 kilometers from the lunar north pole at its closest point, to over 70,000 kilometers from the south pole. A lot of surface infrastructure had been built up along the track of that orbit so simply letting it crash-land was fraught with potential problems. While coming down on a populated zone was statistically unlikely, there was still a sizable chunk of lunar landmass that various other agencies and organizations had laid claim to. If it came down in a sector not controlled by FISA, then this had the potential to be a political nightmare, at best. At worst, they could be sued out of existence.

The other option was to strap a booster to it and send it off into deep space, never to be seen again, assuming it was structurally sound enough to take the stresses without disintegrating and raining space junk down on the lunar surface.

However, at the last moment, the Dizzy Corporation arrived with a proposal. They were in the process of building a theme park in the northern quadrant of Amundsen Crater and wanted to investigate the possibility of salvaging the Lunar Gateway by towing it over to one of the orbital shipyards, dismantling it, and bringing it down to the surface bit-by-bit where it would be reassembled and form the centerpiece of their new Space History Museum. What's more, they would even pay for the structural survey to be conducted to assess the feasibility. FISA jumped at the offer.

Up on the primary monitor, the crew could see the survey drones exit from the underbelly of the maintenance ship and make their way over to the old Lunar Gateway. They soon began to orientate themselves into a preprogrammed configuration and start to run passes along the length of the structure. With each pass, they would look deep into the molecular fabric of the station and build up a detailed picture of the internal structure of the metal struts and beams that held it all together. From this, the crew could then accurately calculate what stresses this ancient space artifact could support. But all this would take time to accomplish—approximately twelve hours, give or take.

Renton glanced at the solar radiation alert timer, ticking down from 3:47:00. By the time it hit zero, the crew would need to be hunkered down in the storage bay, as per the safety regulations. It would be at least a two-hour wait before they could exit again. For the captain, and some of the other crew, it was just more wasted time, time they couldn't afford if they wanted to claim the bonus offered for hitting the project completion deadline.

Yet this was not Renton's primary concern. What occupied his mind most was the repair job he had done on drone Five. He prayed it would hold up and the machine wouldn't start glitching again. Because if it did... well, he didn't want to think about what might happen.

CHAPTER 2
THE NEW LUNAR ACCORD

Selene Mene, Associate Director of FISA, sipped an early morning coffee in the comfort of her accommodation suite on board the Axial Luxor, a luxury orbital lunar hotel with a vaguely Egyptian theme. It had been block-booked in its entirety to host what many described as the most significant international symposium since the Antarctic Treaty back in 1959. Its objective was to redraft the sections of the old Outer Space Treaty of 1967, dealing with the Moon, and produce an agreed legal framework for future exploration. It was to be called the New Lunar Accord. But Selene was under no illusions as to the real intention of this high-level conference, which was to carve up the lunar surface between the main power blocks that had established a significant presence up here and grant them dominion over its resources. In her mind, it was more akin to the Paris Peace Treaty of 1947, which significantly redrew the map of Europe—and to the victor went the spoils.

For well over a century, Earth's space agencies and corporations had expanded the human footprint out into space, and nowhere was this expansion most evident than on the lunar surface. Yet all parties had been operating under a very rudimentary treaty whose signatories had envisioned it as a framework for the exploration of space not the exploitation of its resources, particularly by private corporations. Several ad hoc additions had been made to it over the years, but these were really just sticking plasters—and even then, not everyone that mattered had signed up to these. Something had to be done, things could not go on as they were. What was needed was some legal clarity for all interested parties. And so, after many stalled attempts, the first major revision was being undertaken.

Selene gestured at the large wall monitor, which was currently displaying a real-time image of Earthrise from the lunar surface. This was now overlaid by a series of icons representing all the documents produced from yesterday's sessions. She waved her hand, flipping through each folder until she came to an executive summary that had been produced by her team while she slept. She brought it up on screen and took a bite of the freshly baked almond croissant that had accompanied her room-service breakfast. It tasted surprisingly good, but then again, this was a five-star hotel. She took another bite and began to scan the document.

She was disappointed to see that several of the breakout sessions had been postponed due to these damned solar flare alerts. It seemed that the Sun God was angry with all the meddling humans and was doing its very best to disrupt proceedings. She sighed.

Of the nine sessions that did go ahead, SINO—an aggregate of Chinese and affiliate national space agencies—only showed up for five of them, which was an improvement on the previous day. They were really dragging their feet, and very reluctant to engage with anything outside their own interests. And even then, most of the people they had on these breakout sessions had zero authority to make a decision. It seemed to be just an information-gathering mission. Still, they were here and engaging on some level—progress was being made, even if it was hellishly slow. Selene would take that, for now.

The most active and professional of all the parties involved in the talks were the corporates, particularly mighty industrial conglomerate, Xilinex. They were well prepared, well briefed, had the best people, and enthusiastically engaged with everything. Which is not surprising since they had most to gain out of a successful conclusion to the New Lunar Accord. As Selene digested the summary document, along with her almond croissant, she could see their ultra-professional fingerprints all over yesterday's sessions. Of the ones that had concluded, all topics that were discussed concluded favorably for Xilinex. She sighed again.

An alert flashed on screen. Selene gestured to open up a camera feed from the front door of her suite. It was Nicci Anderson, her assistant, ready to take on another day. Selene gestured again to let her in.

Nicci glanced up at the wall monitor as she entered the

living area. "We've another solar flare alert for today. Long one, two hours."

Selene nodded then pointed at the breakfast trolley. "Help yourself, I'll never eat all that. I've told them a hundred times, just coffee and a croissant is more than enough."

Her assistant put her document bag down on the floor and perused the fare on offer, pouring herself a coffee and snagging a dainty Danish pastry. "SINO came back on the nuclear waste storage session. They agreed to ninety percent of it, so I think we should be concluding today."

"That must be a record. I wonder why they took such an interest in that?"

Nicci didn't reply. She knew Selene well enough to know when she was simply thinking out loud. Instead, she sat in one of the plush armchairs and extracted a tablet from her bag and began to outline the forthcoming day.

"Here's what you've got on." She flicked the face of the tablet screen and Selene's meeting schedule popped up on the main room monitor.

Selene scanned the list. "Gabriel Grando, remind me who he is again," she asked with a slightly furrowed brow as she tried to remember which party he represented.

"Panamanian delegate, aligned with the NSFN, Non-Spacefaring Nations. They're threatening to walk away from the talks. It all blew up last night, some people said things they shouldn't," Nicci gave a resigned shrug. "You know how it is. Anyway, you need to ensure them that we support their rights and are doing everything we can to negotiate a mutually satisfactory outcome."

Selene pursed her lips, her mind working through the political calculus of this stance with the NSFN. They represented most of the nations that did not yet have a footprint on the lunar surface, although some had well-established space industries and even satellite launch capabilities. However, the Moon in its current status was defined as a commons for the benefit of all humankind. If they were now going to divvy it up between the great space powers, then the NSFN were here to ensure their rights were not trampled on. Which, at the end of the day, boiled down to compensation—they would be paid off, with the door left open just a little bit for if and when they had the capability of establishing a colony sometime in the future.

"So, we hear you." Selene began to dictate the generalities of the FISA response to her assistant. "And are acutely aware of the... vital role the NSFN are playing in the... advancement of human cooperation. We're one hundred percent behind you. But we're at a delicate point, just a little more patience and I am convinced we will have a... mutually beneficial agreement that you can hold up as a great achievement for the NSFN."

"That sounds about right," Nicci nodded as she noted her boss's statement. She then carried on to the next item on her list. "INDOCON have added another landing site they claim is of historical significance. And it's near the Sea of Tranquility."

Selene considered this for a moment. INDOCON were a consortium of Indian space interests and affiliates, very powerful, and not going to be pushed around or fobbed off with platitudes. "It's just pushback on the size of our own exclusion zones," said Selene. "It's to be expected. The Historical

Monuments Session deal with that. Tell them our position is the same. Not one inch on Tranquility."

Nicci tapped a note on her tablet, then proceeded on to the next item with her standard efficiency. "This next one is just a rumor, for the moment, but we've got word through one of our backchannels that the Xilinex Corporation are offering CASA, the Combined Arabian Space Alliance, permission to build a new shipping port over at Moretus Crater, if they reciprocate by giving Xilinex their backing on the border control issue."

"Hmmm, I think I'll have a side chat with Dr. Bashir Nasser and see if we can infer a counteroffer. We don't want to lose the principle of free movement. Although, my gut feeling is it's already a lost cause. As soon as we conclude these talks, rest assured the border controls are going up."

Nicci didn't react to this, making no comment. She simply moved on to the final item. "Pompodur Adarok, the Communications Director of Xilinex Lunar, came up from their main base late last night."

"Interesting, the vultures are circling."

"Indeed, and you're having lunch with him, at his request. But we haven't confirmed yet."

"Send a reply back, say I'll be happy to meet. And thank him for the orchid that arrived last night." Selene gestured over at a large exotic plant that sat in the corner of the room. "Apparently, they grow them in their agri-labs. Genetically engineered, I imagine, as I doubt something that bizarre could exist in the wild."

Nicci glanced over at the exotic plant. "Wow, looks almost

alien." She swung back to Selene and went all conspiratorial. "So, what's the message here?"

"Ha, I wouldn't read too much into it. It's just another part of the Xilinex love-bombing strategy. I'm sure everyone has one of these by now. After all, they and the other corporates have most to gain out of these talks," she sighed again. "I fear we are seeing the rise of a modern-day Dutch East India Company."

Nicci thought about this, digging deep into the inner recess of her expensive private education. "Weren't they into coffee or shipping, or something?"

"They were into everything," Selene waved a hand around. "Back in the very early days of the seventeenth century, they started out as a government-sponsored trading cartel to exploit the resources of faraway lands. Sound familiar?"

Nicci nodded.

"But soon they grew so wealthy that they started to invest in their own ports, fortifications, ships, warehouses, to the point where they were effectively a quasi-state empire in their own right. Reputedly the richest company ever to have existed. You see the parallels, don't you?"

"I do. You think Xilinex are heading on a similar path?"

"I don't think so, I know so. The latter half of this century has seen an enormous strain on the concept of the nation state. With the all the challenges of climate, pandemics, wars. The old alliances and institutions are fracturing. It's dog eat dog. People are looking for security and stability and the corporates are beginning to fill that gap. What we're really doing at these talks is not simply setting up a legal framework for the future of the Moon, we are enabling the creation of a new corporate state, with the ability to create its own laws—just like a twenty-second-century Dutch East India Company."

Nicci took a moment to digest this insight into the history of mega-corps. "So how did it all end for them?"

"Oh, like most great empires, death by a thousand cuts."

The wall monitor suddenly flashed an alert, one echoed by Nicci's tablet.

"Another flare alert?" Selene threw her hands in the air. "I'm really getting sick of these, there seems to be no end to them." She glanced over at her assistant. "I hope this doesn't mess up the schedule too much."

Every time there was an alert, everyone on the orbital hotel had to retreat into designated zones with dense, protective shielding and wait it out until the solar radiation passed. Not a big deal, except it seemed to be happening more often and for longer durations. Selene gestured at the monitor to bring up more detailed information on the latest alert. Being a FISA director she had access to more comprehensive scientific data. When she read it, she almost gasped.

Nicci, who was already a little anxious about these solar storms since it was her first time in space, picked up on her boss's sudden alertness. "Anything the matter? Are we okay?"

Selene took a moment to regain her composure. She didn't want to amplify her assistant's general anxiety. "No, nothing important, just the... eh, usual stuff." She flicked off the room monitor. "I think we're finished here." She stood up. "I'll see you at the morning debrief in, say, twenty minutes."

Nicci seemed a little hesitant at first, but finally stood up and started moving for the door. She nodded. "Okay, see you there."

CHAPTER 3
POMPODUR ROSSEN ADAROK

P ompodur Rossen Adarok, Director of Communications for the Xilinex Corporation's considerable industrial interests on the lunar surface, sat his ample frame down on a plush sofa in the Tutankhamen Suite of the Axial Luxor. He had just arrived by shuttle from the Xilinex HQ on the lunar surface and cursed the hotel's 0.8 gravity. It was great for visitors from Earth who lived on a 1G planet—when they came here, they felt twenty percent lighter, like they had finally managed to lose that weight that they had always wanted. But for Pompodur who had spent the last two months, more or less, in a 0.166G environment, it was hell. His back ached, his knees creaked, and his feet were already beginning to swell up. He groaned as he sat down and wiped a bead of sweat from his forehead.

"Be careful with that!" he shouted over at the two young porters that were manhandling his luggage into the room.

"Jason? Some water. And get the room temperature lowered. It's as hot as Satan's anus in here."

"Yes, sir." Jason, his favorite personal assistant bowed and scurried off to fulfill his master's commands.

Pompodur kicked off his traveling shoes, letting his feet breathe a little better, and hoping that the physical adjustment period wouldn't be too taxing. Yet, however much his body was protesting the new demands being placed on it, Pompodur himself was relishing the opportunity to enjoy all the luxury that the Axial Luxor had to offer, starting with a selection of epicurean delights by the establishment's famed head chef, Jean Raul Goutier.

"Jason?" he looked up from massaging his feet. "Where's that damned man?

"He's attending to the environmental controls," said Rachel, his second-favorite personal assistant.

"Eh... okay. Can you see what's holding up the food that was supposed to be ready and waiting for me here?"

"Yes, sir."

He waved a hand to dismiss her, then slowly stood up to test his feet again—still painful but better without the shoes. He walked into the large reception room attached to his suite, headed straight to the bar, and popped the cork on a bottle of *Castello Di Ama Chianti* 2128, an excellent vintage. He poured it into a cut-glass decanter to aerate it, and after a moment, served himself a large glass. It tasted like an Italian opera had just kicked off in his mouth. He sighed, god how he missed the finer things in life, those little luxuries that made it all worthwhile, things that were sadly absent in the Xilinex HQ. He would have to do something about that, especially since they wanted him to do another tour of duty. But that was for another time, now he had a job to do at the New Lunar Accord talks. He had an opportunity to show his true value to the corporation and harvest the rewards that he so justly deserved.

Pompodur was a lawyer by trade, specializing in contract law, and had served his time in the lower levels of the Vermeulen Mining Corporation out in South Africa and Botswana. But his true talents began to emerge when he started dealing with countries that were barely functioning states. Places that were rich in both natural resources and local warlords. He soon honed the craft of negotiating deals that had a veneer of legality yet were anything but.

He took another sip of wine, taking a moment to savor its complexity, before he plonked himself down at a large dining table. Right on cue, Rachel arrived followed by a flock of waiters pushing trollies laden with food. The smells were intoxicating. Pompodur's mouth began to salivate; he licked his lips in anticipation as the waiters laid out the table with a practiced efficiency that he only wished his own team would display. They retreated almost as quickly as they came, leaving only Rachel hovering over him waiting for his next command.

Pompodur surveyed the feast before him, leaning in a little over the table and inhaling the aromas.

"Ahhh... excellent, at last, proper food." He gave a quick glance at his attentive assistant and waved her away. "That's all."

She exited the room with a bow of her head and left him to his meal.

Normally, Pompodur liked to be surrounded by people. It was, he speculated, his natural environment. But once a day, he would shake off his entourage and eat alone if he could. It gave him time to think, to ruminate on the issues, help him see the bigger picture.

He surveyed the delicate arrangement of amuse-bouche, picked up a dainty pastry case filled with crabmeat and capers, and popped it into his mouth. He waved his head around with pleasure, it was delicious—and a long way from the mediocre fare he had been subjected to over the last few months.

Xilinex had transferred him up to their central Moon base around a year ago to sort out the patchwork of deals and contracts they had entered into over the course of their decades-long expansion of lunar mining interests. The most problematic of these were the deals entered into with small states that wanted to have security of resources in an increasingly competitive and fractious world. But as soon as the New Lunar Accord talks started looking like they might happen, these very same states started laying claim to areas and resources they had no right to. Compensation was the name of the game here, they all wanted to be in the strongest position possible going into the talks. Pompodur's job was to ensure that didn't happen.

On top of that, Xilinex had several other fast-growing corporates making moves on territory where they had already established exploratory outposts. Not to mention outright aggression from the Xiang Zu Corporation and their state overlords, SINO. This including a number of incidents that were clearly sabotage of Xilinex infrastructure. These incidents had precipitated fractious internal industrial relations around security—which was probably the intention—and the souring of relations had been growing more problematic with each new expansion of their operation. The whole thing had the potential to turn into a huge stinking lawless mess.

It was all coming to a head, here at the Axial Luxor. These talks would define not just a New Lunar Accord but a new world order, one where the corporates like Xilinex would have power, real power. And Pompodur very much wanted a piece of that action.

He pushed his empty plate aside and gave a satisfied burp, poured the last of the wine into his glass, and considered that he might just have enough room left in his stomach for one last profiterole filled with crème anglaise and a hint of Madagascar vanilla.

He finished the wine in one gulp, set down the glass, and tapped on his comms visor to reactivate it and indicate to his assistants that he had finished and the meeting with the Xilinex negotiating team could begin. They had been the advance party, dealing with a multitude of side-sessions, and formulating the strategy for the final push this week.

The table was cleared with minimal fuss and the team filed in and took up seats around the now bare dining table. Nods and greetings were exchanged and when they were all seated, Pompodur clapped his hands together to get their attention. "So, let's get to it, shall we?"

There was a momentary silence around the table as all heads turned to Dr. Sylvia Syms, the team's science advisor, a stick-thin middle-aged woman with large eyes that gave her face a permanent expression of awe—or maybe it was shock.

"We may have some... complications." She kept her face lowered as if studying the screen on the tablet she had placed on the table.

"Complications? Don't tell me those FISA people are playing hardball again," he glanced around at the faces of the team, but they were silent.

Dr. Syms shook her head. "No, nothing like that. It's just we've just received an alert for another solar event."

Pompodur laughed and waved a hand. "Oh please, how is this a problem, we get them all the time."

"Not like this one, we don't," Dr. Syms shook her head. "If our calculations are correct, then we are looking at a possible Carrington Event."

Pompodur opened his hands in an expression of confusion. "And what might that be?"

"It's the name given to the worst electromagnetic storm ever recorded, way back in 1859. Fortunately, we were not so reliant on electronic infrastructure in those times so disruption was minimal. However, we anticipate that this one could be even more intense."

He considered this for a moment. Clearly his team were spooked by Dr. Syms' announcement, but if he had learned anything from his years of negotiation sessions, it was that most things were never as they seemed. It was quite possible that this was just a scare tactic by one of the other parties to take a regular solar event alert and dial it all the way to the max. The problem in his mind was not the event itself, but who stood to gain from it.

"How do we know this isn't a distraction, a straw man generated by one of the parties involved in these negotiations just seeking an advantage?"

Dr. Syms shook her head. "This originally came from FISA's Astronomical Division, but it has been corroborated by a number of other agencies as well as our own people. But..." her voice trailed off.

"Go on, but what?" Pompodur encouraged.

"But it looks like we might, and I stress might as we don't have the full data yet, escape the worst of it as the Moon is heading for an eclipse around the same time."

Pompodur slapped his hands together again. "Ha, told you. It's a game, someone's just trying to get us all spooked. So, the question is, who gains from amplifying this supposed threat?"

"But this is a real danger. We shouldn't just dismiss it." Dr. Syms sounded a little desperate, feeling that she hadn't quite outlined the seriousness of this event. But Pompodur cut her off with a raised hand. He wasn't about to let this nonsense take up any more time. If anyone was going to take advantage of this situation, it would be Xilinex.

"Thank you for your input, Dr. Syms. If we have any more questions, we will revert," he gave her his best smile, and her cue to leave the meeting.

"Uh, okay, but..."

He raised a hand again and smiled. "As I said, we will revert."

She gathered up her tablet and notes and shuffled out of the room. Pompodur turned to the team and decided it might be best to put a firm lid on this solar flare bullshit before it got out of hand.

"Look, I understand the frustration that these constant solar flares are causing, particularly with all the interruptions, but we know that they are just an inconvenience, nothing more. There's no danger, we are all perfectly safe here," he opened his hands in an expansive gesture.

This seemed to calm everybody down a little.

"We also know," he continued, "that if this most recent alert came via FISA, then it's most likely a plot by them to get us all looking in the wrong direction. So, let's continue on as normal. Let's not fall into their trap."

There was a vaguely positive, if somewhat muted response from around the table. They all knew well enough by now not to argue with Pompodur.

CHAPTER 4
THERE GOES THE BONUS

The countdown timer on the Aurora had just ticked over to 00:27:00 when yet another solar alert flashed up on the primary operations bay monitor. A chorus of groans and sighs emanated from the exasperated crew of the maintenance ship.

"I don't believe it. Not again," Matteo expressed the feelings of the entire crew. "This is going to set us back big time. Now we've got zero chance of collecting that bonus."

"It's just the same bloody crap as always," Mackenzie's voice bellowed out. "The usual FISA health and safety paranoia. They're afraid some random punter is going to sue their asses off if they don't tick all the boxes. Like I said, nobody's ever died from a dose of space sun in all the years I've been out here." The Aussie captain's outburst elicited the usual round of head shaking and eye rolling by the rest of the crew. They were used to her by now, never missing a chance to let them all know how much space time she had under her belt.

"Looks like a standard amber warning for local lunar space, so same procedure as before." Yuna studied the details of the alert on her screen. "We hunker down for 156 minutes—longer than usual, I'll admit. But same old, same old."

"How long before it hits?" Becker asked.

"Eleven hours," replied the flight officer.

"Well, that's going to screw up our bonus for sure." This seemed to be Matteo's main concern.

"Maybe not," said Mackenzie. "If we keep the drones out, keep the scan going, then we'll be back home for tea before that storm hits."

"We're supposed to bring them back in for a reason." Becker clearly wasn't keen on this idea. "They'll be bathed in a lot of nasty radiation, not good for the electronics, we could be introducing errors into the scan."

"We could compensate for that by increasing the sample rate," offered Matteo.

"Possibly," said Becker.

"Eh, I've got an intermittent glitch on drone Five," Renton interjected, a little timidly. "I don't think it would be a good idea to leave it out there."

"So, we lose it, so what?" Mackenzie gave a shrug. "Still means we get the job done on time. So, let's just get on with it, and no more messing around, otherwise we'll be out here until pension age."

Renton wasn't convinced. There were worse things that could happen than simply losing a drone; it could cause physical damage if they didn't have it under control. Nevertheless, he wasn't going to argue with the captain.

By the time the current solar alert countdown hit zero, they were all holed up in an area of the cargo bay that had been packed up on all sides with a density of material. This would absorb most of the solar radiation that was now beginning to bathe the craft and protect the crew. Yuna had also maneuvered the ship into a position that would offer some protection to the survey drones that were still operating, still doing their job. Becker brought a tablet with him into the cargo bay so he could monitor the drones progress and, more importantly, activate a kill-switch should any of the machines start acting weird.

While Becker was focused on this task, Mackenzie, Yuna, and Matteo indulged in idle chatter, swapping war stories of past maintenance jobs gone wrong. Renton sat apart, as did Alice, who had taken herself off to the far end of their radiation bunker and was studying a tablet display, with deep concentration. She was doing that thing she always did when focused, biting the edge of her bottom lip. She glanced up and caught Renton looking at her. Yet, she wasn't looking at him. She had that thousand-yard stare, looking at nothing in particular. He instinctively rose and floated over to her.

"Everything okay? You look like you've seen a ghost."

She looked around at him, seeming to only notice him when he spoke. "Eh? Oh, well yes, you could say that." She angled the tablet so he could see the lines of data displayed on the screen.

"See this? This is the source data, direct from FISA, for the current solar storm that's hitting us now," she gestured at it, flicking through screen after screen of more dense data. "And these are all the reports of all the other storms I've been tracking."

"That's a lot of data." Renton was getting the feeling she was leading up to something, and it possibly wasn't good.

"The thing is, I can't access any source data for the next solar storm—the one that's due to hit Earth in a few hours—because it's been restricted."

"Is that unusual?" Renton wasn't sure how these things worked.

"It's weird. I've never seen that before, and I've been nerding out on this stuff for a long time. If it's just a run-of-the-mill solar storm, then why restrict it?"

"Because it isn't run-of-the-mill. And maybe FISA want to control the flow of information?" Renton felt his anxiety rising.

"That's exactly what I was thinking. Maybe this next one is a real blowout, a Carrington Event, or even worse." Her eyes widened and her eyebrows were reaching peak levels.

Renton felt his stomach tighten. "Eh, should we... be doing something?"

Alice sighed and seemed to relax a little. "Well, here's the thing. As luck would have it, the Moon will be in eclipse while this passes over Earth. So, we'll be in shadow, in the umbra. The Moon will be protected. That's probably why Central only issued us with an amber alert. We won't be much affected by this."

Renton felt his stomach relax a little. "But, if it is a big one, then that's going to cause some serious outages back on Earth."

"Oh, for sure. Major technical mayhem. There's going to be plenty of work for maintenance crews after this storm—if it's actually as bad as a Carrington Event," she managed a smile, then her face turned serious again. "Listen, I could be reading this all wrong, so don't go freaking out or telling anyone else what I just told you."

"Sure, understood," Renton nodded. "It would just make Mackenzie mad. And we don't want that."

"Yeah, and like I said, we'll be back behind Earth's shadow by then anyway."

When the current storm passed, the crew moved back to the operations bay, and began focusing all their attentions on the performance of the survey drones. They were still tracking along the main body of the Lunar Gateway within acceptable tolerances. Everyone breathed a sigh of relief, none more so than Renton.

Alice resumed analyzing the incoming data, monitoring for noise and gaps that would mean doing a second pass, which would mean spending more time out here. Becker and Matteo were busy plotting out the most efficient drone flight patterns for the remainder of the scan.

The captain and Yuna had taken themselves off to the flight deck to dial in some return transit options depending on when the scan was complete. Yuna was anxious to get a good view of the lunar eclipse when it happened. It had the potential to be a spectacular visual event. The Sun, Earth, and Moon would be in alignment, with Earth completely blocking out the Sun with only a deep red halo around its circumference where the sunlight shafted through the atmosphere. The lunar surface would turn a deep red also. For those people looking up at the dawn sky from Earth, they would see a Blood Moon. But now a new element had entered the equation, a massive coronal mass ejection would be bombarding Earth's atmosphere at almost the same time. This would create a spectacular aurora over Earth's poles stretching far toward the equator. The potential for this unique celestial spectacle had got the flight officer very excited and she was determined to find an opportunity to maneuver the ship into the best vantage point.

Renton found himself getting distracted. The drone seemed to be behaving itself and so his mind began to work through Alice's reaction to the new solar storm data. It had clearly spooked her, even if Central Maintenance—the FISA division that oversaw all maintenance crews in lunar space—had not made a big deal of it. But if she was right, then a Carrington Event would cause mayhem to electrical systems back on Earth, especially any Sun-facing space infrastructure in Earth orbit. That would almost certainly be a big deal. But then again, things were built to withstand these events, it was par for the course in the design framework he had learned. You built in redundancy, and then some. Still he couldn't shake the feeling that there was more to this next storm than the authorities were letting on.

He was about to message Alice when his screen started flashing alerts.

"Shit."

"Renton, drone Five is moving out of alignment," Becker said, glancing over at him from his screen.

"I see it, I see it." Renton flipped on a new camera feed, brought it up on a second monitor, and started tracking the rogue drone. He began to analyze the alerts. The drone had started deviating from the preprogrammed flight path and the alignment software was not autocorrecting. It was trying, he could see that, but it was as he had feared, the range sensor on the pitch axis had started glitching again. The secondary sensor was dead and had been for a while. He knew this before he sent it out there. His thoughts of design redundancy came back to him as he tried to compensate with a quick software update. But this only seemed to make it worse.

"Renton," Becker shouted over at him. "What's happening? Are we losing that drone?"

"I can't stabilize it."

"Then decommission it. Get it out of there before it does some damage."

"Crap, that's going to slow us down." Matteo was now taking an interest in the ongoing drone drama.

"Can't be helped, too risky to leave it there," said Becker, shaking his head. "Just kill it, Renton."

"Will do." Renton issued the return-to-base command to the probe, keeping one finger on the kill switch just in case he had to take manual control. On screen he could see the drone execute a quick burst of its forward thruster to slow its forward momentum. But for whatever reason, this action introduced a tumble in its Z-axis, which sent it dramatically off track.

"Renton, what the hell are you playing at?"

He didn't reply, he was frantically trying to get some control over the drone that was now tumbling toward the large aft solar array on the Lunar Gateway. He hit the kill switch and took manual control but it was not responding. He tried again.

"Renton!" Becker shouted as the crew held their breath watching the probe spin ever closer to the solar array.

Renton could do nothing except watch it smash into the array, causing the entire panel to detach itself from the body of the ancient space station, and taking with it one of the ion thrusters that had been recently retrofitted to the outer structure.

No one spoke in the operations bay of the Aurora. They all floated mute, staring wide-eyed at the carnage unfolding before them as a vital section of the old Lunar Gateway tumbled off into space.

"Well, there goes our bonus, I guess," said Matteo.

CHAPTER 5
HELIOPHYSICS

Selene Mene took an elevator down to the ground floor of the hotel—which, by the strange disconcerting physics of centrifugal force, was in reality the level closest to the outer hull of the vast rotating doughnut that was the Axial Luxor. This ground floor level, as with most conventional hotels, accommodated most of the public areas: bars, restaurants, conference rooms, a theater and cinema, nightclubs, swimming pools, gyms, spas—everything one would expect in a luxury hotel. Above this, the middle level was where most of the rooms and suites were located. There was also a third level above this, the inner ring of the doughnut, where all the utilities were housed: power management, life support, environmental controls, waste processing, storage, maintenance, workshops, and more.

This vast three-level ring was connected to a central hub via eight spokes housing elevator shafts, and a few thousand kilometers of wiring, ducting, and cabling. On either side of the hub were two long docking gantries. One of which currently accommodated two of the huge Starliner spacecraft, each having the ability to transport over two-hundred passengers to and from Earth. The gantry on the opposite side housed a vast array of much smaller spacecraft, many of which were owned or operated by the plethora of space agencies and corporations attending the talks. But for anyone standing in the lobby on the ground floor of the Axial Luxor, provided you didn't look out through the wide panoramic windows at the lunar surface glistening in the sunlight, it would feel like any other ultra-luxury hotel anywhere on Earth.

Selene immediately spotted her group milling around along with some new FISA arrivals that had joined them for the big push to get the talks concluded. Dale Graham, the negotiating team's Liaison Officer, saw her from across the lobby, waved, and strode over.

"All set for the strategy session this morning?" he asked in his standard breezy manner.

Selene paused studying the newcomers in the group. They had arrived very early this morning after a long eighteen-hour journey from Earth. Some she recognized, FISA heavy hitters, here to help get the negotiations over the line. "Is that Professor Henriksen from the Heliophysics Division?" she nodded in the direction of a tall, thin man in his late fifties.

"Yes, the very same. He came up with the team this morning."

"I didn't know he was en route," she gave Dale a questioning look. "I wonder why he's here?"

"No idea. He's certainly not known for his negotiating skills —which are nonexistent."

Selene considered this for a moment. "I suppose we'll find out soon enough. Come on, let's get to the meeting."

FISA, like all the other parties involved in the talks, had a suite of conference rooms put at their disposal. They assembled in the biggest of these, their main boardroom, around a large oval table with enough seating for twenty. But with the newcomers and their staff, the room was full, with some having to stand against the surrounding walls. It was a standard FISA morning debrief, where everyone would be brought up to date on developments from the previous day's sessions. After that they would reformulate their strategy and move forward from there.

Selene glanced at the newly updated agenda and noted that Professor Henriksen was now penciled in to give a presentation after the debrief, but before any discussion on strategy. Indicating to her that whatever he had to say, it was going to affect how they progressed with the negotiation. *I wonder what that's about,* she thought, *something's up for sure.* She called the meeting to order and immediately handed over to Dale for the debrief.

Nothing much had changed. Negotiations were still bogged down in a number of areas. Pressure was being put on the FISA for concessions regarding the size of the exclusion zone around historical sites. Since the United States of America had the most sites and also the primary partner in the agency, they were not conceding any ground. The arrangements for the new Lunar Council were also deadlocked around the issue of vetoes for the primary agencies. Compensation for the NSFN had moved forward a little after it was agreed that they could have representation on the new Lunar Council.

Then came a brief update on the thorn in everyone's side, which was the long-abandoned Moon Base Delta. It had been constructed almost four decades ago during an unprecedented period of international cooperation. All the major space agencies, and many of the minor ones, took part in its design and construction. The end result was a testament to what could be achieved when humans come together and act as one. A vast, self-sustaining, scientific research base built into an ancient lava pit in the Sea of Tranquility, capable of sustaining up to five-thousand personnel. It had been regarded as the first true wonder of the lunar world.

But it was not to last. Soon, humanity returned to its old ways and the cycle of division and conflict began again—just when people had thought it was over for good. As the various Earth-bound conflicts grew ever more aggressive, national agencies began to pull out of the moon base, reflecting their respective government's political posturing. This put the remaining agencies in a tricky position, they could not remain because Moon Base Delta was legally only partly theirs to operate. A stop-gap solution was found where the central AI core that controlled the entire base would be shut down and the base broken up into individual sectors, operated by each of the agencies involved in its original construction. This lasted for a while but was fraught with political tensions and it soon became clear that the base was simply no longer viable. In the end, an agreement was reached for Moon Base Delta to be vacated, put into low-power maintenance mode, and left empty until better times. That was around a decade ago, and things were only getting worse.

It was hoped that these talks would finally resolve the issue. The proposal outlined was that it could be partly reactivated and used as the seat of the new Lunar Council, but this would mean diluting ownership to accommodate the vast array of new agencies and corporates that now had claims on Luna—the official name for the Moon. But there was just no way that SINO or INDOCON were going to agree to that. From Selene's point of view, it seemed that they relished the fact that they were denying the FISA access to the jewel in their crown. She despaired. It was a project close to her heart but she had to face the reality that these talks would probably end without resolving this issue. There was too much history there, too much bad blood.

The debrief ended on somewhat of a subdued note; it was clear that little had been achieved in the previous day's sessions, where everyone had been digging in, hoping the other side would blink first. But Selene, ever the professional, quickly moved on to the next item on the agenda, and handed the floor to Professor Henriksen, from FISA's Heliophysics Division.

He stood up, always a bad sign. "Thank you," he nodded to Selene. Then leaned in and activated the holo-screen in the center of the boardroom table. It enabled 3D images and animations to be presented as if they were hovering just above the tabletop. Being a very recent technology most people were still very much in awe of it. It was a great way to get someone's undivided attention. The tabletop came to life with a projection of the Sun–Earth–Moon system slowly rotating as they normally would. The room went silent. Henriksen began.

"As you all know, we've been experiencing an unprecedented level of solar flaring coupled with coronal mass ejection over the past few months." The 3D image showed plumes of solar matter being violently ejected into space. "This has been very disruptive for us all, having to hunker down in shielded areas for the duration of each storm. It's also causing considerable disruption to electrical systems, particularly satellite communications."

There was a low murmur of agreement around the room.

"This activity is generally regarded to be cyclical in nature, having an eleven-year peak, as the sun's magnetic field shifts polarity. We are currently experiencing this peak, also known as the solar maxima. However, our predictive modeling has improved dramatically over the last decade to a point where we can now more accurately forecast future activity."

The room was silent, each person anxious to hear what the future held.

"These models are now showing us that there is an even longer cycle operating in tandem with the standard eleven-year period, and that both of these are now coming into synchronization. We have loosely classified this moment in time as the solar apex."

There was much murmuring and seat shifting at the mention of this.

Henriksen raised a hand to quieten everyone down. Then continued. "The model also predicts that during this solar apex, there is the potential for a dramatic rise in both the number and scale of coronal mass ejections."

"So what are you saying? Are we heading for the big one?" Dale couldn't contain himself and spoke for everyone in the room.

Henriksen again raised a hand. "I'm getting to that." He pointed at the 3D projection, currently displaying the Sun spewing out massive plumes of irradiated mayhem in all directions.

"No matter how massively charged a solar eruption is, it is of no danger unless it is heading in our direction. The odds of this happening are statistically quite low. But, of course, these odds change as solar activity increases. Yet, even if Earth is in the direct path of a solar storm, we are still protected from the worst effects by both our magnetic field and atmosphere."

Over the holo-screen, a wave of highly charged particles spewed out from the Sun and began to impact a stylized rendering of the magnetosphere, diverting and neutralizing most of it. The image then zoomed in on Earth's atmosphere showing spectacular aurora dancing at both poles, gaining in intensity as the storm hit, and dissipating slowly as the storm passed.

"But what about us, out here at the Moon?"

The projection zoomed out again to this time showing the Moon as it passed behind Earth.

"Yes, good question. The Moon lacks Earth's defenses so is totally exposed. Ironically, it is this exposure that has created the abundance of Helium-3 in the surface regolith. But I digress," he waved a dismissive hand. "By a stroke of good fortune, this latest storm will hit when the Moon is in full eclipse, so it will be protected by Earth."

The projection showed the shadow cast by Earth with the Moon slowly moving into shade, then to full shadow. "We will have some refraction through Earth's atmosphere but nothing to concern us."

There was an audible sense of relief around the room at this assurance from the professor.

"So you're saying this next one is a super storm, but not to worry, as we're protected?" Selene summed up the professor's presentation.

Henriksen hesitated, his eyes flicking over to Alan E. Dyson, current Head of FISA, who had also just arrived up this morning.

Dyson then took up the baton and responded by opening his hands in an expansive gesture. "Yes, this next one is going to be a doozy, but we'll be okay up here. However, we're at a delicate juncture in the talks and what we don't want is everyone reading more into this than there is. So we've made the decision to restrict the data set for this next solar storm."

Selene raised an eyebrow. "Is that wise? You know what people are like. As soon as you restrict something, they'll always think it's worse than it is."

"True, and some people will be anxious to return to Earth as soon as possible. This can't be helped," Dyson gave a shrug.

Selene had known the head of the agency for a long time, so

she knew his ways. She understood that he was trying say something to all of them—without actually saying it.

"Of course," Selene responded. "This... desire to return home would also put pressure on people to conclude the talks as soon as possible. Maybe cut quick deals now that time is of the essence."

Dyson smiled, "It's possible, sure."

Selene considered this for a moment. Far from trying to calm everyone down, the FISA top brass were using this latest storm data to ramp up the paranoia levels in the hope that it would unlock the negotiations. It was a dangerous gambit in Selene's mind. One that could backfire if not controlled very, very carefully. But she wasn't about to voice her concerns here.

"So, no change in strategy, then," she finally said. "We keep pushing, stick to our red-lines, and hope the others fold first?"

Dyson nodded. "For today at least. We can revise tomorrow, after the storm has passed."

The meeting broke up eventually, people gathered up their stuff and headed out the door ready for what was gearing up to be an interesting day. Dyson caught Selene's eye and gestured that he wanted a quiet word. They made their way out of the boardroom to a small alcove that was jokingly referred to as *the cone of silence*.

"Dangerous strategy, Alan. Are you sure you've thought this through?

He gave a disarming sigh. "Agreed. But we see it as a last throw of the dice. Things are stalled, we need something to break the deadlock. Maybe this is it. If not, what have we lost?"

"Hmmm... I suppose we'll soon find out."

"But there's something else I need to tell you." He glanced around to make sure they were alone, then leaned in and whispered, "we may concede on Tranquility."

Selene raised her eyebrows. "I thought that was sacrosanct? Not an inch, and all that?"

Dyson shrugged. "Apparently not, but it's your call on how far."

"That could be a poison chalice you've just handed me, Alan. So, what do they want in return?"

"Some movement on the Moon Base Delta issue would be good."

Selene laughed and shook her head. "Ha, not a hope. For SINO and INDOCON, that would be like handing over their first born. Seriously, Alan, what's the real deal here?"

"The bottom line is you've been cleared to concede to the five-hundred-kilometer mark for historic sites—if that will unlock progress and clinch a deal. The moon base would be the icing on the cake, but we're all being realistic here. This is a once in a lifetime opportunity to finally get some clarity on lunar governance. Time to go the extra mile—or in this case, kilometer."

Selene nodded. She was finally being given some room to maneuver, but it was up to her how to use it. She let that sink in for a beat before turning back to Dyson. "Tell me, this latest storm could cause a lot of damage, couldn't it?"

"Back on Earth, for sure. But systems are designed to handle these types of events so it probably won't be as bad as the predictions. Anyway, we'll all be safely tucked in behind Earth's shadow," he gave her his best disarming smile.

She spotted Nicci hovering at a discreet distance, trying to catch her attention. She nodded to her, then turned back to the agency head. "Gotta go. I'm having lunch with his excellency, Pompodur Bombast of Xilinex."

"Well, from what I've heard, at least the food should be good."

But Selene was not thinking of her lunch meeting when she joined up again with Nicci. She was going to have a look at the data for herself. It may be restricted but she had the clearance to read it. Then she was going to break protocol and get a message to her nephew, Renton Hicks, and make sure he understood what was heading his way.

CHAPTER 6
A LOT OF FRYING PAN

C entral Maintenance were not happy. Hard questions would be asked as soon as the crew got back to base. This was a vital operation for the FISA and now they looked like a bunch of amateurs. The crew needed to rectify the situation and fast, meaning that they weren't going anywhere until they got the mission back under control.

Becker and Matteo had already sent out a salvage droid to chase down the rogue solar panel and thruster pod assembly. It wouldn't do to have that adding to the space junk already piling up in lunar orbit, and they were going to need that thruster pod. Alice and Yuna continued on with the survey using the remaining drones.

Renton, however, was no longer employee of the month, far from it. There was now open hostility from Mackenzie who seemed to relish the opportunity to berate his incompetence.

"You screwed up big time, Renton. You shouldn't have put a faulty drone out there."

Renton couldn't believe that she was now blaming him; he was seeing another side of her. Still, he tried to fight his corner. "You wanted that bonus, you said it didn't matter if we lose a drone, so..."

"Not if it meant premature disassembly of the station while it's still in orbit."

He glanced over at the others, hoping for some support, but they all looked to be very busy, except for Alice, who looked just as perplexed as he was as to the captain's reaction.

"Now we've no chance," Mackenzie continued, her face a picture of anger and frustration. "We've no hope of getting that bonus. So you just park yourself in a corner and don't touch anything. The adults will have to sort out this mess."

"Hey, Captain? We may have a bigger problem." Becker was staring intently at a screen displaying orbital data.

"What now?"

He pointed at a stream of digits. "These numbers are showing a significant orbital deviation of the station."

Yuna floated over and scanned the data, then started gesturing frantically above an interface, running the numbers. "Not good," she finally said, floating back from the deck shaking her head.

"What? Tell me," Mackenzie gesticulated wildly in frustration.

"It looks like that drone impact had enough momentum to alter the station's orbit significantly." She checked the numbers on screen. "It's now in a death spiral and will impact the lunar surface in..." She did another quick calculation. "Six hours." Yuna looked over at the rest of the crew, and then to Renton.

He raised his hands. "Hey, I did say it was a bad idea."

"It is what it is," said Matteo. "Shit happens. What we gotta do now is get that station back onto the correct orbit."

"Easier said than done," Becker still had his eyes glued to the data readouts. "We need to retrieve that thruster pod first, then check it to make sure everything is okay, then reattach it."

"Well that's just bloody great," Mackenzie was winding up again. "Not only have we blown the bonus but now we're going to be stuck out here for another half a day—at least," she glared at Renton, who tried to make himself invisible. Then let out a long sigh as if decompressing, trying to get a grip on things. "Becker, how long on that retrieval?"

The Chief Engineer tilted his head this way and that, doing the math. "Another forty or so minutes until the robot catches up with it. Then say, another twenty to snag it, plus the time needed to bring it back. All told, probably the guts of two hours."

Mackenzie did her own calculations. "Then we'll need to bring it into the maintenance bay to check it over, fix it, reattach it, and get the station back on track. All that's gonna take a while," she decompressed again.

"Something you should be aware of, Cap," Yuna looked around from her screen. "That solar event is due in five hours, and if we stay on this flight path then we're way past the lee of Earth. We're going to be exposed. That means hunkering down for a few hours."

Mackenzie threw her hands up in the air causing her body

to drift in the zero-G environment before she reached for a hand grab. "Bugger that, we'll have to work up until the last minute. We need to get this done even if that means bending the regulations," she glanced around from one to the other. "Anybody got a problem with that?"

No one did, or they weren't saying.

Renton went back to working with Alice and Matteo on the station survey. That was the job they came out here to do and it was still continuing with the remaining drones. Although, if they didn't get the station back on track, then it would all be for nothing. But he didn't want to think about that. If the historical treasure that was the Lunar Gateway was lost, and it turned out to be because of him pushing the envelope, his aunt would never forgive him. It was she who had intervened to get him this job, so there would be blowback for sure. Renton pushed the thought away to focus on the task at hand when he got a ping on his personal comms unit. He glanced at the screen. His heart nearly stopped; it was from Selene Mene—his aunt.

His first thoughts were that she somehow must have heard of the screw up, but he relaxed when he saw she was just sending him some data.

Renton, restricted data attached from Heliophysics Division regarding imminent solar storm. Very high energy profile, largest ever recorded. However, you should be okay if you keep inside the umbra during the eclipse.

Make sure you do. Stay safe.

Selene.

He gestured at an icon to bring the attached data up on one

of the many monitors he had in front of him and quickly scanned it. It was written in a scientific lexicon that he was not familiar with. He sent it to Alice.

Just got this. Should we be worried?

He saw her glance over from her bank of monitors when his message popped up. As she studied the data Renton could see her expression slowly change from neutral to wide-eyed shock, and she began to chew her bottom lip again—not a good sign. Alice knew this stuff, and if she was concerned, then so should everyone else. She looked over at him and held his gaze. He would have left his station and floated over to her but, after taking his eye off the ball the last time, there was no way he was doing it again. A message popped up on his screen.

This is mega. Take over my station for a few minutes while I go and inform the Cap.

Before Renton could react, Alice had floated away from her station, and out of the operations bay.

Goddamnit, he thought. *Now she's going to get the captain even more pissed off at me.* He shook his head, then tapped in a few commands to take control of Alice's station—and waited for the inevitable.

"Everybody, listen up." Mackenzie flew into the operations bay like a shuttle on reentry, only to deftly grab a handrail and bring herself to an abrupt halt facing the crew. Yuna and Alice followed in her wake.

"It looks like this latest solar storm is a bit more serious than Central is letting on. Now you all know me, and what I think of all this solar storm crap so believe me when I say

49

this, but it looks like a right royal radiation shitstorm is heading our way," she glanced over at Alice. "And kudos to Alice here for digging up the data and raising a flag. Otherwise those useless buggers over at Central would have left us out to fry."

Alice caught Renton's eye and gave him an almost imperceptible nod. She had kept him out of it, much to his relief.

"So, here's the beef. Central assumed we'd be home in time for tea long before this solar storm hit, hiding behind a big fat Earth, hence the low-grade amber alert. But because of the screw up with the drone," she glanced over at Renton, "we've been chasing that heap of space junk way out past Earth's shadow. Anyway, Yuna's been running the numbers on this," she nodded to the Flight Engineer to take over.

Yuna gestured at her tablet and the data set that Selene sent Renton flickered to life on the primary monitor. "We're looking at a very high X-class event. Estimates put it at possibly an X200, way higher than a Carrington Event."

This had the effect of producing wide-eyed shock from Becker and Matteo. "Holy..." Becker's expletive trailed off. "That's a serious amount of radiation. If that hits Earth then we're talking major blackout territory."

"Not if," replied Yuna, "when. But that's not our problem. Our issue is that we'll have to ride this out. We can't abandon the Lunar Gateway. If we don't get it back on track then it will crash-land on the lunar surface."

"Can't we just head for the shadow, wait it out, and come back and sort out the gateway then?" asked Matteo.

Yuna shook her head. "Not enough time. We have to do it now—preferably before we need to hunker down."

"That level of electromagnetic radiation is going play havoc with the ship's systems."

"Listen," Mackenzie interjected. "For what it's worth, I've been through a lot of intense storms before. Now, while I'm not saying it's nothing, these things are never as bad as they make out."

"Maybe. But just look at the data," Becker jerked a finger at the screen. "This is... unprecedented. This is serious."

"We could suit up," said Renton, surprising even himself. He had not meant to open his mouth, but it just happened, almost unconsciously. "Then we could take all the ship's systems offline. Completely power down."

The crew stared at him for what seemed like a very long time, perhaps calculating just how insane that idea was.

"Now you're just being paranoid," Mackenzie was first to reply, and first to dismiss his suggestion.

"It's not completely crazy," Becker scratched his bottom lip, working through the procedure in his head. "That level of radiation could induce a lot of unwanted eddy currents. It makes sense to power down as much as we can."

"Yes, I agree," said Yuna. "It is better to be safe than in the frying pan," she gave a rare smile to accompany her strange mixed metaphor. No one corrected her, they all knew what she meant.

Mackenzie took a deep breath and rocked her head a little before asking. "Who else thinks we should take such drastic action?"

"It would be a pain in the ass for sure," said Becker, "and would take more time. But that's a lot of frying pan heading our way," he winked at Yuna. "So, yeah. Let's do as Renton suggests."

"Anyone else?" Mackenzie continued her survey.

"I'll run some calculations on potential inductive current," said Matteo, more to Becker and Yuna than Makenzie. "That'll give us an idea of what to power down."

"Absolutely," said Alice, giving Renton a quick glance. "I've never seen figures like these before. I'm pretty sure everything's going to glitch if we don't power down. That last storm could be why that drone went haywire."

Renton felt as if the operations bay just suffered a massive decompression, like the atmosphere had just been sucked out of the area. The others noticed it too, except for Yuna, and all eyes flicked from Mackenzie to Renton. After all, it was Mackenzie's decision to keep the drones in operation during the storm. He held his breath. But the captain didn't react. Maybe she didn't hear it or she decided to let it lie, for now.

"Okay," she finally said. "We've got five hours to get this station back on track, power down whatever systems you think need shutting down—and be all suited up in the cargo bay," she looked around from one to the other. "Let's get to it, ladies."

CHAPTER 7
TIME IS OF THE ESSENCE

Pompodur Rossen Adarok moved toward Selene Mene like a great ship coming in to dock. His silk shirt and trousers billowing around him as he advanced. A row of brilliant white teeth exposed in a wide smile.

"Ah, Selene. You look as radiant as ever," he offered a hand. She took it, almost without thinking. It was warm and slightly moist.

"It seems that the Xilinex Corporation has seen fit to allow you out for the day, Pompodur," she quipped.

"Ah, you mock me. But you're not far from the truth, Selene. Sometimes I feel like I have been banished to the lunar equivalent of the Siberian wastelands for my past misdeeds." He gestured over at the restaurant table all set up for their lunch meeting. "Shall we?"

Selene nodded. "Lead the way."

Their table was situated within a broad alcove, isolated

from the other tables so that conversations could be conducted in relative privacy. While their meeting was officially classified as informal, in truth it was simply a way for two sides to get a better feel for the other's position. Nothing would be said that contravened their respective negotiating positions, but things could be inferred, hinted at, probed.

As Selene took her seat, she could see several of Pompodur's entourage occupying a nearby table—too far to eavesdrop, but close enough to keep an eye on their man. This was to be expected. Her own secretary, Nicci, and a few others of her team occupied another table within line of sight.

Pompodur flopped down in a plush, high-backed seat with a groan. "Please forgive me. Having come up from the lunar surface, the gravity here is cruel on the body. I still haven't acclimatized to it yet," he made an apologetic face.

"How long have you been down there?" Selene asked, by way of conversation, not taking her eyes away from the lunch menu she was perusing.

"Six months too long," he leaned in a little and lowered his voice as if to impart a great secret. "As I said, I fear I've been banished to Xilinex Lunar HQ so that I can contemplate the superior virtues of the stoic life."

Selene gave her order to the waiter that had been hovering over them and turned back to Pompodur. "And how's that going?"

For a moment he continued to give a complicated set of instructions to the waiter along with a brief discussion on the best wine to accompany his dish. The waiter took note and retreated.

"As you can tell," he jerked a thumb at the retreating waiter. "It has only served to make me appreciate the finer things in life even more. It appears my superior's attempt at reprogramming has been a failure," he said with a look of mock abjection. "But enough of me. What of your good self? While I am suffering for my past, you, it would seem, are rising in the ranks of the Federation. Associate Director, no less."

"It has its upsides and downsides, like everything in life." Selene kept her response as vague as possible not wishing to give Pompodur any ammunition he could use against her. Their exchanges continued in this vein for a while until a flock of waiters arrived and began serving the food. They retreated as efficiently as they had arrived except for the head waiter who began to hover over them, wringing his hands; never a good sign. Perhaps Pompodur's choice of wine was not available and the waiter now had the odious task of breaking the bad news. But it was not that. Instead he informed them that they would have only forty-five minutes before all personnel needed to be evacuated to the shelters to ride out the current solar storm heading their way.

When the waiter departed, Pompodur shook his head and sighed. "These storms are such a bother."

"Yes, very disruptive to the talks," Selene agreed.

"Indeed, but I can't help wondering if all this hiding away in shelters is really necessary?" He waved a fork in the air, a plump pink prawn skewered on its prongs.

"People need the assurance that they're not going to be bathed in solar radiation."

"Well, correct me if I'm wrong, but I've never heard of someone dying as a result of a solar flare."

Selene was intrigued by this admission from the Xilinex director. Did he really believe this or was it some ruse to trap her into saying something she shouldn't? She decided to dig a little deeper. "You think it's all nonsense, then?"

"I wouldn't say nonsense, Selene," he said as he snared an asparagus spear. "It has a function. But not to keep anyone safe. It's simply to make the bureaucrats feel like they have a purpose, that they have power," he leaned in again. "It keeps the little people off-balance."

Selene resisted the impulse to laugh. Instead she bit down on a celery stick and took a moment to compose herself. "Have you seen the data for the next storm that's shortly heading our way?" This was her sending out a probe, just to see if Xilinex had taken the forthcoming threat seriously.

Again, Pompodur waved his fork in the air. "Yes, I did get notice of it, and yes, it might knock out a few satellites or some cell towers back on Earth. But we're protected by an eclipse—nothing for us to worry about, wouldn't you agree?"

She nodded. "Let's hope so."

"However," he continued. "What intrigues me is why FISA decided to restrict the data at the eleventh hour of these negotiations?"

"We felt it wouldn't be... productive to unnecessarily panic the general population since, as you say, we'll be in eclipse so no big deal."

He smiled. "Very civic-minded of you. Still, there are now

some of the more feeble-minded amongst us thinking the worst, getting anxious."

"Really?" Selene's face exuded a look of surprise. "People can be so... unpredictable."

"Indeed," he leaned in a little and lowered his voice. "Rumor has it that some now want to expedite these discussions sooner rather than later so they can all get back home to Earth."

Selene shrugged. "Oh, I wouldn't read too much into rumor, Pompodur. We all want a successful conclusion to these talks, and as quickly as possible. If the rumors are indeed true, then consider it a side bonus," she raised her glass and took a sip.

Pompodur was quiet for a moment as he dispatched the last of his crème brûlée. "To tell you the truth," he said between mouthfuls, "I wouldn't mind staying here a lot longer. The food back in Amundsen is sadly lacking in almost every respect." He pushed the empty plate aside, then wiped his mouth with a napkin, and gave Selene a considered look.

Here it comes, she thought. *Now we'll find out what he really wants.*

"I have something that I think might interest you."

"Oh?" Selene tried her best to feign disinterest.

He pursed his lips, considering his next words. "It's no secret that there is, how shall I put it, a certain reticence to corporations such as Xilinex sitting on the proposed New Lunar Council—with all that that entails. It's understandable that the other nation states, and their respective space agencies, would have reservations around a commercial entity having the same rights and legal powers of a sovereign country. But..." he opened his hands in an expansive gesture, "... here we all are ..." he paused.

Selene stayed silent, prompting him to continue.

"So, as you can imagine, any support we can muster to get this fundamental requirement across the line would be most appreciated."

Selene considered this for a moment. Having a corporation ensconced in such a position of power was indeed a major sticking point to the entire negotiations. Yet, it needed to be addressed or the talks would ultimately fail. And there was no escaping the reality that Xilinex, and the other corporations, were the economic engine that made lunar colonization a reality. Without them, there would be nothing other than scientific research and tourism—paltry industries by comparison. But the corporations also laid claim to relatively large areas of the lunar surface and the mineral resources therein. To grant them parity with a nation state would in effect give them complete legal control over these areas. A troubling proposition for many and a bitter pill to swallow, not least for FISA and its national sponsors. Yet, any carve up of lunar resources had to include the corporations—this was the reality.

"And?" she replied, raising a questioning eyebrow.

"And, well..." he fumbled with his napkin. "How would you like to have Moon Base Delta back in operation?"

Selene tilted her head and gave him a suspicious look.

"I know it's close to your heart," he continued. "You were a project director, I believe, one of those who drove the vision for FISA. I'm sure you hate to see it just rotting away, falling into dereliction?"

Selene lifted her glass and took a sip of water, more to compose herself than to quench her thirst. Yet, she had no doubt she had already revealed her shock at this proposal from Pompodur. He clearly knew what would get her heart racing; the prospect of reactivating the base. She studied the rim of her glass for a moment, running her finger along the edge trying to get a grip on this outlandish offer.

"That's... very interesting," she finally said. "Please enlighten me how you propose to achieve this seeming feat of magic?"

He dispensed with the napkin, clasped his hands together, and leaned in. "Your problem is SINO, they're ideologically driven. Back on Earth, they've become extremely confrontational and lash out at any country or organization that opposes them. They are paranoid, aggressive, and despise FISA and everything you stand for. Even the innocent act of wandering into any SINO territory on the lunar surface would be enough to ignite an international incident. So they're more than happy to let Moon Base Delta turn to dust just so you guys can't have it. However," he jerked a finger in the air, "the one thing they're more paranoid about than ideological confrontation is access to resources."

The wheels in Selene's mind suddenly began to turn. *Resources,* she thought, *of course.* The reason SINO were up here was access to mineral resources, but they had lagged far behind the corporations in this regard. Xilinex, on the other hand, were awash with mining concessions, many of which were yet to be exploited. *Was the deal a direct swap?* She wondered. Xilinex would give SINO some of these valuable mining rights and they would hand over their control to their sector of the moon base? Which would also mean that Xilinex would be the new partner, and whatever may be said about them, at least they were not ideologically driven. Presumably they had tested this deal with not just SINO but the other parties as well. INDOCON would also need to be on board.

Selene could see how this could play out for Xilinex. Since she was chief negotiator for FISA and their sponsor nations, if they could get her vote on granting the corporations nation status, then most of the other agencies would fall in line. And Pompodur had picked the very thing that might make her go for it, to see her passion project, Moon Base Delta, back up and operational again. She looked over at Pompodur and realized that he wasn't quite the decadent dandy she had pegged him for, it was just an act. There was a cunning mind at work in that expensively groomed head of his. *Good to know,* she thought. She would need to factor that into any further interactions. But for now at least, he was offering her the seemingly impossible.

She nodded her acknowledgment that she understood what he was offering and how it would be achieved. "I see. So, for this breakthrough over the moon base issue, you would want what exactly?" She already knew the answer, but she wanted to hear it from him.

He gave a disarming smile and opened his hands. "That when the final vote comes, the Federation of International Space Agencies gives due consideration to our entreaties."

The meaning was implicit. A vote by FISA would carry the day, the corporation would get their sovereign status.

Before Selene could react, the waiter arrived again to clear the table. "Sorry to bother you, but we need you to go to the safe area now."

Selene glanced over at the other diners and saw Nicci approaching. Pompodur's people were also up and moving.

She turned back to him. "Thank you for the lunch. You have given me much to think about."

"My pleasure. But don't take too long, time is of the essence."

CHAPTER 8
CARRINGTON EVENT

Renton tugged at the tether connecting him to the hull of the old Lunar Gateway and pulled himself closer to where the reclaimed and repaired thruster pod was currently being fitted. The team had been working flat out for the last few hours to get to this point. Now, they only had a few minutes to get it reattached, powered up, and get themselves back to the relative safety of the maintenance ship before the advancing solar storm started to bathe them in radiation.

He had volunteered for the refit operation, much to the protest of Chief Engineer Becker, who tried to argue that he didn't need to take unnecessary risks; although Renton suspected it was because Becker didn't want the responsibility of looking after him if he got into trouble. But Renton insisted, arguing that more hands would get the job done quicker. Yet deep down he knew that he needed to get back out there, sort out the mess the drone crash had caused, and show the others that he was willing to take responsibility. Maybe it was foolish. Maybe Becker was right. Yet Renton felt he needed to do this, for his own sake, if not necessarily for the needs of his fellow crew.

The salvage droid had chased down the errant thrust pod and solar array, snagged them, and brought them back to the maintenance bay on board the ship. Becker, Renton, and Matteo worked nonstop to assess the damage to the pod, and fix anything that was broken—or looked like it might break. Fortunately, as this was a self-contained, bolt-on unit that had been retrofitted to the station only a few years back, everything was still intact and functioning, except for the actual attachment points. These had been engineered so as not to damage the structural aesthetic of the station. This was what the runaway drone had taken out. But the good news was that the xenon gas tanks that provided the propellant for the advanced ion thruster pack were undamaged, as was the power supply. All they had to do was strap it back on to the old station, along with the repaired solar array, and power it up.

Renton nudged the base of the thruster pod into its final position, slotting it over a mounting truss that they had just finished repairing. Becker then went to work with a small laser welder, laying down a few tacks to quickly secure the pod in place. He raised a thumb to inform him he could let go. Renton then floated gently around to where Becker continued working with the welder. He was lying flat on the station's outer hull twisting his arm under the mounting truss to get at an awkwardly positioned join.

Renton suddenly began seeing light flashes. He blinked a few times and closed his eyes—he could still see them.

"You alright, Renton?" Matteo's voice resonated in his helmet. He was coordinating from inside the operations bay.

"Yeah, just experiencing a photon burst, flashing light specks."

"It's the outer edge of the radiation storm, you'd better get back inside as soon as you can."

"Working on it," Renton glanced down at Becker who was struggling to get the last weld done in the bulky EVA suit.

"How's that looking?"

Becker gave an exasperated sigh, then shuffled out from under the thruster pod. "Can't get it. Going to unclip just for a second. Might be able to squeeze in better."

Renton was about to suggest that this was a really bad idea. But it was not his place to tell the Chief Engineer what to do, or how to do it. So he gave him the thumbs up.

"Hey, guys," Matteo's voice came over the comms again. "You'd better pick up the pace. The outer edge of that storm is nearly on us."

"Going as fast as we can," Becker responded with note of frustration. "Renton, you can start heading back. I don't need you anymore. Go," he waved a hand at him, then unclipped the tether, and bent down again to work his way under the mounting truss.

"It's okay, I'll stay," Renton replied, just as another series of flashes perforated his vision, and he found himself getting a little disorientated.

The same thing must have happened to Becker as he

seemed to miss the hand hold he was aiming for and went tumbling sideways. He scrambled to find something to grab on to but his fingers couldn't find purchase. He slipped off the edge of the station and out into open space.

"Becker," Renton shouted out as he watched the engineer drift away. Without thinking, he propelled himself off the station aiming for his floundering colleague. His vector was straight and true, and within less than a second, he had caught up with Becker, who was now hopelessly flailing. Renton slammed into him and wrapped his arms around his colleague, just as his own tether had reached its limit. He felt the tug bring him to a halt and it was all he could do to keep Becker from slipping out of his grasp.

They took a moment to orientate themselves. "Thanks, buddy," Becker's breathing was labored. "Glad you stuck around. Otherwise you'd have to go chasing me down with a salvage droid."

Renton smiled, not that Becker could see it as both men had their reflective gold solar visors down, offering them some protection from unfiltered sunlight.

"Ha, yeah. Twice in one mission. Mackenzie would be going nuts." He started tugging at the tether. "Hold on, I'll pull us back in."

"What the hell are you two doing out there?" the captain's voice barked over the comms.

"Sorry, Cap. Bit of a slip up. All good now."

"Get your asses back here now. You're holding everything up." The comms went dead.

Renton pulled them back on to the station and Becker clipped himself back on. "I still need to make that last weld."

"I'll do it. I'm smaller, should be able to squeeze in."

Becker didn't argue. He was probably still a bit rattled from the experience of losing his tether. "Okay, just make it quick. I'm already seeing a universe of stars with my eyes closed."

Less than a minute later, Renton had made the final weld and the two engineers were letting go of the station and pulling themselves back to the maintenance ship. They piled into the airlock, repressurized, and made their way to the operations bay.

Yuna, Mackenzie, and Alice were gathered around a bank of monitors as Yuna entered in the parameters for the initial burn of the station's thrusters.

"Jeez, you two were making hard work of that. Thought we'd have to leave you out there," said Mackenzie.

"Yeah, fortunately Renton came to the rescue," Becker replied as he unclipped the EVA suit helmet.

The captain didn't reply, just gave him an appraising look.

"How are we looking?" Renton asked Yuna, as he scanned the readouts.

"Haven't initiated it yet. Just moving us out of the way first. Better hold on to something."

Renton felt himself drift as the ship began slowly moving away from the old station.

"Here we go. Let's hope those welds hold." Yuna initiated the orbit correction burn. The numbers on screen began to change, and the orbital schematic began to redraw. "Looking good," Yuna said, eyes fixed on the data. "But it will take a few minutes to know for sure. Best get down to the cargo bay, we've no time to waste."

"Are we shutting down ship systems?" Renton asked, even though he could see everyone was in full EVA suits.

"We've set up a kill switch procedure," Matteo said. "We'll hunker down in the cargo bay; Yuna has offered to stay here. Once she's happy with the realignment of the station, she'll then take everything we can offline."

"No she won't," Mackenzie announced. Everyone looked at her as if she had lost her mind. "You lot bugger off, I'll stay. The captain needs to have something to do on this bucket of bolts," she turned to the flight officer. "Show me what I need to do, then you all get lost. That's an order."

They did as the captain asked, moving down into the belly of the maintenance ship to a small space they had created, surrounded by as much material as they could muster between them and the outer hull. This would hopefully absorb and block much of the solar radiation heading their way.

Less than a minute after settling in, the lights went out, and the pervasive background hum of electrical and mechanical systems that pervades all ships dialed down to almost complete silence, leaving Renton and the other crew with nothing but their EVA suits keeping them alive. A moment later, the cramped space was swept by the headlight on the captain's suit as she squeezed in beside them, giving them all the thumbs up. She flicked off her headlight and they were left in complete darkness.

As Renton's eyes adjusted to the darkness, the phantom

lights that he and Becker had experienced out on the old station returned. But they seemed different now, less of a popping spark, more of a diffused glow. He moved his head around and blinked several times only to realize that the flashes were not emanating from his retina but from his surroundings. He looked around the cramped, dark cargo bay and saw flashes arcing across areas of exposed metal. The solar storm had begun and the electromagnetic radiation was setting up eddy currents and standing waves in the metallic hull of the ship which were propagating through to the internal structure. The others had noticed it too as all were looking over at the patch of bare metal that fizzed and sparked.

As an engineer, Renton understood what was happening, they all did. But as his brain started doing the math on how much radiation there must be to provide such a light show, he got a deep worrying feeling that this was much worse than even he had feared. As another flash popped overhead, he wondered what damage was being caused to the delicate electronics of the ship's systems. It was going to be an anxious time spent cooped up in their makeshift bunker. And after, would the ship's systems be dead? No power, no life support. And if so, how long would they have before they all died out here?

CHAPTER 9
NOT GOING ANYWHERE SOON

I t was the longest few hours in Renton's life, and he doubted he was alone with this feeling. A palpable sense of anxiety radiated out from his fellow crew members. At its peak, even his EVA suit began to glitch out. On several occasions, the head-up display flickered and buzzed momentarily, only to settle down again, much to his relief.

No one spoke a word during the entire ordeal.

Eventually, the storm passed, as they do. There was no more suit glitching or pyrotechnics being induced in the ship's hull. When the estimated time had passed, it was the captain who was first to speak. Uncharacteristically, it was not to bark an order or bawl someone out. It was a simple question.

"Alice?" her voice was low and uncertain. "You think it's over?"

Renton wondered why the captain was directing this question to Alice. Perhaps more had been said when she went to deliver the FISA data that Renton had received from Selene. Whatever the reason, the captain now considered Alice as the authority on solar storms.

"Yes. It should have passed below ten percent of the peak around twenty minutes ago."

"Okay then," Mackenzie began to move. "Time to get this tub back up and running She flicked her helmet light on, as did the others. It took a moment for Renton's eyes to adjust, then he followed them out of the bunker.

Yuna and Mackenzie moved into the flight deck, Becker headed to the rear of the ship where the main power control was located, and the rest of them returned to the operations bay, took up their respective stations, and waited for Becker to reboot the power. Nobody spoke.

Suddenly, the ship blossomed back to life, lights flickered on, systems booted up, and the background hum of the life-support systems kicked in. Renton, like the rest of the crew, breathed a long slow sigh of relief, then flicked open his suit visor and unclipped his helmet. This was followed by much cheering and fist bumping. So far so good, the old ship had survived. Alice glanced over from her station and gave him the thumbs up. He smiled back, happy that his worst fears had not been realized. Everybody started stripping out of the bulky EVA suits and Renton offered to gather them up and return them to storage.

"I'll give you a hand," said Alice, as she slipped out of her own suit.

"Sure, thanks." He began moving out of the operations bay with two suits trailing behind him.

They made their way over to the primary airlock where the main suit dock was located. Renton pushed one into its nook, connected the services, and booted up the check routine. He hit the button to initiate—and all power in the ship went down.

"Oh shit," he heard Alice say in the darkness. But before he could reply, the lights flickered back on again as the power returned. They gave each other a long anxious look.

"That's not good," he finally said, reflexively looking around the area.

They paused for a moment, waiting to see if the power would go out again. When it didn't Renton slowly resumed the task of stowing away the EVA suits.

"What do you think that was?" Alice asked, as she hooked up the last of the suits.

Renton had a few ideas, but none he was going to share with Alice—why make her more anxious. "Eh... I don't know. Could be just a simple circuit breaker not liking the power surge," he glanced over at her. "It's an old ship, things are a bit clunky." This seemed to satisfy her... for the moment.

They made their way back to the operations bay in silence only to find everyone gathered around the primary monitor. Yuna was explaining something but stopped when they entered.

"What's up?" Renton asked.

"We've got a problem," Mackenzie replied without looking at him. She nodded at Yuna. "We may have lost flight control."

"You're joking me?" said Alice as she tried to make sense of the screen data.

"Nope," Yuna was matter of fact as she pointed at the

monitor which showed a mess of characters that looked like rows of hieroglyphs—in other words, major data corruption.

"Navigation, flight control, positioning—totally fried, complete junk."

"Can we fix it?" Alice asked the obvious question on everyone's lips.

Yuna gave a long slow sigh, is if she was physically preparing herself for the answer. "Yes and no."

"And what's that supposed to mean?" Matteo sounded jittery.

"We can replace the physical components; we have the spare parts. But we need to rewrite the data set and we don't have a backup."

"We could get Central to send us a data set," Renton offered.

"We could," said Mackenzie. "Except we don't have comms either. It's fried too."

"And we can't fix that," Matteo shook his head. "Just in case you're about to ask. It's the antenna array on the outside of the ship," he jerked a thumb over his shoulder. "That, we don't have the parts for."

"Alright," Mackenzie barked out. "Let's not go all soft in the middle. We've got power, we've got life support, and as far as I know, the engines still work. Even better, we've got a ship full of engineers. So, let's figure out a way to get home."

"I'm pretty sure I could fabricate a rudimentary antenna, might get us voice comms over VHF," offered Renton, although without delving into the exact problem he was just spitballing.

"I think you've done enough helping out for one mission, Renton. I'd rather you not touch anything from now on. Best you just sit this out," Mackenzie again spoke without looking at him.

"What's that supposed to mean?" Renton could feel the bile rise in his belly.

Mackenzie turned to face him and backed herself in beside Yuna and Becker as if seeking their support. "Let's face it, Renton, everything you've touched on this mission has turned to rat-shit. Hey, maybe it's just bad luck, but I rather you just take a back seat. The rest of the team can handle it from here."

"That's crap." Renton had had enough, he wasn't going to take this from the captain, but Becker floated his body in front of him. "Woah, just cool it. We're in enough of a mess already without starting an argument. That's not going to get us anywhere."

"But this is totally unfair," Renton waved a hand in the direction of Mackenzie.

"Unfair!" Mackenzie barked. "I'll tell you what's unfair. Being stuck out here with a crippled ship, not to mention losing our bonus, all because you thought operating a faulty drone was a good idea."

"That drone would have been fine if you had let us pause the operation during the first solar storm." There, he had said it, he finally got it out. This whole shitshow was down to a gung-ho captain who thought being bathed in electromagnetic radiation was just another day at the beach. Mackenzie's face turned a deeper shade of red, and Renton could feel the anger building up inside her. He had done it now, there was no going back from this.

"You're way out of line, boy. Maybe if we hadn't powered

down the ship's systems we wouldn't be in this mess. That was your idea too," she jerked a finger at him. Becker raised a hand. "Okay, okay, let's just cool it down," he looked at the captain, his hands out in a gesture of conciliation.

"Agreed, this is not getting us anywhere," Yuna piped in. She turned to Renton. "Maybe you should just take some time out, Renton. Go to the galley, grab a coffee. Take a break."

A rage was building in Renton that he had not experienced in a very long time, if ever. It would consume him if he let it, he knew that. He had said his piece, there was nothing more he could do. He looked around at the others, they were all on edge, all anxious about their situation. And all he was doing was adding to that. So, he took a deep breath.

"Fine," he said. Then turned and floated out of the operations bay.

CHAPTER 10
FALLOUT

Selene and her team had just emerged from the storm shelters on the Axial Luxor Hotel when the first reports started coming in. Massive power and communications disruption across most of Earth's northern hemisphere. Still, this did not come as any great surprise. Most people had expected that a storm of this magnitude would leave some disruption in its wake, yet Selene couldn't help feeling that the reports she was getting were on the upper end of this expectation. Soon the conference delegates were abuzz with the news, and a palpable air of concern began to settle over the various parties assembled for the talks. However, most hoped that it would soon sort itself out when maintenance crews got down to work and commenced the repair process.

The primary session that afternoon was on historic sites and Selene had been given a lot of leeway on this by Dyson at their early morning debrief. But things had moved on considerably since then. Her lunch with Pompodur had left her with an offer that needed to be teased out first. There was still an hour before the next session kicked off so she convened a quick meeting with Alan Dyson and Dale Graham along with a conference link to Samantha Bersin—Director of Operations, back at FISA HQ on Earth. What Xilinex was offering was big, so she needed buy in from the main decision makers.

Dale Graham drummed his fingers on the edge of the boardroom table as they all waited for the tech to establish a comms connection with HQ.

"I wish you would stop doing that," said Selene with just a hint of exasperation. "It gets annoying very quickly."

He raised his hands in the air and gave an apologetic smile. "Sorry, bad habit."

"What's the hold up?" Dyson directed his question at a very flustered tech, who was pecking at a keyboard, clearly confused that he was not getting the response he expected.

"Our normal comms link is down, probably because the storm disrupted the Earth-side satellite network. I'm trying to route us through another channel."

"Well, can you hurry up. We don't have all day."

The tech glanced over at him, then paused what he was doing, and gestured at the terminal. "Would you like to try?"

Selene raised a hand. "Just cool it. Let the guy do his job. Okay?" she scowled at Dyson.

"Fine," he shrugged. "Just wondering why it's taking so long, is all."

"It's not just one network that's out of commission, it's several," offered the tech by way of clarification. "Those that are still operational are experiencing extremely high traffic. Wait..." he leaned into the terminal. "There. Got it. Might be a bit laggy, but we're connected."

"Thanks. Appreciate your efforts," Selene gave the tech a nod.

The main monitor flickered to life and the head and shoulders of Samantha Bersin materialized.

"Hi, Selene. You'd better make it quick. We're maxed out at the moment dealing with the fallout from that Carrington Event. Got a lot of infrastructure down."

Selene paused for a beat. "How bad is it?"

"Bad and getting worse. Can't hang around too long. So what's up?"

Selene then proceeded to outline the Xilinex offer.

Bersin rubbed a hand over her forehead. "Seriously? Moon Base Delta? How?"

"My guess is they've offered SINO, and maybe INDOCON, a deal on access to mining concessions. But I've nothing to back that up."

"I don't trust them, and certainly not that Pompodur fop."

"Neither do I, who knows what double dealing is going on. But it's on the table, what do we care how they do it."

"And what do they want in return?" asked the operations director.

"Our vote on corporate sovereignty."

"That would be a difficult sell to the board, not to mention the sponsors. It would mean that Xilinex would be co-partners in the moon base. Why would they even want that?"

Selene was about to reply when Bersin's attention was diverted by some off-camera alert. She stared at it intently, rubbing her chin as she digested the information then screwed her face up and turned back to Selene. "Gotta run. Just got a preliminary damage report and it's worse that we thought."

"What about the offer?"

Bersin waved a hand. "Eh... I'll run it by the board. Just sit on it for the moment."

Selene really needed something better to go on than that. "No can do. I need something, even if it's provisional."

"Eh... now's not the time. Sorry. Just do your best."

The connection ended. Selene looked around at Dyson and Graham, a question on her face.

"What sort of fallout is she talking about?" asked Dale.

Dyson tapped the side of the slim augmented reality visor reminiscent of old-school glasses. "Just been scrolling through messages. Looks like there's significant satellite damage. And I don't mean just FISA. It's everybody." He tapped the side of the unit again and gave a gesture to broadcast it to the main boardroom monitor.

"This is the live incident list from Central Maintenance up here in cislunar space. I had them send it to me."

Line after line of maintenance alerts scrolled down the screen. All triaged by severity. Selene was alarmed to see so many flagged as critical.

"We're talking mostly infrastructure in local space:

communications, navigation, refueling depots, maintenance droids, and a whole bunch of other stuff."

"My god, and we were protected by Earth during the eclipse. I can't imagine what's going on down there," said Dale, his eyes wide.

"Wait a minute," Selene shouted and started gesturing wildly at the screen. "Back up, can you go back a few lines."

"Sure." Dyson gestured in mid-air and the scrolling lines on the main monitor reversed direction.

"There, stop," Selene pointed at the screen, then got to her feet and read the message.

SLT - 04:27:13 | Maintenance vessel Aurora: Mackenzie | LOC: LOP-G 68,000 | Status: Comms Failure | Action: OBSERVATION

"Aurora. That's my nephew's ship."

Dyson gestured again to drill down on the detail. "Looks like they lost comms with the ship somewhere along the old Lunar Gateway orbit," he glanced back at Selene.

"Can you escalate that?" she asked, although it was more of an order.

"Hey, I'm sure it's nothing. And I don't want to go pressurizing Central. They've got enough on their plate."

Selene thought about this for a moment. "Yeah, you're probably right. But, just for me, can you at least mention it to them. Get them to keep an eye on it?"

Dyson pursed his lips and nodded, "Sure."

Selene sat down again and tried to gather herself together. She had a distinct feeling that things might just slip away from her if she wasn't careful. The FISA directorate back home were too preoccupied dealing with the fallout from the solar storm to make an executive decision on the Xilinex offer. Then again, Samantha Bersin did say, *do your best*. That gave her some wiggle room. But if FISA were knee-deep in technical firefighting, then all the other parties at the conference would be in the exact same position. That meant a lot of mental bandwidth was now redirected to internal affairs. Not a good place to be if you're looking for a breakthrough. And then there was Renton. His ship had lost comms. One more worry to occupy her mind.

She was about to call the meeting to a close when Nicci's head and shoulders materialized on the main screen. She looked frazzled, and it took a lot to get her into that state.

"Eh... we may have a major problem," she said.

Selene rolled her eyes. "What now?"

"It's CASA, they're leaving."

"What? Walking out of the session?"

"No, not the session, the hotel. They're heading back to Earth. They're saying it's not safe here."

"But they can't do that. Not before the vote in two days."

"Well, you all better get down here and try and persuade them, otherwise they're on the next shuttle home."

Selene was on her feet again, along with Dyson and Dale. "We're coming. Just do whatever it takes to keep them from leaving until we get there. Understood?"

Nicci nodded. "I'll try my best."

"I don't care how you do it. Lock the doors if you have to."

The cracks were beginning to appear. Selene could feel them building all around her. If CASA were running scared then others would be feeling the same. She had to handle this, otherwise it could turn into a stampede and all that work would be for nothing. She couldn't let that happen. Not when Pompodur had virtually handed Moon Base Delta to her on a plate. It was all that mattered, and she was not going to let CASA, or anyone else, screw up that dream.

CHAPTER 11
CONTAINMENT

Renton jabbed an agitated finger at a button on the coffee machine in the galley. He badly needed a pouch of joe to settle himself down after his angry exchange with the captain. He shouldn't have lost control. Why did he do that? Because now, even if they did get out of this mess, he was back to being jobless. Worse, he'd just blown all chance of working in cislunar space again. No one was going to hire him after this. Not even his well-connected aunt could sort this one out.

He sighed and jabbed at the button again—nothing happened.

"Goddamnit," he shouted at the machine and jabbed the button a few more times, without success. He was about to slam his fist into it when Alice floated into the galley.

"More mechanical trouble?" she asked, coming to a halt beside him, and glancing down at the errant coffee dispenser.

Renton stayed his hand and took a deep breath. "It seems

like everything's falling apart on this ship," he gave her a feeble smile.

Alice carefully leaned over the machine, unclasped a side panel, and extracted a pouch of coffee. "Here," she said handing it to him. "It's cold, but I think you probably need to cool down anyway."

He took the pouch, snapped the cap, and sucked on the tube. "So, what's the mood like?" he jerked his head toward the operations bay.

"They're still assessing the damage. Yuna's doing an old-school flight plan, and Matteo's fabricating a makeshift antenna for wide-spectrum broadcast—as you suggested."

Renton nodded a little sheepishly and took another belt of coffee. "I think I might have got on the wrong side of the captain."

Alice raised an eyebrow. "That's putting it mildly. You basically accused her of incompetence. How did you think she was going to react?"

"Yeah, I suppose. It's just... I'm sick of taking the blame for other people's shit."

"Look, Renton," Alice glanced back in the direction of the bay. "I'm not disagreeing with you," her voice was low, almost a whisper. "With hindsight, there might have been one too many risks taken for the sake of the bonus. But it was just a bad call, that's all. What's done is done. We need to keep it together now."

Renton screwed his mouth and nodded a vague acceptance of Alice's assessment of the situation. "Yeah, but—"

"But nothing," she cut him off. "For what it's worth, if you hadn't gotten hold of that storm data from FISA, then we could be in a much worse situation."

"Thanks, but that's not how Makenzie sees it. Everything's my fault as far as she's concerned. I don't know if she's got a chip on her shoulder or what, but she just doesn't like me, maybe it's the fact that I got this job through family connections rather than working my way up through the ranks," he waved a hand. "I don't know."

"Maybe you're the one with the chip on your shoulder. Ever think of that?" Alice countered.

He gave a resigned smile. "Yeah, I have. Plenty of times."

He then gave Alice a conspiratorial look. "You made sure not to mention where you got that solar storm data from when you were talking to the captain, didn't you?"

Alice looked taken aback, like she had been caught out. "I was just trying to keep you out of it."

"It's fine, you were right not to mention me, otherwise Mackenzie might not have taken it seriously." He really didn't want to get on the wrong side with Alice, he liked her, she was smart. But more than that, she was looking out for him.

Suddenly the lights in the galley flickered and went out and a dim red emergency light kicked in. Both of them stopped talking and looked at one another. "That's a little concerning," said Renton, stating the obvious.

Alice said nothing, just glanced around at the dimly lit galley interior, a worried look on her face. The power kicked back on again, and both of them breathed a sigh of relief.

"That's the second time that's happened," she said. "What the heck is going on?"

"I have a few ideas, but you probably don't want to hear any of them."

"Why, are they bad?" The worried look on her face dialed up a notch.

"If it is what I think it might be then yes, it's bad."

"I think we should both head back to the others and see what's going on."

Renton hesitated, not sure if he was ready to keep his cool if Mackenzie started up again. Alice pulled on his arm. "Come on. We're all in this together, whether the captain likes it or not."

Makenzie cast him a dismissive glance when he floated in after Alice, but otherwise just ignored him. Renton reckoned that this was probably progress.

"What's going on with the power?" It was a general question from Alice, directed at no one in particular.

Becker looked up from his screen. "Could be just a problem with the regulator. I'm trying to track it down."

"The good news is we managed to contact Central," said Matteo. "I cobbled together an antenna and got our comms kinda working," he looked over at Renton and gave him the thumbs up. "However, the bad news is it's mayhem over there. Lots of stuff out of action, so they can't get to us for at least a day."

"A day?" Alice exclaimed. "Why so long?"

"They've got bigger problems than us," said Makenzie. "It doesn't matter anyway, because Yuna's calculated our route back. It'll be slow and steady, but we're good to go as soon as everything's stored away. So, let's get to it."

"I wouldn't do that if I were you." Renton just couldn't help himself. If he was correct in his assessment of the power problem, then firing up the plasma engines could pop the reactor. Then they would be in real serious trouble, assuming they were still alive.

Mackenzie glared at him. "I don't remember anyone asking for your advice."

"Renton's right," Becker raised a hand. "The problem could be more serious than we think. And the last thing we need is to completely lose all power. So let's not do anything hasty until we give it a thorough once over."

There was a brief moment of silence as the crew waited on Mackenzie's reaction.

"Okay," she finally said, with a hint of frustration. "Go check it out. But whatever the problem is, we need it fixed pronto. I don't want to be out here a moment longer than I have to." She turned and floated back toward the flight deck.

Becker nodded to Renton. "Follow me. Let's get down to the reactor bay."

They floated out of operations and worked their way past the cargo bay, moving steadily toward the rear of the ship where the fusion reactor was located.

"So what do you reckon?" Becker asked as they moved.

"Eh... I could be wrong, I mean, it's just a gut feeling, nothing more."

"Just spit it out. I'm not the captain. I won't bite," Becker turned and gave him a grin.

"Containment," said Renton. "I think we might have a problem with plasma containment."

"Yeah," Becker sighed. "I've been thinking that very same thing. Just didn't want to mention it back there. You know how people get when you start mentioning plasma containment."

"I know. It's serious business. Especially if it fails."

"Well, let's hope we're both wrong about it." Becker came to a halt in front of the reactor room door. He punched in the security code, spun the locking wheel, and cracked the door open. Immediately they were assaulted with a strong smell of ozone.

"Smell that?" said Renton.

"I do, ozone. There must have been a lot of ionization going on in here during that storm. Better leave the door open and let some air circulate in here."

The reactor itself was toroidal in shape, like a doughnut, and orientated to fit the circular curve of the ship's hull. As Renton and Becker entered the room, they were effectively looking at the dead center of this reactor ring, which was behind a protective bulkhead. Mounted all across this bulkhead wall were a bank of systems used to monitor the functioning of the reactor. Becker headed over to one, booted it up, and started running diagnostics.

"Woah," he said as he paused a screen full of scrolling data and pointed. "There. Look at the voltage in the electromagnets during the storm. It's off the charts."

Renton moved closer and looked at the log data. "That's three times what they're rated for. What's the current draw now? How much power are they consuming?"

"Holy crap," Becker shook his head. "I've never seen anything like that before," he glanced at Renton. "It's worse than we thought."

"How bad?"

Becker scratched his chin. "Looks like the plasma containment subsystem has been damaged due to a surge in energy from the solar storm. Their efficiency had been degraded. Now the electromagnets need considerably more power to keep the reactor stable."

"Then there's no way we can fire up the plasma engines. We'd need, what... a few hundred megawatts just to get moving?"

Becker nodded. "The reactor is barely able to maintain containment," he leaned in and pointed at a set of numbers. "And if I'm not mistaken, it's getting worse." He was silent for a moment as he studied the data readout and did the mental calculations. "Seven hours," he finally said, looking at Renton as if he'd just seen a ghost. "We've got seven hours before..." his sentence trailed off.

Renton took a deep breath and sighed. "I think it might be best if you were the one to break the news to the captain."

CHAPTER 12
LOP-G

As expected, Mackenzie did not take the news well. A long string of foul-mouthed abuse was hurled at no one in particular. It ended with the captain flinging a handheld comms unit across the operations bay, where it slammed off the far wall and smashed into pieces. So for the next few minutes, while the captain calmed down, the crew busied themselves collecting all the floating debris.

Mackenzie gripped the edge of a workstation, her head down, trying to regain some composure more befitting a captain of a FISA maintenance vessel.

"Options," she finally said.

"Can we shut it down and wait it out on backup power until Central get here?" suggested Alice.

"We can't shut down a fusion reactor. No one on this ship has that knowledge. Once it's up and running, it stays that way. Yes, we can take it offline, but it's still operating." Becker shook his head. "Even if we tried, the most likely scenario is we vaporize the ship and all of us along with it."

"Well that's just great. Just bloody great," Mackenzie waved an arm around.

"There's... one possibility." Yuna had strapped herself into one of the workstation seats, and she swung it around to face them. "But it's a bit tricky."

No one spoke. They all just looked at her expectantly. Yuna looked from one to the other, then swung her seat back around to operate the workstation. She gestured at the control interface and an orbital chart blossomed up on the main monitor. It showed an elliptical line scribed around Luna. She pointed at it.

"We are currently in the same near rectilinear orbit as the old Lunar Gateway, LOP-G. The storm hit us at the apogee, around 70,000 kilometers out. Since then we have been tracking back toward Luna. In approximately five hours' time we will be passing over the north pole and at the closest point in the orbit to the surface, by then we will be only 3,000 kilometers away." The chart zoomed in to show a more detailed image of the polar region.

"We still have retro-thrusters," she continued. "The ones we use for landing on the surface. These are old-school hypergolic so we don't need electrical power for ignition. It's simply aerozine and nitrogen tetroxide mixed together, which self-ignite. Foolproof technology, used for well over a century."

"Go on," prompted Becker.

She pointed at the image. "If we do a long burn here, at the closest point to the surface, I think we can slow the ship down enough to allow Luna to pull us out of orbit."

"You mean crash-land?" asked Matteo.

"We would need to leave enough in the tanks to do a second burn, enough to slow the ship down so we can land. Just keep in mind that I'm working the math out on this without the aid of our flight control system."

There was a long moment of silence as the crew digested Yuna's radical plan.

"Well, screw me sideways on a maintenance droid, Yuna. But that's the craziest plan I've ever heard in all my years out here in the black hole of space," Mackenzie shook her head in disbelief.

Yuna, as usual, was completely unfazed by the captain's response. "Does anyone have a better crazy plan?" she glanced around.

No one did. But that didn't mean they were happy about this one.

"We should just broadcast a mayday on repeat. Maybe there's a ship close to us." Alice clearly wasn't onboard with this plan.

"We're already doing that," Matteo jerked a thumb at the comms monitor. "But what we've got back from Central is that there are simply no ships in this region of cislunar space and the soonest they can get anything here is eleven hours."

"Do we have enough fuel to pull off this maneuver?" Renton focused his attention back on Yuna, since she was the flight officer and the only one amongst them with the ability to calculate orbital mechanics without the aid of a computer. He was also acutely aware that this ship had not landed on the surface of Luna for over a year, so fuel for the retro-thrusters would probably be a low priority during resupply.

"If my calculations are correct, then I think I can get us down in just under seven hours."

"That's cutting it tight," said Becker. "We could lose containment before that."

"What if we reduce power consumption elsewhere on the ship?" said Renton. "Deactivate everything we can, maybe even including life support? We can use our EVA suits. It could buy us more time."

"Hmmm..." Becker thought about this for a moment. "It could possibly buy us another thirty or forty minutes."

"It would be enough," said Renton.

"Woah," the captain held a hand up. "Let's all just back up a pair of moments here. Assuming we all agreed to this crazy plan, has anyone considered where we might land. Because if you track east of that flight path, that's all SINO territory," Mackenzie pointed at the line scribed along a north–south axis overlaid on the image of the lunar surface. "I for one would prefer being vaporized in a reactor meltdown than being used as a political pawn by those guys. Because that's exactly what they will do to us. We're talking about spending time in Lunar Siberia."

"Ah... Siberia gets a bad rap. It's actually one of the last great natural wildernesses on Earth. And it's much warmer there these days," Matteo grinned as he tried to lighten the mood.

Yuna tapped a few commands on her workstation screen

and a geopolitical map of the lunar surface zoomed out on the main monitor.

"This is our predicted flight path, traveling north–south. Unfortunately, I cannot predict with any great accuracy exactly where we'll land along this line. But we need to come down at least a few kilometers from any population center," she turned to Becker. "Just in case the reactor does go boom. We don't want to cause any collateral damage."

"We're skirting mighty close to the badlands," Mackenzie studied the flight path that mirrored the intersection of SINO to the east and a patchwork of other territories to the west: Xilinex, FISA, INDOCON, and a few others. Most of these areas were peppered with mining stations, research facilities, and a host of other outposts and bases, all populated.

"We have to avoid all these areas," Yuna pointed out most of the western side. "Which leaves us no other option but to aim for the very edge of SINO territory."

"And what then?" Mackenzie mocked, gesturing at the map. "We make a run for the border?"

"What's that?" Alice pointed at a small area, highlighted in a different color, centered in the Sea of Tranquility.

Yuna glanced up, then tapped in a command to zoom in on the area.

"That's Moon Base Delta," said Renton.

"The old international research facility," said Matteo. "That's been out of commission for decades. It's probably derelict by now. Not much use to us."

"It's not derelict," Renton corrected him. "It was mothballed, put into maintenance mode back when all the various agencies involved in it fell out with each other. But I know they maintain an emergency shelter there. It was part of the deal when they decommissioned the base that a shelter be maintained."

The others remained silent for a beat as all heads turned to look at this mysterious blob on the lunar map.

"How do you know all this?" Becker finally asked.

Renton hesitated, wondering how much he should reveal about himself and his connections to the highest echelons of FISA. Under normal circumstances, he had kept very quiet about it. But these were not normal circumstances, and in a little over seven hours, unless they were rescued or Yuna managed to land the ship intact, they were all going to be dead. And by the look of things, getting to Moon Base Delta might be their only chance of survival.

"My aunt is Selene Mene; she was deeply involved in the Moon Base Delta project. I became fascinated by it when I was younger, hearing all the stories. It's the reason why I wanted to go into space."

"Is that the same Selene Mene that's a director of FISA?" asked Becker, a little incredulously.

Renton nodded.

"Holy cow," Matteo was genuinely shocked. "So how come you're working on this tub and not in one of the fancy research bases? I know I would be if I had those family connections."

Renton shrugged. "It's a long story."

"Yeah," Mackenzie added, turning to address the rest of the crew. "Renton here has a bit of a history of screwing things up."

Renton surprised himself that he didn't rise to the captain's taunting. Less than an hour ago, he was filled with rage, but now it was simply not worth the effort.

"You think you could land us there?" he turned back to Yuna, ignoring Mackenzie.

"Possibly," she changed the elevation on the map, studying the terrain. "That whole area is relatively flat, and within FISA boundaries. I could get us down somewhere that's far enough away so as not to damage the facility if the reactor goes critical."

"But how do we know we can get into the base even if we do land?" asked Alice, who now seemed to be acquiescing to the idea.

"We don't need to enter the base, just this section here," Renton leaned over and tapped some commands into the interface and the map zoomed in on a close-up view. He pointed to an isolated domed structure. "This here is an emergency shelter. It should have life support and comms. We can wait it out there until they send a rescue shuttle."

Again, the crew were silent as they all looked at the gray blob on the lunar surface that now represented a potential life raft.

"So are we doing this?" Yuna finally asked.

One by one they all nodded agreement, leaving just Mackenzie.

"Do we have any other choice?" she said by way of an answer.

"Okay," said Yuna as she swung her seat back and started tapping commands on her workstation. "We head for Moon Base Delta."

CHAPTER 13

MASTERM

D r. Han Sundar, Senior Analyst at the Meteoroid and Space Debris Terrestrial Environment Reference Model, aka MASTERM, has a version of an old quotation framed and mounted on the wall behind his desk. It reads—*A butterfly flaps its wings in the Amazon, and very soon someone somewhere will be having a really bad day.*

It's a reference to the *butterfly effect* in chaos theory, where a small change in one state of a system can result in large differences in a later state. Meaning that small, seemingly insignificant actions can have an enormous effect further on down the line. It was first postulated by an American mathematician and metrologist Edward Norton Lorenz with reference to a seagull flapping its wings causing a slight ripple in the air, that when amplified, could cause a tornado a few weeks later.

But in reality, Han had no interest in either seagulls or

butterflies. His job, and those of the hundred plus people who worked at MASTERM, was in cataloguing and modeling space debris. Their collective function was to know what was out there, how fast it was going and where it would be in the future —but most importantly, if it was going to hit somebody's very expensive space infrastructure and destroy it.

This vital task took place within a nondescript, low-rise office campus on the outskirts of Denver, Colorado. The epicenter of this campus was a 5-Zetaflop supercomputer, nicknamed MasterMind, that took in data from a myriad of sources including a number of FISA orbital debris observatories and a host of other ground-based systems located all over the globe. The upshot of all this data acquisition was to model, as accurately as possible, the whereabouts of every object in Earth orbit bigger than one centimeter in size.

And this is where the butterfly effect reference comes into the equation. Because Han Sundar, and every other person involved in the business of launching and maintaining space infrastructure in Earth orbit, knows that even a tiny pellet of frozen rocket fuel, traveling at an average speed of 25,000 kilometers per hour, could shatter something like a solar panel into several larger pieces, which in turn could go on to cause some serious damage to an orbiting space craft. And if that were to happen, then someone somewhere is going to be having a really bad day. So, the job of MASTERM was to provide advance warning to space infrastructure operators of potential collisions so that they would have time to move their assets out of harm's way.

At any moment in time, their model was tracking over one

million objects, both artificial and natural. There was also estimated to be another hundred million or so smaller fragments in orbit: paint flecks, micrometeorites, and such like —but these were much too insubstantial even for MASTERM to track. The objects that they did track, however, ranged from small shards of broken satellites and pellets of frozen rocket fuel, up to dead spacecraft and spent rocket stages, as well as all active space infrastructure currently whizzing around Earth.

LEO, or Low Earth Orbit, is the high traffic zone. A region, around 500 to 2,000 kilometers up, where most of the global communications constellations exist—each consisting of thousands of small satellites and generally referred to as the Datasphere. Situated between 2,000 and 35,000 kilometers up is the Medium Earth Orbit, aka MEO, where the space stations, refueling depots, and space hotels all live. Further up, above 35,000 kilometers, is the Geosynchronous Earth Orbit, aka GEO, and is populated by mostly global weather and Earth observation assets, space-based solar power stations, and quite a number of older communications satellites. All this space infrastructure is tracked by MASTERM and kept safe—every single day. Except today. Today, a butterfly flapped its wings.

When Dr. Han Sundar awoke on the morning after the Carrington Event, it was to an alert from HUB, his household AI, informing him that the local power grid was down. This did not surprise him; it was not uncommon for the ancient grid to go offline intermittently. He also knew that the solar storm that had occurred while he slept was certain to have caused havoc with Earth-based electrical systems. And since this was the most intense solar storm ever recorded, there were bound to be a few infrastructural casualties. But he was fortunate that his house had ample solar power—the very best, multi-spectrum panels with very high efficiency, and enough energy storage to keep all his household systems running for weeks. So the grid being down did not unduly concern him. What did concern him, however, was the thought of what might face him when he arrived at work in MASTERM that morning. It had the potential to be a total shitshow.

He checked his other alerts with a sense of foreboding. But, to his great relief, no one on the nightshift at MASTERM had pressed the proverbial panic button, yet. If things were really bad, they would have let him know. But his alerts this morning were all just routine. His wife, Sheneese Richmond, had already left for work at the university, around an hour earlier, and had sent a message saying that the traffic was crazy and he should give himself some extra time.

He got up and began to get dressed.

"HUB, can you check if my transport is on its way," he asked the household AI as he made his way to the kitchen to prepare some breakfast.

"Autocab has informed me that they are experiencing some minor network problems this morning and will not be able to fulfill your request. However, they are working hard to resolve the issue and apologize for the inconvenience. Would you like me to inform you when the service has been restored?"

"No, I don't have time to wait. Looks like I'll be using my own car this morning."

"Would you like me to run a diagnostics check?"

"Yes, please do. And could you put my newsfeed up onscreen."

"Certainly."

Han sat down at the kitchen counter with a large mug of coffee and took a bite out of a warm croissant as a section of the faux wooden countertop flickered into life and displayed the current headlines. As he suspected, almost all were details of various power and communications disruptions being experienced all across the northern hemisphere. The severity of the disruption seemed to be collated with the age of the infrastructure. Some areas had complete grid collapse, while others only suffered isolated outages. GPS was being affected in some regions, while others using different geo-positioning constellations were operating just fine. Banking and payment systems were also suffering disruptions and at least two stock exchanges had ceased trading temporarily.

"Han, I'm happy to inform you that I've run the diagnostics check on your car and everything looks normal. However, the autopilot is returning a network error, so you will have to employ manual override if you are planning to use it to get to work."

Manual override, he thought. *It was a while since I had to do that on city streets. Should be interesting.*

"What's the traffic situation like?"

"I assume you want an estimate on travel time to your place of work. Unfortunately, I am having difficulties in accessing this information. My apologies."

Han finished his coffee and rose from his seat at the

counter. "That's okay. I imagine it's going to be chaos if everybody has to manually drive this morning."

"Indeed," replied HUB.

It took Han over an hour to manually do what would normally take thirty minutes on auto-drive. Even though there were far less cars on the road than normal, they all moved slowly and erratically as most people were not accustomed to the mental strain of manually piloting a one-ton machine and trying not to crash into anyone. By the time he got to the MASTERM campus, he was frazzled—not a good start to the day.

He parked the car and made his way to the Control Room building, a large semicircular space with rows of workstations radiating out from a large monitor array that covered the entirety of one wall. As he entered, the scene was a hive of activity. Instinctively, he glanced up at the main monitor that displayed a schematic of Earth almost completely enveloped by thousands of data points, each one an orbital object being tracked in real time. The first thing he noticed was that they had stripped out all data points in MEO and GEO, and were completely focused on LEO, where the mega-communications constellations orbited. This made sense because this was where the vast majority of space hardware was located.

Ted Norton, another of the Senior Analysts, caught his eye and waved at him from one of the workstations down on the central floor. He then jerked his head in the direction of the conference room, signaling to Han that the morning's debrief was about to start. Han grabbed a coffee from a vending machine on the way to the meeting; he was going to need it.

The glass-walled conference room was situated at an elevated position overlooking the main workstation area, with a clear view of the large monitor array. Ted took the floor, quickly glancing at a tablet screen, then at the small group of MASTERM managers and directors—those that were coming off shift, and those that were about to take over.

"Okay, here's the situation as of oh-seven-hundred hours this morning," he paused, took a breath. "I'm not going to sugarcoat this, it's a shitshow." The conference room monitor flickered to life mirroring the primary control room schematic.

"We've been taking in data from early this morning, updates from the main agencies and operators on satellite damage. So far, we have an estimated 3.7 percent attrition rate in LEO... nothing major in MEO... and several of the solar power stations confirmed unresponsive in GEO. Our big concern is what's happening in LEO as this 3.7 percent figure can and will change as the day progresses. All agencies and operators have maintenance crews in orbit and are working to either repair or replace these dead satellites."

Han did a quick calculation in his head: 3.7 percent of approximately fifty-thousand satellites was a boatload of newly created space junk. Even if there were double the maintenance crews working twice as fast, it would take them weeks to tidy up the mess, and a dead satellite was a danger to the entire constellation. The longer it stayed up there, the greater the likelihood something would hit it.

"Any collisions?" he asked.

Ted wiped his forehead. "Yes. There's been quite a few. But our primary concern is that this collision rate is escalating. Therefore, we need to identify and prioritize the debris most at risk of causing an immediate strike to enable the cleanup crews to deal with this efficiently."

All satellites in LEO had small ion thrusters enabling operators on the ground to instruct them to move out of the way in the event of a potential strike. But a dead satellite was a sitting duck. If it was struck, and shattered, then that only increased the danger to all nearby satellites.

"Have we run a simulation yet?" Han asked. Since he was about to take over the day's operations, he would need to run a simulation of potential future events, if one was not already running.

"Yeah, eh... that's the next thing I need to talk about," Ted gave a sigh. "And you're not going to like it." He turned to face the screen, which now displayed a similar schematic but this time speeded up, along with the addition of several numerical values, the most prominent of which read 6.25 KS. Where KS stood for Kessler Syndrome, and the number represented the percentage probability of such an event occurring. This was the highest Han had ever seen it.

The Kessler Syndrome was outlined by NASA scientist Donald J. Kessler in 1978 and considered the possibility of a cascading scenario where debris from one collision caused multiple other collisions and so on, resulting in a runaway event culminating with the complete destruction of all manmade objects in Earth orbit. Effectively rendering these orbital zones unusable.

However, no one back then could possibly have conceived of the hundreds of thousands of objects that now occupied the space above Earth's atmosphere. The Kessler Syndrome was no longer just a theory but a potential reality if alert systems like MASTERM did not perform their function. And the risk was not just the total loss of an orbital plain, but the creation of an impenetrable barrier for all space travel to and from Earth. It was an ever-present existential threat that literally hung over the heads of human civilization. If all communications satellites were to suddenly become extinct, with no way to rebuild, then the prospects for humanity would be catastrophic.

The simulation on the main screen began to progress through time, and as it did, the KS number began to increase dramatically. At fourteen hours out, its rate of increase began to slow. At twenty-six hours, it leveled out at 16.52 KS, then began to drop.

Ted paused the simulation at this point. "As you all know, we are obliged to issue an advisory evacuation of all nonessential personnel in Earth orbit, once the KS number reaches ten. If this simulation pans out, then that will be issued in seven hours."

There was a collective gasp in the room as this potential reality sank in with the group.

"And Luna, what about all the people up there?" someone asked.

Han answered this one. "We just issue the advisory. It's up to the agencies and operators to act on it."

"And where do we need to get to for a compete evacuation. I mean everybody, all personnel?" someone else asked.

"When KS hits 17," said Ted.

"So potentially we could reach that in a little over twenty-four hours?"

"Potentially," he confirmed.

"Oh my god, this could get serious real quick," someone said. A concern that was echoed around the room.

Ted raised a hand to settle everyone down. "It could, but it would be wise for us not to overreact. Let's just stick to the data and keep our heads cool. And it goes without saying that we don't broadcast this information inadvertently to any unauthorized individuals, especially family. You all know how the messaging grapevine works, before you know it, the press will be publishing apocalyptic headlines, causing unnecessary panic."

The meeting ended shortly after with Ted handing over to Han with a handshake, heavy with solemn gravitas. "Good luck, Han. Hate to be leaving you with all this to deal with, but I'm just dead on my feet." He leaned in a little closer and said, almost in a whisper, "Eh... it might be wise to take a closer look at the input data for that simulation," he broke off, giving Han what he could only describe as a conspiratorial look, as if, based on his years of experience, he knew that the simulation was not telling the whole story. He turned and walked out of the Control Room, not once giving it a second glance. Han retreated to his work-desk and began doing exactly as Ted suggested.

The first thing he noticed was not all tracking stations were online, which could potentially introduce a margin of error. Yet, he was not overly concerned with this as there was plenty of redundancy built into the system. Having multiple data sources simply acted to confirm observations by another. He then turned his attentions to the ongoing cleanup operation. Multiple maintenance crews were already in LEO servicing dead satellites, and they took instructions from MasterMind, as it worked tirelessly to calculate the optimal schedule. Along with physical crews there were also a swarm of autonomous sweeper craft that cleaned up smaller debris on an ongoing basis. All seemed to be working as expected—or were they?

He wondered if the MasterMind simulation could be working under the assumption that all these sweeper craft were operating as normal. If one of the machines got its brains fried during the storm, then the simulation wouldn't know until the ground operators fed it the data. He then checked the feed for this data input and was stunned to find that it was still offline. That would mean the simulation was working with potentially erroneous data.

"Shit," he said out loud as he sat back in his seat and stared at the screen. *I wonder,* he thought. *What if the sweepers suffered the same attrition rate as the satellites?*

He bent to the interface again and instigated a new simulation, privately, for his eyes only. This time he gave it a 3.7 percent attrition rate for the sweepers and sat back. He didn't have long to wait. After twenty minutes, it was clear that they were in a runaway cascade of orbital destruction. The KS number was rising exponentially, there was no slowing down, it just kept going. He didn't need to keep running the simulation to know the ultimate outcome. Han hit the kill icon to stop it, sat back, and took a moment to think this through.

But he was not trying to figure out some clever solution that would tip the balance and halt the destruction happening up in Earth orbit, some way he could single-handedly prevent the oncoming communications apocalypse. No, he was trying to figure out the conversation he was going to have with his wife, very soon, and how to not sound too crazy.

CHAPTER 14
NO GOOD OPTIONS

Selene spent most of the afternoon in crisis management mode dealing with the walkout of the CASA delegation from the Historic Monuments session and their desire to return to Earth immediately. They had somehow got into their heads that the Axial Luxor had sustained significant damage during the solar storm and that the life support systems were failing. It had taken Selene almost an hour of probing until they finally came out with it.

She suspected that someone had got to them by providing faked data reports and convincing them that the danger was real. Who was responsible for this misinformation they wouldn't say, but she had her suspects, chief among them being the anti-Luna factions that had been disrupting talks for years. The very reason that the grand session was being held up here was so that the interference by these reactionaries would be minimized. Yet, they had still found a way.

How many others have been infected? she wondered. How much erroneous information was slushing around in the background of these talks and how much was being taken seriously? It was a problem. Not because some people believed this garbage, but because most people suspected all information, even that which was true. This made the business of coming to a collective agreement all the more difficult when most of the time was taken up on simply getting alignment on all the versions of reality that existed between the different parties.

In the end, Selene had managed to get all the other parties around the table to assure the CASA delegation that the hotel was perfectly safe and that there was simply no truth to these rumors. However, it helped that Selene offered a concession that now brought two of their own sites on to the protected monuments final list. It was effectively a territorial gain for them, albeit a small one.

By the time Selene had dragged herself back to her hotel suite later that evening, she was utterly exhausted by the day's proceedings. Yet, despite all the turmoil, she was still buoyed up by the prospect of reclaiming Moon Base Delta. The final vote was in two days' time, and if she could persuade FISA to move on Xilinex demands, then a new Lunar Accord would be achieved, and her legacy secured. She kicked off her shoes, slumped down on the sofa, and let her mind and body relax for a moment before checking her personal messages. She was hoping to get an update on the status of her nephew and his fellow crew out at the old Lunar Gateway. The wall screen opposite her flickered to life and a stream of message alerts started scrolling up. She gestured at one from Jean Reizen over at Central Maintenance and tapped to view it. His head and shoulders appeared.

"Hey, Selene. I've just got an update for you on the Aurora maintenance ship. The good news is we have reestablished contact, and you'll be happy to hear that they're all okay. However, the ship did suffer some damage from the storm. Comms is out, but they jerry-rigged an antenna for VHF. Other subsystems are also out, including navigation and flight control. But..." he paused for a moment, collecting his thoughts. "They have a major problem with their fusion core," he let this sentence rest for a beat before continuing. "We're working through the options at the moment. But as soon as you get a chance please contact me and I can talk more freely." The message ended.

More freely. What does he mean by that? she wondered.

She gestured at the screen to bring up Jean's details, then instigated a call. A few seconds later, he appeared on screen.

"Selene," he nodded.

"I've opened a secure channel."

"Good. Eh... we have a... potential situation."

"Go on," Selene was not liking the sound of this.

"From what we can gather, the Aurora maintenance ship has suffered significant damage to the plasma containment subsystem of its fusion core. We've not been able to assess the extent of the damage as we have no data connectivity with the ship. All we've got is voice telemetry over VHF. However, by their own estimates, they've got around seven hours before... containment failure."

"You're joking me," Selene sat bolt upright on the sofa. "I presume Central has a plan to rescue them before that happens?"

Jean screwed his mouth up and took a breath. "Eh... it turns out the soonest we can get a rescue ship out there is ten hours, maybe nine at a pinch. Everything was grounded during the storm, we've just got nothing out there," he shook his head, then raised a hand. "But... they have a plan. They're currently in a LOP-G orbit, five hours from perigee over the lunar north pole. That's the closest they'll be. So they're going to execute a retro-burn to drop them out of orbit and land down on the surface. They estimate they can do it in six hours."

Selene stood up and moved closer to the screen. She looked at Jean for a moment. "You think it will work?"

"High probability, and Yuna Djinn, their flight officer, is very experienced. If anyone can do it, she can."

Selene nodded, "Okay, I see. So where do they come down? Do we have any resources close to them?"

"Eh, yes... well, that could be a bit tricky, considering the ship might... violently disassemble an hour or so after they land, they are opting for a more isolated area."

"Well, that makes sense. So what's the issue? Just get a rescue ship out to them."

"We will, absolutely. In fact, we're getting one ready as we speak. The issue is that they have limited landing options, considering most of the eastern side of their flight path is SINO."

"Oh god, they don't want to land anywhere in that territory, you know how paranoid they are. SINO would just use it against us any way they can. We could be negotiating for a long time just to get them released. Emergency landing or not."

"Agreed, and the crew are acutely aware of this. So they've opted for the area surrounding Moon Base Delta."

Selene froze. While she was seriously concerned for the safety for her nephew and his fellow crew, landing at that base could cause some real problems for her negotiations. "Eh... that option also comes with its own set of problems. It's a politically sensitive site."

"But it's effectively neutral territory. And there's an internationally recognized shelter maintained there. It's clearly the best option."

"Yes, yes, of course. But it's only neutral because nobody can go anywhere near it without universal agreement by all the agencies that were involved in building it. And..." Selene wondered how much to reveal to Jean around the Xilinex offer. "There are, let's just say, very delicate backchannels at work at the moment."

"Be that as it may, Selene, but we're not the ones flying the ship. It's up to the crew to decide what's best for their survival. If they have to land there, then so be it."

"Yes, yes, you're right. It's just... oh, never mind. Just keep me posted."

"Will do. And don't worry. Yuna has got this, they'll get down okay."

"Thanks, I hope so." The call ended.

Selene began to pace, something she always did when there

was a complex problem she needed to work through. After a while, she decided her best bet was to try and head off any political blowback from this unscheduled landing at the Moon Base Delta site by informing Xilinex and SINO immediately. She would also need to communicate with the other agencies, but they were a lot easier to deal with. None of them possessed the stratospheric levels of state paranoia that SINO did. She gave a long sigh, sat back down on the sofa, and sent a message to her assistant, Nicci, to get her ass in here pronto.

CHAPTER 15
LUNA

Mackenzie was possessed. Now that she had accepted the decision of the crew to try and land the crippled craft at Moon Base Delta, she threw herself into the mission with amplified gusto—maybe that's why she was a ship's captain. There was a myriad of tasks that needed to be accomplished even before Yuna attempted the initial retro-burn. She cracked the whip and got everybody to work.

Alice ran the numbers on power consumption and containment degradation, identifying any subsystem, no matter how insignificant, that could be safely powered down—anything that could buy them more time. It was a similar process to the one they employed during the solar storm, when they hunkered down in the cargo bay, but this time, Alice was taking no prisoners, everything was a target.

Renton, along with Becker, spent their time physically shutting down each of the various systems. Some they could do simply from a workstation, but for others they had to get their hands dirty—removing paneling, tracing wiring, and manually isolating systems.

Matteo liaised with Central over their only functioning radio channel. They would be sending a rescue ship to that location to pick them up. However, this wouldn't arrive for at least two hours after Yuna had estimated their touchdown at the moon base.

Their plan was to evacuate the ship as soon as they landed, head for the shelter—which would be a few kilometers away—and hold up there until the rescue ship arrived. That meant making sure that everyone's EVA suit was fully resourced. It was Mackenzie who volunteered for this task. It seemed she needed something to do other than hovering over everyone else, ramping up their anxiety levels.

Yuna took up residence on the flight deck and checked and double-checked her calculations. By her own admission, she had never manually calculated a flight path since her days back in training, nobody did. All this was done by AI, and for the most part it was fully automated. Mostly she flew the ship by simply entering predefined cislunar coordinates and the onboard systems did the rest. Even docking was automated. Rarely did any flight officer manually operate a craft, except for where minor adjustments might be needed in negotiating a congested shipyard, and even then, she would just be using the tiny gas reaction thrusters.

An hour before the scheduled retro-burn, they all assembled on the flight deck and strapped themselves into their respective seats. All had full EVA suits on with the visors open. The deck was dark, with the only light coming from the instrument panel. Through the windshield, Renton could see the bright daylight surface of the moon speed by as they approached the perigee of their orbit.

"Ten minutes to retro-burn!" Yuna shouted out. "Reorientating the ship."

With that, she nudged on the gas reaction controls and the craft began to spin around to face the opposite direction of travel. They were now in effect flying backward. Through the forward window, the Moon's surface stretched out behind them.

"Get ready!" Yuna shouted out again. "In three... two... one..."

Renton felt himself being slammed back into his seat as the thrusters ignited, decelerating the craft. The burn continued for quite some time as he carefully watched the data on the central flight deck monitor. The craft's speed over the ground was dropping, as was their elevation. Lunar gravity was now acting on the ship, pulling it down toward the surface. The other metric that he, and all the others, kept a close eye on was their fuel reserves. They were burning through it at an alarming rate. It was as if Yuna had decided to simply fly the ship to its destination using brute force, rather than a slow gradual de-orbit. But time was not on their side, she had to get the ship down, and soon; there was no room for fancy orbital mechanics.

Renton experienced a sudden physical release as the engines finally cut-off, and he began to feel the downward gravitational pull of the Moon. Outside, through the forward window, the lunar surface filled the view, still speeding away from them.

"Time to suit up," Yuna announced. "Switching to suit comms." She closed the visor on her EVA suit helmet, as did the rest of the crew.

Renton monitored his suit stats, checking for any alerts as it booted up. All okay, he was good for at least five hours.

"Get ready for second burn," Yuna's voice crackled through the helmet comm, and again Renton felt himself being vacuum-packed into the back of his seat. The landscape outside slowed noticeably.

"Coming up on Tranquility," Mackenzie announced.

The engines shut down suddenly.

"Shit," someone said. Renton thought it must have been the captain as he'd never heard Yuna utter an expletive—ever. Yet, it did sound like her voice, and if that was the case, then something was very wrong.

"Yuna, we're coming in too fast." That was definitely the captain.

"I've lost power... I've lost power... no engines... I can't slow us down," Yuna was clearly panicked. She was frantically stabbing at various cockpit controls. "Damnit."

The engines fired back up again but sounded different. "Okay, we've got landing engines. Going to flip us around and put our nose up. We'll be coming in at a very steep angle."

Renton had no clue what was going on. He just gripped the armrests and tried to breathe. The craft began to shake violently and he felt as if his teeth would fall out. Outside, the lunar surface rose to meet them at an alarming rate.

The engines died again.

They hit the surface with a bone shattering thump only to be bounced back up off the surface and there was a moment where time seemed to stand still. Renton gripped the armrests tighter waiting for gravity to do its thing. They slammed back down onto the surface again, this time sliding along, gouging out a deep furrow in the soft lunar regolith. The landscape outside was replaced with utter blackness. Then another bone shattering thump as the ship slammed into something solid. He was pressed hard against the seat's restraining straps almost to the point of breaking ribs. He felt the rear of the ship rise, and rise, and finally the entire craft seemed to flip over on its side and come crashing back down again with a sickening cacophony of crunching metal accompanied by a violent swirl of flying debris—some of which slammed into the side of his helmet. He blacked out.

CHAPTER 16
INCARCERATION

Consciousness came to Renton in waves of slowly increasing clarity. First came muffled, distant sounds, then voices, calling his name.

"Renton, Renton?"

Then came pain, searing pain, stabbing at his temples. The reality of it pulled him into full consciousness. He opened his eyes and took a moment to orientate himself. He was not on the flight deck of the Aurora. He was somewhere else, some other ship—strange and unfamiliar.

He raised a hand to his temple to assess the damage but was prevented by another hand gripping his arm. Words were spoken to him that he didn't understand, yet the meaning seemed to be that he should lie still. He turned his head instinctively toward the voice, blinking to try and clear the fog of his vision and gain some clarity. The source was dressed in a medic's uniform with what looked to be the insignia of Xiang

Zu, a corporate mining concession of SINO, displayed on the breast pocket.

Renton tried to speak but his jaw hurt when he tried to move it. "Others?" he managed. "The others?"

"Renton. Thank god you're okay." He turned his head to see Yuna's face hover over him. Her helmet was off and her EVA suit stripped to the waist, her left arm was in a sling.

"I'm sorry, so sorry," she touched his shoulder with the hand of her good arm. "I shouldn't have tried to land. Now..." her sentence trailed off and she lowered her head shaking it at the same time.

The fog of Renton's vision was dissipating and he glanced around to get some understanding of his surroundings. It was an evac-shuttle, medical, but clearly not FISA. Several figures moved around, similarly dressed to the medic that was attending to him. He could see some of his crew lying on gurneys.

"Becker..." Yuna spoke again. "Becker's dead," she shook her head again. "Should not have tried to land."

"Finish. No touch." The medic attending to Renton pointed at the dressing on his head and wagged his finger. He moved off, content that his patient had been satisfactorily addressed.

Renton lifted himself up on one elbow, with considerable effort, and tried to engage with the clearly distraught flight officer. "The others?"

"I'm okay." It was Matteo who now spoke. He came into view behind Yuna. "Alice too. She's just a bit shaken. Resting, sedated. But Mackenzie, she's bad, as far as we can tell."

Renton tested his body by sitting up on the gurney. Finding

that it didn't hurt too much, he swung his legs over the edge, and did exactly what the medic had told him not to. He touched his head and felt a mass of bandages circumnavigating his skull. Behind these was nothing but pain ranging from dull to sharp depending on where he prodded. He glanced around and asked in a low voice. "Is Becker really dead? What happened?"

Yuna wiped a tear from her eye. "Yes. His EVA suit failed, loss of oxygen. He was dead before these people showed up," she nodded over at the medics, who were scrutinizing scans of what Renton assumed to be Mackenzie.

"We had a hull breech, lost our environment, and his suit failed. That's what... killed Becker, we think. We were trying to evacuate everyone from the wreckage when these guys showed up. Thank God, otherwise..." Matteo shook his head.

"We overflew the target landing zone and ended up in SINO territory," Yuna shook her head again. "I shouldn't..."

"It's not your fault," Renton stopped her. "We all agreed. Anyway, what choice did we have. Attempt a landing or get vaporized."

Yuna wiped her face.

Matteo gestured toward the medics. "These people are from Xiang Zu, one of SINO's corporates. Not very friendly, but at least they got us out before the ship blew."

"Where are they taking us?" asked Renton.

"No idea. But I'm pretty sure it's not where we want to go."

"What a mess," Renton shook his head and regretted it.

"I'm sorry," Yuna was clearly taking it hard.

"Yuna," Renton reached out and clutched her hand. "Blame

the solar storm, or all the mishaps that led up to it. But this is not your fault."

She sniffed.

"Where's Alice?" he asked.

Matteo turned and gestured behind him. "She's on a gurney in there, getting a chest x-ray. Broken ribs, we think."

Renton felt a sudden change in the motion of the craft. A medic approached them waving his hands and shouting. "Sit, sit. Landing. Now!"

Matteo and Yuna returned to their seats while Renton was unceremoniously pushed back down on the gurney by the medic and strapped in. He felt the craft drop in altitude, bank to starboard—the tone of its engines shifting, mirroring his own shifting mood. It was all messed up. Becker dead. How could that be? He had trouble getting his head around it, imagining that at any moment the chief engineer would wander in and crack a joke. But, it was not to be; he was gone. As for Mackenzie, even though he really didn't like the captain, he still felt for her precarious medical condition. She didn't deserve that, nor did any of the rest of them for that matter. No one had escaped injury, either physically or emotionally. *So what now?* he thought as he heard the airlock doors open and the trample of feet.

Several armed SINO operatives barged into the medbay where Renton was being untethered by a medic. At the head of this incursion strode a SINO official, unarmed and dressed in what must have passed for a business suit in these here parts. He observed Renton over the edge of a pair of old-school gold-rimmed glasses, as if he were a specimen in a lab. Some instruction was given to the armed operatives, followed by a momentary argument with the medics. Seemingly, the Xiang Zu people who operated the ship were not happy with this intrusion.

A few moments later, the rest of the crew who were capable of walking were assembled in the central medbay, prompted by several weapons of a compact railgun design pointed in their direction. Renton was happy to see that Alice looked okay, aside from a thick bandage wrapped around her waist. He was hauled off the gurney to a standing position alongside the others. Glances were exchanged between the crew, but no one spoke. There was a palpable air of threat emanating from this SINO official and his cadre of guards, not just directed at the FISA crew but also at the medics in the rescue ship, whose captain was currently being berated by the official. An argument of sorts had erupted, the details of which were hidden from Renton and the others, as it was being conducted in Mandarin. Clearly, the medical commander was not happy about what these guys were up to and was letting them know. But the argument suddenly ended when the official produced an identification badge along with a small document, which the commander quickly read. Her eyes widened, she took a step back, and bowed to the official. It seemed the argument was well and truly over. The official now turned to face the crew, who had been pushed and prodded into a standing line.

"You will be taken now for processing," he gestured to one of the operatives to lead the way.

"Where are you taking us?" Renton ventured.

The official gave a disarming smile and raised a hand.

"Where you can be more comfortable. A place where we can talk. Come," he gestured with a ringed index finger.

They were marched out of the medevac ship through an airlock tunnel that opened out into a cavernous but spartan loading area. It had a bleak industrial feel, all concrete and steel, and harsh lighting. They moved along this area through a series of corridors, each one slightly less bleak than the last, until finally they entered a large windowless room that seemed to be an accommodation module. Several bunks occupied one wall, along with some utilitarian furniture: a long table, bench seating, storage lockers, and a sanitary facility.

The official gestured at the table. "Sit."

The crew did as instructed, still exchanging glances at each other. The official sat at the head of the table; two operatives stood at the door. He took out a small comms unit and placed it carefully on the table in front of him.

"My name is Chen Gongbo, Director of Internal Security for all SINO facilities both here on the lunar surface and in orbit. You will remain here for the duration of the investigation."

"What do you mean by *investigation*? Our ship was damaged during the solar storm, we crash-landed, and we need to get back to base." Renton found himself speaking before he had even thought about it.

"The reactor onboard your ship went critical shortly after you were all extracted from the wreckage. As a result, we cannot rule out that you were on a sabotage mission that went badly wrong."

"That's ridiculous," Matteo jumped up from his seat and jerked a finger at Chen. He was rewarded for his outburst with the butt of a railgun being slammed into his back, then being forced back down on the seat by the two operatives.

"It would be wise," continued Chen, "for you all to comply with my requests or I will be forced to restrain you." He cast a cold eye at each of them in turn.

Renton felt the anger rise up inside him, wanting to lash out at this officious prick, but his rational side got the better of him and he remained still and silent, as did the others.

"This is unacceptable," said Renton in a measured, matter-of-fact voice. "You know our ship was compromised. You are just playing politics, using us as bargaining chips."

Chen stood up, ignoring Renton's accusation. He pointed over to a shelf where several jumpsuits were stacked. "You will need to remove your EVA suits and change into the garments we have provided for you. Guards will return in twenty minutes to collect them. Make sure it's done." He strode out the door, leaving the crew to contemplate their incarceration.

CHAPTER 17

DATASPHERE

I t hadn't taken Dr. Han Sundar long to figure out what he needed to do, apart from having a long conversation with his wife, Sheneese—but that would be later. First, he packaged up the data from the simulation he had run earlier, encrypted it, and sent it to Professor Lars Henriksen of the Heliophysics Division at FISA—with a note for a second opinion. Assuming that his analysis held up, he trusted that Henriksen would disseminate it to the necessary people and hopefully they could act on it before it was too late for the lunar population.

Second, he sent the same files to Lieutenant General Philip Grant who oversaw Strategy and Analysis at Space Division, the military wing of FISA. Again, he knew that this would then be forwarded to the necessary departments, both up and down the food chain. He also referenced the FISA professor for authentication, as he himself would be uncontactable for a while.

Then he cleared out his bank account, transferring all his money to his personal area network. Since most in-person transactions were still done over near-field communication, he could still pay for things even if the wider networks were down —for a time. He then purged all his personal data on the local area network.

Finally, he picked up a photograph of himself and his wife spending time at their weekend retreat up in the mountains and shoved it into his bag along with the framed quotation that hung on the wall behind his desk.

It was lunchtime so no one commented as he left the building and made his way to the parking lot. He got into his car and immediately contacted Sheneese. To his surprise, she was at home. Then again, it shouldn't have come as that much of a surprise. The university where she worked as an associate professor of physics did not have an independent energy supply, so it was one-hundred percent reliant on the grid, which went down in that area around mid-morning.

"The power went just as I got in this morning. Part of a rolling blackout they said. Took me hours to get back, no auto-cabs, people driving manually. Absolutely nuts. In the end, one of the students drove me. Very nice of her," her voice sounded weary. "But what about you? You must be having a pretty bad day over there after the storm."

"Eh, yeah, it's been hectic. Listen, Sheneese, I think it might be a good idea if we head off to the observatory for a few days. Just until things settle down."

"Now? Don't they need you over there? Wouldn't you just be running out on them?"

"The AI, MasterMind, is mostly running the show now. Remember I'm just an analyst. So, why don't you pack a bag and I'll be back in an hour or so depending on the traffic."

"I'd love to, but will they really let you go at a time like this?"

"Yes, yes, it's fine. See you soon."

"Well, okay then."

That would be the easy conversation, the crazy one would come later, when they got to the observatory.

The observatory was a rather grandiose term for what was in essence a collection of rudimentary concrete buildings clustered atop a mountain, accessed via a long and winding dirt track, around two-hundred kilometers from the city. It had at one point in its life been an actual astronomical observatory belonging to the university. It still had the Equatorial room, a great metal dome that opened and rotated to observe the nighttime sky.

The original structure came into being around two centuries ago, through a substantial endowment to the university. Back then, the sky was less polluted by the lights of the city, but over the years, even with upgrades to bigger and better telescopes, the city eventually won out. The observatory was decommissioned, the astronomical instruments removed, and the buildings sold to a property developer with more imagination than good sense. It lay empty for decades as its new owner failed to find a way to circumvent the strict planning laws surrounding the property.

That was until Han's father had bought it as a derelict wreck and turned it into a weekend retreat and summer getaway.

When his father passed away, three years ago, most of his estate was liquidated to pay off debts, and what was left was split up between the siblings. Since no one in his family wanted this crazy old place, it ended up in Han's ownership as his portion of the estate. Initially, he tried to sell it, but all the realtors he contacted said the same thing: the property was complicated, meaning there was no market for such an odd building, in such a remote place, with such restrictions on what could be done to the structure. In the end, he kept it, and he was damn glad he did.

Traffic was not quite as bad as he had feared. GPS was still glitching so most of the delivery vehicles had not been operating, which freed up a lot of road bandwidth. Also, the traffic cops were out in force, directing, keeping things moving. Still, he passed a lot of accidents. A lot of irate drivers standing by their crumpled cars wondering when this nightmare day would end.

Sheneese was already packing a bag when he got back. So it didn't take them long to get themselves organized and back into the car. That was when she started asking the hard questions.

"What's going on, Han? And don't tell me it's all under control because it clearly isn't."

He sighed, gripped the steering yoke, and considered what to say. He then reached behind to grab his bag from the back seat. He pulled out the framed quotation he had hung behind his desk. He handed it to her. "You're familiar with chaos theory?"

She glowered at him, for asking such a stupid question.

"Okay, well a butterfly has just flapped its wings."

"Meaning?" she replied, still glowering.

"Meaning a cascading chain of destruction is now happening in Earth orbit," he pointed upward.

She stopped glowering, her face morphing into one of incredulity.

He activated the car and began moving. "An advisory has just been issued by MASTERM for the evacuation of all nonessential personnel in Earth orbit and cislunar space."

"You're joking me."

"That advisory was based on a predictive model that they ran this morning. But the thing is..." he paused for a beat as he entered onto the main highway, traffic was heavier here, and moving slow. "When I checked the model. I found a number of errors. I re-ran the simulation, correcting for these errors, and found... eh... a significant difference in the rate of entropy," he looked over at her. "We're looking at a full-blown Kessler Syndrome."

She raised a hand to her mouth, staring wide-eyed at him. "Are you sure? Could you have made a mistake in the calculations?"

He shook his head. "No, if anything I was being conservative. I was only looking at the network constellations that make up the Datasphere. Before I left, I did a quick check on the status of assets in GEO, where the solar power stations are."

"And?"

"Most of those in the northern hemisphere are down. That's

partly why we're experiencing rolling blackouts. But all the rest will be gone soon, there's no way they can escape destruction."

"My god. Do you know what this means for..." her sentence trailed off.

"That's why I think it might be a good idea to head for the hills," he gave a wry smile.

Sheneese was quiet for a while as she digested this news, no doubt working through all the ramifications. "We're going to need to stock up," she finally said. "And I don't mean enough for the weekend."

"I've been thinking about that. The reality is things are only going to get worse, and probably very quickly. But we have a window of opportunity before the payment systems grind to a halt. I suggest we make a few stops, procure as much as possible, and wait it out until some semblance of control has been re-imposed."

"You're talking social breakdown. Do you really think it will come to that?"

"At any moment in time, there is only around two weeks' worth of food stocked in the stores in any big city. Restocking is automatically routed through the distribution warehouses, then packed by robots, delivered by autonomous vehicles, and paid for by electronic funds transfer—and all that infrastructure operates through the Datasphere. Once that link is broken, the entire house of cards collapses," he looked over at her again. "My guess is we've got less than two weeks before society begins to turn very, very nasty."

CHAPTER 18
KESSLER SYNDROME

Selene Mene studied the 3D holographic map of the lunar surface as Alan E. Dyson outlined the area where the FISA maintenance ship had crash-landed. They were in a hastily convened emergency meeting with a few other FISA people, all gathered around the boardroom table in their sector of the Axial Luxor.

"This is the exact spot where they came down," Dyson pointed at an illuminated pulsating marker on the 3D map. "East of the Couchy I Rille on the edge of Tranquility, around five kilometers inside SINO territory. Most of this region is under concession to the Xiang Zu Corporation, the Helium-3 mining consortium. They claim some of their equipment was damaged when the ship's fusion core went boom..." he paused for a moment before continuing his brief report. "Becker De Havilland, the chief engineer, is reportedly dead, and Captain Mackenzie

Arnold is critical. The rest of the crew are a bit battered but will be okay."

"What a goddamn mess," Dale Graham shook his head. "Has De Havilland's family been informed?"

"Not yet," Dyson shook his head. "We thought it might be best to sit on it for a day or two."

"Well, since we all know that the spying and sabotage charges are just a load of crap, the question is what do they want?" Selene threw this out to everyone.

"Nothing official, as yet," said Dale.

"And the backchannels?" Selene prompted.

"Too early," said Dyson. "I suspect they're still formulating their shopping list."

"Could they pull out of the talks?" asked Dale.

"Unlikely. If they wanted to, they would have done so already," Selene replied. "They need this accord just as much as everyone else. All we can do now is keep the backchannels open and wait for the demands to arrive. The final vote is in less than two days, so it won't be long in coming."

"Eh... we may have another problem." Everyone looked over at Professor Henriksen, from Heliophysics. They had all assumed he had joined the meeting for no other reason than by virtue of his seniority in FISA.

"What sort of problem?" prompted Dyson, with a note of frustration in his voice.

"We've just got a notification from MASTERM, the space debris tracking network." He looked up from his tablet screen, his eyes wide. "They've just issued an advisory evacuation alert for non-essential personnel in Earth orbit."

No one spoke for a moment; everyone's jaw dropped. Dyson slumped back down on his seat. "Seriously?"

Henriksen gestured at his tablet and brought the alert up on the main monitor for all to see. "Look for yourself. I kid you not."

Again, a momentary silence permeated the room as they all tried to comprehend this bombshell.

"Just be aware," he continued, in a decidedly academic manner, "that this is an advisory notice. Not an actual command. No point in getting people panicked. You know what chaos the media can create with this type of information if taken out of context."

"Professor, be straight with us," Selene leaned forward in her seat and gave the Director a measured stare. "How bad is it back on Earth?"

Henriksen screwed his mouth up, hesitating. "Well... it's both good and bad."

"Good and bad," said Selene, with a hint of sarcasm.

"If you've been following the newsfeeds on the Datasphere, you've all seen and heard the reports of outages, blackouts, brownouts, communications disruptions, and so on. Meaning that a significant amount of ground infrastructure was damaged during the solar event. Now, while that's a pain in the rear-end, it's still manageable—maintenance crews can get it all back working again over time. That's the good part," he shifted in his seat. "The bad part is when we get to orbital infrastructure. Specifically, how fast it takes to repair dead satellites before they become a danger to other spacecraft."

"I think we have to face the facts. This advisory is going to get people panicked, no doubt about that," said Dyson, clearly frustrated by this new development.

"It's just a precaution, nothing more," Henriksen gave a gesture of appeasement with both hands. "It's based on a projection, a model of the future. It has not actually happened yet. In fact, they could reverse it in a few hours as new data comes in."

"Either way, we'll need to convene a meeting of the full FISA board immediately and decide how we're going to action this," said Dyson, his frustration lessening a little.

"You can't start sending people home just yet, not until after the vote," Selene looked from one to the other, searching their faces for confirmation.

"Selene's right. What we need to do is keep calm, push the message that it's just advisory, no big deal." Dale was doing what he did, managing the story. "We've come this close, only another day and a half and we've got the New Lunar Accord."

"What if we urge that the vote be moved forward?" suggested Dyson.

"It's possible, but would it just be feeding the panic if we did that?" cautioned Dale.

"It would," said Selene. "Also, the other parties might think we're just playing games, that this alert is simply a fabrication by FISA to get a quick compromise resolution," she sighed, then saw that Henriksen was more interested on something on his tablet than the discussion. He had been gesturing at it continuously as if he were manipulating a data set.

"Professor, what do you think?"

He glanced up. "Eh... sorry. But I've just been digging a little deeper into this alert. A good friend of mine, Dr. Han Sundar, is one of the senior analysts over at MASTERM, and he's sent me an alternative model for a second opinion. This is his own projection, which he claims is more accurate, and... well, it's... eh... troubling," he looked up from the screen.

"What do you mean, troubling?" Dyson asked, with a note of trepidation in his voice.

Henriksen looked back at his screen for a moment, frowning and shaking his head. "I can't quite believe it myself, but Dr. Sundar's model is showing a sufficient density of orbital debris to create a collision cascade, a runaway event, a point of no return," explained Henriksen. "The destruction of almost everything in orbit."

"That's impossible. It can't be," Dyson sat up, his face a mask of shock.

Selene's mouth hung, she struggled to get any words out. "Are... are you absolutely sure?"

Henriksen went back to the screen, rubbed his chin, and shook his head. "That's what it's projecting, one-hundred percent."

"How long, before this happens?" asked Selene.

"It's already happened. New collision debris is being created faster than it can be cleared by the crews and robots. We're looking at an exponential graph," he gestured at his screen with a quick deft-hand movement and a chart blossomed out on the main monitor.

"According to Dr. Sundar's model, we have approximately ten days until the debris cloud becomes impassable. Anything traveling up or down to Earth after that has an extremely high likelihood of being impacted."

There was complete silence in the room as all present simply stared at the graph trying to find a way to prove it wasn't true.

"My god." Dale, who had been standing up for most of the meeting collapsed back down on to his seat.

"Are you saying that Earth orbit will be nothing but a cloud of dust, and that nothing can pass through it?" Dyson asked, clearly not fully comprehending the enormity of the situation.

"In a word, yes. You need to understand that the general speed of an object in that debris field will be traveling at approximately seven meters per second. Even a fleck of paint can cause damage at that velocity."

"Wait a minute," Dale raised a hand. "How do we know this information is true, that it's not some... I don't know... hack. Someone feeding us false data so we get all panicky and do something stupid."

Selene sensed that Dale was just clutching at straws. Yet the ramifications of this analysis were so existential that she began to clutch at this same straw herself.

Henriksen shook his head. "Dr. Sundar is a personal friend of mine. This came in over our secure channel, quantum encrypted, extremely high probability of authenticity."

"Then maybe he got it wrong, a miscalculation, a program error?" Dyson was also clutching at straws.

"That's what he thought too, hence the reason he sent it to me for a second opinion. But I can find no fault," Henriksen shook his head. "You need to consider that these analysts at MASTERM have been doing this for a very long time. Their tracking data has been keeping Earth orbit safe and functioning for decades."

Again no one spoke for a moment, as each searched for another passing straw.

"Who else has this analysis?" Selene finally asked.

"Everybody has the official evacuation advisory data, that's now public knowledge. This..." Henriksen pointed at the monitor. "This... is just us, and... Lieutenant General Philip Grant over at Space Division, for the moment."

Dyson stood up and leaned on the back of his chair. His face resolute. He looked at the chart for a moment. "I think we have to face some hard facts here. We need an emergency meeting immediately, but..." he said while gesturing at the screen, "the reality is we'll have to start evacuating people from Luna as soon as possible."

"What?" Selene stood up. "Abandon the talks, abandon everything we've built up here? You've got to be joking me."

"I have to agree," said Henriksen. "The writing is on the wall. Anyone who stays here could potentially be trapped with no way to return to Earth."

Selene ran a hand through her hair, slumped back down on her seat, then turned to the professor again. "How long are we talking about? How long before they can clear the debris and get things back to normal?"

Henriksen screwed his mouth up. "Eh... hard to give an exact answer but we're talking years, possibly decades."

"Decades?" Dale looked stunned.

"Yes. You see, eh... there's possibly an even greater threat."

"Than this?" Dyson exclaimed, gesturing at the monitor.

"Yes," Henriksen nodded. "We're talking about the complete destruction of all communication networks in Earth orbit. Think about what that will mean. It could be catastrophic."

"Good god." Dyson sat back down and put his head in his hands. "I can't believe this is happening."

"It's over, isn't it?" Selene said more as a statement than a question. "You're right. The talks, they're finished. All the other parties will be figuring this out just as we are and coming to exactly the same conclusion."

"Agreed, the talks don't matter now," said Dyson. "We've all got bigger problems on our hands."

Again they all were silent as each of them tried in their own way to rationalize this new paradigm shift in the fortunes of humanity. The enormity of what was about to occur needed time to sink in. As Selene considered this, she slowly began to realize the true scale of the catastrophe that was about to befall human civilization. All dreams of creating an interplanetary civilization would be smashed to pieces within a cloud of orbital debris. It would be the end of an era, the end of all that she had worked for her whole life. It was truly hard for her to process.

Then her mind went to Renton, locked up with his crew in some godforsaken mining facility. How would SINO react to this impending disaster? Would they release the crew in time to evacuate?

"We need to find a way to get the maintenance crew out now, before it's too late," she said. "There has to be a way."

The others glanced at her, a little absentmindedly. They were all still processing.

"They'll probably just release them now," said Dyson, waving a hand. "What would be the point of keeping them as a bargaining chip, if there's nothing to bargain for?"

Selene thought about this for a moment. But the more she did, the more she got the feeling that SINO might just see this impending disaster as an opportunity to expand their presence.

"What if SINO don't evacuate?" she said finally. "What if they see it as a strategic opportunity, a way to take total control of Luna?"

"Don't be so dramatic, Selene. That would be suicide," Henriksen almost laughed. "They'd be trapped up here for years, decades, they would probably all die up here."

"I'm not sure that Luna is self-sustaining, Selene," Dyson added. "And without supplies from Earth, how long would they last?"

Selene gave them both a cold look. "You clearly have no concept of the mind of SINO, and some of the other regimes up here—corporate or otherwise. I wouldn't put it past them. But at this point, I really don't care what they do. All I care about is my nephew, Renton. He's my responsibility. I took that on when his parents were killed in a car crash five years ago. My older sister was his mother. I've looked after him and his siblings. I'm not abandoning him. There has to be a way to get him out?"

Dyson shrugged. "You could appeal to SINO's better nature, humanitarian evacuation, you know the drill, go through the backchannels."

Selene thought about this, it seemed like her only option.

What did SINO have to gain by keeping them now. Yet, what she really needed was a plan B.

"We have people embedded with SINO, don't we?"

Dyson gave her a hard look. "That would be a military matter, Selene. That's Space Division. I can't say."

"Then I assume that Space Division will want to get their people out very soon, or they'll be left stranded up here."

Dyson gave her a cautious look. "I would imagine so. Why, what are you getting at?"

"Plan B, just in case SINO decide to bring it to the wire."

Dyson considered this for a moment. "I'll make some... enquiries, but I can't promise anything, you know what the spooks are like. They can be..." but he never got to finish his sentence. At the other side of the table, Dale's face went pale, his forehead beaded in sweat. Suddenly he fell off his seat and made a lunge for a trashcan. Then he threw up.

CHAPTER 19
OPPORTUNITIES

Pompodur Rossen Adarok fumed with barely restrained violence at the vagaries of fate. One minute he was on the cusp of pulling off a deal that would see him, and Xilinex, take a controlling interest in the Moon Base Delta facility, as well as getting the vote of sovereignty for corporate organizations passed unopposed. But no. Some bunch of FISA idiots had to go and crash a maintenance ship into SINO territory and start an international incident. Worse, one of the crew just so happened to be a nephew of the lead negotiator for FISA, Selene Mene. Now SINO had their backs up and had gone completely cold on the Xilinex offer. Maybe they reckoned they could extract everything they wanted from FISA and still keep the moon base parked firmly in limbo. Goddamnit, he had come so close to pulling this off, setting himself up for a position of power here on Luna, and now it was all gone, blown away in a cloud of lunar dust.

FISA, for their part, were reacting badly to this incident. The smug smile had been wiped from their respective faces. As soon as word of the crash, and the subsequent incarceration of the crew on spying charges, had gone public, FISA responded with the release of some hastily crafted bogus evacuation advisory. What the hell were they playing at? Did they really think anyone was going to fall for that bullshit?

Pompodur knew exactly what they were up to, of course. He could see right through it. They used the reports of damage from the solar storm to get everybody panicky, convince them that they had to evacuate—*just a precaution for safety*. No doubt hoping that SINO would release their people on some supposed humanitarian grounds. It was ludicrous.

Yet, he was slightly impressed with the speed at which they got this fiction out into the public domain. Normally, being such a ridiculously bureaucratic organization, it would take them forever to put something like this together. There would be meetings, and discussions, and votes, and buy-ins from all their subagencies and governments. But this came out in double-quick time. *They must be freaking out,* he thought.

It looked desperate, it looked weak. SINO were never going to fall into that trap. Nevertheless, other simple-minded agencies were beginning to take the bait. Idiots. And now that the newsfeeds had got hold of it, the whole thing was being dialed up way past max. There was even talk of a mass evacuation of everyone, not just nonessential personnel. Even talk of social breakdown back on Earth. Fools. But none of this really mattered to Pompodur. SINO now had leverage over FISA and they were going to use it.

Xilinex HQ were disappointed, to say the least. He had failed and he would pay dearly for this almighty screw up. Already, the Xilinex board back on Earth were convening an emergency meeting, no doubt to give him a grilling and he wasn't looking forward to it. He glanced up at the wall monitor in his suite on the Axial Luxor and wondered what was keeping them. The connection should have been established a half hour ago, but there was still nothing popping up on screen. He stabbed at his comms unit and called the local Xilinex techs that were supposed to be getting the conference call up and running.

"What the hell is taking so long? This is the board you're dealing with; you can't keep them waiting like this."

"Sorry, sir. The problem is at the Earth end, satellite disruption, we're working on rerouting, won't be long now."

"It better not." Pompodur stabbed the comms unit again and closed the connection.

He was about to pour himself another drink, just to steady his nerves, when the screen flickered to life and a checkerboard of faces materialized—some quite fuzzy, some still just an avatar. There then ensued a confusion of pixelated chatter before the connection finally stabilized and Lane Zeebos, the current President of Xilinex, opened proceedings. Much to Pompodur's dismay, the first order of business was the rapidly developing situation on the lunar colonies. Pompodur decided to take the initiative—go on the attack and get his word in before anyone else.

"It was just one of those... unfortunate events that can't be predicted. I mean, what are the chances of an FISA maintenance ship crashing in SINO territory?" But he was cut off by Zeebos with a raised hand.

"We know what happened, and yes, it was just an unfortunate random event. But we're not here to talk about that —things have moved on."

Pompodur breathed a sigh of relief, yet it was short lived as he began to consider that the Xilinex board might be taking this FISA evacuation advisory seriously.

"As you know, the solar storm has had a detrimental effect on Earth's orbital infrastructure and our own analysis has indicated this is only going to get worse."

"You're not seriously falling for this FISA evacuation ruse?" he scoffed. Almost as soon as the words were out of his mouth, he began to regret saying them. He needed to get a grip, not show his hand, let the meeting play out.

Zeebos didn't reply. Instead he gave Pompodur a curious look. "You think it's... fictitious?"

"Well, eh... it would seem more like an act of desperation on their part."

There was a split second where Pompodur considered he may have said the wrong thing as the channel's audio muted and the board members conducted a quick discussion amongst themselves. He waited and sweated.

"You're not completely wrong in your assessment, Director Adarok," said Zeebos, when the audio channel unmuted. Pompodur allowed himself to breathe again.

"However, there is a core of truth in this... advisory. The information comes from MASTERM, and although they are affiliated to FISA, they are as close to being an independent entity as it is possible to get these days. Our own analysis supports their assessment. Increasing collision debris has the potential to become a major threat to crewed traffic—hence the advisory notice to evacuate. These collision events are projected to escalate to a point were crewed transit through this debris field will be... impossible.

Pompodur eyes widened. "Seriously?" He couldn't believe it. It was not possible. Then a twinge of panic began to bubble up from his gut.

"But where our analysis diverges is in the length and severity of this event. We suspect that FISA and their associates are pushing the narrative that it will be a decades-long isolation. This suits their agenda, to force SINO's hand. Yet, this is not true. Our analysis shows an isolation period of less than two years, that's how long we estimate it would take to clear up the mess."

"Two years? Oh, I see." He wasn't sure if he did see, he just wanted to sound like he wasn't completely confused at where this was all going.

"In reality, the talks are dead. Panic has set in due to FISA propaganda and many of the agencies operating on and around Luna are withdrawing their people. This is set to dramatically escalate over the next few days."

Pompodur now wondered if he should ask about plans for his own evacuation.

"However, this presents us with a once-in-a-lifetime opportunity. One that we on the board think that you are uniquely positioned to lead."

The twinge of confused panic rumbling in Pompodur's gut

now receded, to be replaced by one of cautious curiosity. What opportunity?

"With lunar facilities denuded of people and effectively left stranded, this will expose them to potential takeover by those agencies that intend to remain."

"SINO," said Pompodur, almost to himself.

"Precisely. Through our intelligence, we have concluded that they will not evacuate, no one is leaving. Furthermore, only a few of their directors know of the true severity of the solar event, they are hiding all knowledge of it from their people. We suspect they are planning to execute a complete takeover of all stranded assets once the evacuation is complete."

Pompodur thought about this for a moment and realized he would do exactly the same thing if he was in their position, it was an obvious next move.

"Needless to say, we are not going to let that happen. To that end, we have dispatched a cohort of... eh, specialists. People who can protect our interests, militarily. We also seek to undermine SINO's cone of silence and begin spreading our own propaganda about the impending disaster throughout their ranks. This will cause them plenty of headaches and will, hopefully, diminish their number."

There was a momentary pause as the board let all this sink in with Pompodur, who had a million-and-one questions running around his head, too many to formulate a coherent response just yet.

"We feel that you are the person best placed to head up this operation since you have leadership experience, you are on the ground—so to speak—and are suitably qualified in the propagation of disinformation. You would, of course, be handsomely rewarded for your loyalty to the Xilinex Corporation."

"Eh," said Pompodur, as his brain tried frantically to make sense of this proposal.

"We understand that it will mean a two-year commitment, there will be no way to return to Earth during that time. But when you do, you will be very, very rich. Not only that, but you will have complete control over all Xilinex operations and facilities while you are on this assignment.

"Eh, I'm... flattered that you would consider me for this position. I don't quite know what to say. There's a lot to process here."

"We understand, it's a bolt from the blue. But time is of the essence, so we need your decision by the end of this meeting."

"Two years, you say?"

"At most."

"I see. And during that time, I have complete control?"

"Absolutely. You will be elevated to the position of President."

"And the objective is to undermine SINO, and whomever else is left up here, and protect our interests."

"Correct. However, there is a secondary objective."

"Oh?"

"Yes, other opportunities may present themselves as the situation unfolds. Opportunities to, eh... acquire assets. It would be a shame to see them going to waste or fall into the wrong hands."

"Would Moon Base Delta fall under that category?"

"It would."

"Even if that means butting up against SINO?"

"The specialists that have been dispatched will advise on when and where military advantage may be progressed."

Pompodur's mind was now running at breakneck speed, parsing all this data and formulating future projections—mostly centered around the awesome power that the board were now conferring on him. And then he finally saw the big picture.

"It's not just stranded assets, is it? You're talking about all assets, including those controlled by SINO and their associates. The ultimate goal is for complete control of all lunar resources."

There was a sudden outbreak of smiling amongst the board members. "We knew you were the right man for the job. You will do it?"

Pompodur leaned forward, smiled his best smile, and said, "Where do I sign?"

CHAPTER 20
SINO

Chen Gongbo, Director of Internal Security for SINO, considered the official diktat that had just been issued to all high-level operatives in the lunar colonies.

A severe solar storm has occurred that has caused some damage to low Earth orbit constellation networks, but no significant lunar infrastructure has been affected. Any rumor that there is a threat to crewed space travel and that personnel need to be evacuated is nothing more than dangerous disinformation being spewed out by FISA and their puppet allies designed to pressure the feeble minded into rushed compromises during the current negotiations. This devious propaganda needs to be banned to prevent it from infecting the wider SINO lunar population. Any persons found spreading these malicious rumors will be seen as an enemy of the state and will be dealt with in the harshest possible manner. All travel from the lunar colonies, except on official business, will cease forthwith until the current situation is deemed to have stabilized.

Unofficially, Chen knew that the situation was much more complex. The damage from the solar storm was significant and could potentially affect all space flight to and from Earth. That being said, senior SINO aerospace engineers were confident that a ship could be built to withstand all but the most severe debris impacts. They estimated that this would take no more than a year to develop. The bottom line was that whoever was currently on Luna would stay there for at least another year.

However, there was a once in a millennia opportunity opening up for SINO, and for those loyal to the regime. If the spineless simpletons who led FISA, INDOCON, JAXA-KARI, and the other decadent regimes who were expecting their lunar infrastructure to still be here when they got back, then they were more deluded than even Chen could imagine.

With a little military persuasion, SINO could conceivably take complete control over the entire lunar surface and the surrounding orbital space. They would effectively own the Moon along with all its mineral resources—and no other agency could possible gain a new foothold without an all-out war.

The only kink in this potential future that FISA, in their wisdom, had gifted them, was the corporate entity known as, Xilinex. These people were no fools, there was a good reason why they were the largest conglomerate on both Earth and Luna—and they weren't going to miss out on a colossal opportunity like this. They had already started to amplify the paranoia levels, spreading doom-laden disinformation, hoping to persuade more people to leave for Earth. And no doubt they would be targeting the general SINO population with the same message hoping to sow discontent. Chen and his operatives needed to be on top of this and stomp it out now. Yet, the most worrying development was the report of Xilinex ships leaving Earth with a company of mercenaries on board. They were laying down a marker; they would not be pushed around. Perhaps they even had delusions of total lunar domination.

But what troubled Chen the most was FISA's almost complete capitulation—so soon. Officially, they were simpletons, but in reality, they had always played a straight game. If they were leaving, as it seemed they were—no doubt handing over to their military wing—then they must know something that the SINO officials either didn't know or were not telling any of their operatives up here. Chen pondered this for quite some time and eventually came to the conclusion that the only way they would surrender all they had built, is if they had calculated that there would be no going back. At least not until all those who stayed behind were long dead, and that was a much, much longer timeline than the official SINO estimate of one year. He hoped this wasn't so, hoped that they had got it wrong, that in reality they really were just simpletons.

He put it out of his mind and focused on his more immediate problems, of which there were five. Four locked up tight and one strapped onto a bed in the intensive care unit— the crew of the crashed FISA maintenance ship. The humanitarian thing to do, now that the talks were well and truly over, would be to release them and allow them the chance to be evacuated. But that's not the way Chen looked at things. The way he saw it was that he had probably been condemned to die up here by diktat of the regime, and if so, then why should FISA get away without any collateral damage? No, the five-surviving crew of the crash would also die up here—probably much sooner than him.

CHAPTER 21
CODES

The meeting ended abruptly when Dale threw up. At least he had the good sense—or good luck—to use the trashcan designated for organic material. No doubt it would be saved and recycled into... whatever. Selene really didn't want to think about that. Nicci was waiting for her outside the boardroom, a worried look on her face. She stood up as soon as she saw her, came over, and whispered in her ear.

"Eh, sorry to bother you with this, but we are having some problems that may need your input." She then proceeded to list off a whole host of problematic sessions. Selene wasn't listening, she already knew the root cause—people were panicking. She turned to Nicci and raised a hand to stop her midsentence. "Okay, I got it," she gave her a matronly look, "But what I really need now is a drink."

Her assistant raised an eyebrow, then calmly resumed professional mode. "Of course. I understand, what with the...

crash, and all," she looked down the long corridor that ran the length of the FISA sector. "There's that lounge down at the end," she pointed. "It's usually quiet."

Selene nodded and started walking.

They didn't speak again until they were sitting beside a faux observation window made from an enormous high-definition wall monitor, displaying a real-time image of the lunar surface as the space-station passed over. Selene took a sip of bourbon, gave a long sigh, and looked at the image of Luna. Her mind went to Renton and what he might be feeling now.

"Meeting didn't go well, then?" Nicci said, with a hint of sarcasm, interrupting her thoughts.

"You could say that."

Nicci shifted in her seat and lowered her voice. "Is it true, everyone's being evacuated?"

Selene took another sip of her drink and wondered how her assistant knew this. "What have you been hearing?"

"Just rumor and increase in satellite debris around Earth or something like that. It's got people spooked."

"Who did you hear that from?"

"Some of the Xilinex people. But it's doing the rounds, everyone's talking about it."

Xilinex. That figures, thought Selene. *That Pompodur slime-ball is stirring it up.*

"Well, it's true. And it means game-over for the talks; we've failed," Selene gestured at Nicci's tablet, where she had been reading off all the issues with current discussions. "None of that matters anymore," Selene raised her glass. "Now you know why I need a drink."

Her assistant sank back in the chair, visibly deflated. "Maybe I'll have one too."

Selene's comms unit pinged, it was Dyson, looking for her. "I'm in the lounge at the end of the hallway."

A moment later, Dyson walked in looking very stern, like he was building himself up for something he'd rather not be doing. "I need a word," he glanced at Nicci. "Alone, if you don't mind."

Nicci rose. "Of course..." then hesitated. "What should I be doing? Now that..." she let the words trail off.

"I think you should go and pack."

Her assistant took a second to realize that her boss wasn't joking. She nodded then headed out of the lounge.

Dyson sat down. "Some developments you should be aware of. Space Division are taking over. Just been informed."

"SD, the military? Taking over what?" Selene couldn't see what the space marines could possible achieve now that everyone was leaving.

Dyson waved a hand around. "All this, whatever this ends up being. A ship has just departed from Vandenberg, with a load of hardballs on board."

Selene's eyes widened. "Seriously? Don't they know that's a one-way ticket to Palookaville. I mean, there will be no going back home after this tour of duty."

"They know that, it's what they signed up to, it's in the contract, apparently. Probably it's the reason for all the trillions that have been spent on SD over the years..." he paused, then took a quick look around the lounge even though there was nobody else in there, except the barman, busy minding his own business.

"We talked about the crew situation."

Selene immediately sat up. "Can they get them out? Do, what do they call it, an extraction?"

"They said that the situation with the crew is being closely monitored. But they would like all diplomatic options explored before considering any military action."

"But that's bullshit. There are no diplomatic options. I've put the feelers out through the backchannels and nobody is responding, not even an acknowledgment. It's like they're all spooked. Something's changed with SINO, like they're digging in for the long haul. I'm getting nothing, Alan."

He shrugged sympathetically. "It's what they said, and they were pretty emphatic about it."

"It'll be too late by then. You heard what Henriksen said, we're talking days. And it's going to take Space Division over a day to just get here."

"There is one thing," Dyson began. "It seems you were correct, SD have some people already embedded with SINO. One is in the same facility where they're holding the crew. Her code name is Spider, I think. Anyway, it might be possible for you to get a message to your nephew via that channel."

Selene gave him a hard look. "And say what? Hi, Renton, this is your aunt. Sorry for your troubles, but I'm off back to Earth. Have a nice life."

"I know, but the option is there if you want it. Just don't take too long thinking about it."

They were both silent for a beat. Selene finished her drink, then ordered another.

"The only thing I can think of," she paused, choosing her words carefully. "And this is going to sound nuts, is to offer SINO the reboot codes for Moon Base Delta."

Dyson's eyes widened, and he leaned back, seemingly to get a better look at this crazy person. His mouth opened in a silent gasp. He was about to speak when Selene's drink arrived. She took it, then nodded her thanks to the barman.

Dyson waited until he was gone before talking. "What makes you think such a thing even exists?"

"You forget how much I was involved in that project. When the AI core was deactivated and the base split up into sectors, there was talk of a... backdoor, just in case we ever needed it again. So don't go all coy on me, Alan," she looked him straight in the eye.

He considered her for a moment. "Let's say, hypothetically, that such a thing existed, and I'm not saying it does. What do you think would happen if I were to just hand them over to SINO?"

Selene didn't reply.

"I'll tell you," he went on. "I would be handing them the entire base. They could reprogram the security, lock everybody else out. That's a treasonable offense. I'd go to jail for life, and so would you."

"But if it gets Renton and the crew out?"

Dyson shook his head. "I'm sorry. But even if these, so called, codes did exist. I can't do it. And I can't believe you're even suggesting it."

"What use is it to anyone if they're all going to die up here anyway?"

"Not the point, Selene. You know that."

Selene stared into her glass as if looking for inspiration from the melting ice cubes.

"I know, Alan. I just thought I'd ask."

"We're all doing everything we can for that crew. But you need to start thinking about yourself, Selene. There are two FISA ships leaving tomorrow evening on direct flights back to Earth. Just make sure you're on one of them." He rose from his seat. "I mean that. Be on one."

Selene gave him a nod. "Okay."

"And let me know about that message before then."

She raised her empty glass at him. "I might need a few more drinks for that."

CHAPTER 22
SPIDER

Selene didn't have any more to drink. Instead she switched off her comms unit and went dark, she needed to be alone. She could not remember another time in her life when the situation seemed so hopeless. Even when her sister died in that car crash, it was a tragedy, it was an emotional storm, but it was absolute—no action could change it. This was different, Renton was still alive, but trapped, and Selene felt powerless to do anything about it even with all her supposed power and connections. The world had changed utterly in the space of a day, wiping away everything that had mattered to her. Now, what could she do? She needed to think.

For some reason, she found herself wandering, the act of walking helping quiet her mind. She vaguely headed in the direction of her room but for some reason she found herself being drawn toward the cavernous hotel lobby. As if the mass of people gathered there had its own gravitational force, pulling her in. It was a strange place for someone who wanted to be alone to end up. Yet, as she entered the lobby, she felt a detachment, as if she were simply an observer.

It was packed, and a palpable air of urgency rippled through the crowd. Everyone seemed to be on the move, and in a hurry to get there. Gone was the easy murmur of conversation, with people gathered in knots at the bars and cafes, all enjoying their time on board the Axial Luxor. Now, the vacation was well and truly over; it was time to get out.

Through the huge observation window, she could see an armada of ships drifting out from the central docking hub. Some were shuttles taking people on to the main orbital spaceport from where they would catch flights back home. Others were the big private ships that would power up their main engines once they were out past the safety zone and point their bows for Earth.

Across the lobby, she spotted Pompodur and his entourage. His vast bulk and garish clothing made him stand out in the crowd. But there was something else, Selene thought, he seemed utterly delighted with himself, in complete contrast to the concerned looks of everyone else. *What's he so happy about?* she wondered. *What's he plotting?*

Her instincts wanted her to engage him in conversation and try and read between the lines, get some hint of what he and Xilinex were up to. But her heart just wasn't in it anymore, what would be the point, he would probably just gloat. He saw her, lifted his hat off his head, and gave an exaggerated bow, like some musketeer in an old movie. His way of saying, *so long, loser.*

She arrived at her suite, not really remembering how she got there. Once inside, she poured herself a stiff drink, and slumped down on the sofa. That's when she saw it. Sitting on the coffee table was a small box wrapped in gold-colored paper, tied with an artfully crafted bow of white silk. There was a note resting against it, in a small white envelope. Selene picked up the envelope and opened it. It read: *We may never get another chance.*

She flipped it over, hoping for some clue as to who sent this. It was blank. She flipped it back. Was it from some secret admirer? A past lover? Or maybe that pompous prick Pompodur having a last laugh?

Selene picked up the box. It was light. She opened it. Inside was a tiny earpiece, a standard unit, the type used if you want to be discreet. Selene turned it over a few times in her hand. It was unremarkable. She inserted it into her right ear. A voice message began.

We don't have much time. It was a woman's voice, clear and precise. *I can get the crew out within the next twenty-four hours. But I need a way off the lunar surface. I will bring them to the emergency shelter near Moon Base Delta. You need to have a shuttle waiting for us. Someone in FISA will offer you a way to get a message to your nephew, Renton Hicks. Mention the phrase, "Remember Shackleton and the voyage to South Georgia Island." Once I hear this, I will trust that you will have a shuttle waiting. Do not talk about this to FISA or Space Division, they must be kept in the dark until the operation is complete. This is critical, as they will not help you. I await your message.*

Selene pulled out the earpiece and stared at it like it was a mysterious artifact, which in many ways it was. Questions tumbled through her mind, and each one came with even more questions. Was someone trying to set her up? If so who, and to what end? Was this the SD operative codenamed Spider? If so, why the secrecy, and could she really do what SD said they couldn't? How was Selene going to organize a shuttle without help from FISA? Who brought this artifact here? How did they get it through security?

All these questions and more buzzed around in her head like a hive of angry insects. She stood up and began to slowly pace around her suite, thinking this out. After ten or so minutes, she had narrowed all the questions down to just one. What did she have to lose by sending the message? And the answer was: nothing.

She reactivated her comms unit and a sea of messages came flooding in. She ignored them all and called Dyson. He answered quickly.

"Selene?"

"I'll send that message to Renton. Do I still have time?"

"Yes. Record something and send it to me within the next hour. I'll get it over to SD."

"Thanks." She closed the call. But before Selene could record the message, she needed to be sure she could commandeer a shuttle. She called Jean Reizen over at Central Maintenance.

"Hi, Selene." Jean's head and shoulders popped up on the main monitor in her suite.

"It's just terrible what's happened to Renton and the crew,

just terrible. And what are those SINO bastards playing at? Why won't they just release them?"

"Yes, terrible, Jean. However, there might be an option, but I'll need your help."

"Name it."

"I need a shuttle to go to the emergency shelter near Moon Base Delta in the next few hours and wait there for... as long as they can."

"A shuttle? Are they getting out?"

"It's a possibility, no guarantees. And we gotta keep it quiet. FISA can't find out until it's done. You need to keep knowledge of this to as few people as possible."

Jean took a moment to think about this, then nodded. "Okay, I won't ask. Only glad to be helping to get our guys back. But commandeering a shuttle is a bit tricky, most of the crews are busy with this sudden evacuation. Let me see," his eyes flicked off to another screen, checking something. "Alright, I think I've found the perfect crew, ex-colleagues of Mackenzie and Yuna. They'll do it, no problem, and they'll wait as long as they can."

"Thanks, Jean. And remember, this is all on the QT."

"You got it."

The call ended. Selene sat down again on the sofa and began to record a voice message for her nephew.

CHAPTER 23
THE WAITING GAME

Matteo paced up and down, ranting and raving at the sheer arrogance of SINO, and that this affront to international treaties would not go unpunished. Yuna, who was sitting on the edge of a bunk, periodically nodded in agreement. But the person Renton was most concerned about was Alice. She had withdrawn into herself and sat on the floor in a corner of the room, arms wrapped around her knees.

For Renton, acceptance of their current situation came sooner than any of the others. The moment when they stripped off their FISA EVA suits and donned the jumpsuits that their captors had provided, that was when Renton had fully accepted his situation. Matteo, on the other hand, was still in the anger phase, Yuna in transition between anger and acceptance. But Alice had slipped straight into depression.

He also realized that he was probably better equipped to

deal with this trauma than the rest of the crew. After all, he had a lot of experience in dealing with loss. When his parents died in a car crash five years ago, he went through the full range of emotions: anger, guilt, despair, depression. Bizarrely, he only arrived at acceptance after watching an old, twentieth-century martial arts movie one night alone in his room at his aunt's house. The hero, a combat master, was battling his way through the evil lord's castle, dispatching the hordes of feeble fighters with ease, only to walk straight into a trap as a steel cage sprung up around him. Realizing that he was now trapped, with no possible way out, did he react with anger or descend into despair? No, he simply sat down cross-legged on the floor of the cage, conserved his energy, and waited.

This scene was a revelation to Renton at the time. The hero had accepted his situation, yet he wasn't powerless, he wasn't without agency. He had a choice, he could sap his energy through rage, or anger, or despair. Or he could conserve his physical and mental self and wait for an opportunity to present itself for escape. He would be ready for when that opportunity occurred. Renton had instantly understood the lesson; perhaps his mind had been ready for it at the time. Nevertheless, he too realized that he had a choice. Acceptance of the hand that fate had dealt him or shrivel up in self-pity and despair. He chose the former, and it became a kind of mantra for him for a time. Yet somehow, he had forgotten the lesson and had been slipping back into his old self-deprecating ways—like when he was on the FISA maintenance ship, letting doubt creep in, letting the captain get under his skin. Now, here he was, trapped in a cage, no way to get out, nowhere to hide, and like a switch going on inside his head, he had to accept it, conserve his energy and marshal his resources. He also felt he needed to pull the crew together somehow, starting with Alice.

He slumped down on the floor beside her. She didn't move, her eyes fixed on some point on the floor.

"How are you holding up?" he tentatively asked.

For a moment she remained silent, her eyes still fixed on that same point. "I can't stop thinking about Mackenzie. I wonder how she's doing; if she'll survive?"

"For what it's worth, I think they'll do everything they can to save her. They won't want her to die on them."

Alice flicked her head to look at him. "You really think so?"

"Sure, it makes sense. They're holding us here on fake charges so we can be used as bargaining chips—leverage for the talks that are going on. They won't want Mackenzie to die on their watch. That would be... bad for business."

"Your aunt is high up in FISA?" Yuna called over from her bunk. She had her arm out of the sling and was testing its level of movement. Fortunately, she had not broken it.

"Yeah. Actually... she's leading the negotiating team at the talks."

Matteo finally stopped pacing and swung around to face him. "She will help us, then, won't she?"

"It's a double-edged sword, Matteo. Yes, it means we have someone at the top table fighting our corner. But it also means we're more valuable to SINO. They might hold out for more concessions."

"These talks," said Yuna, "I don't know much about them, are they a big deal?"

"Oh, for sure. We're talking about a New Lunar Accord, the creation of nation states up here on Luna. They're a really big deal. SINO will want to get the most out of them."

"So, we're being traded for a few square kilometers of territory?" Matteo scowled.

"Yup, that's sounds about right," Renton nodded.

"Bastards." Matteo shook his fist at the ceiling, where he assumed there were hidden cameras watching their every move —which there probably was.

"The thing is," continued Renton, "we have to accept that we'll probably be here for some time. We need to stay cool and wait it out—and try not to die of boredom," he smiled.

"Ha, that would be ironic, after everything that's happened," Matteo sighed and finally sat down on a bunk. "You're probably right. Renton. We need to keep our heads."

"Yes," said Yuna. "And try not go crazy, Matteo."

He gave a hint of a grin in reply. "I'll try."

Alice said nothing. She simply slipped her arm in through his and rested her head on his shoulder.

"How are the ribs?" he asked.

"Fine, as long as I don't breathe."

They talked for a time. He told her about the accident, about losing his parents, and about how he coped. She listened, squeezing his arm every so often.

"We will get out of this, Alice. It will end."

"I hope so," she said, with a yawn.

He disentangled himself and stood up. "Probably best get some rest."

"Yeah," she looked up at him. "And thanks."

He nodded, went back to his own bunk and dozed off.

He woke a few hours later to the sound of the door opening and a trolley of food being brought in.

Alice, asked about the captain. "How's Mackenzie? Is she okay, is she still alive?" But there was no reply. The guards remained steadfastly mute. They transferred the food onto the table. One of them picked up a small bowl of fruit and looked over at Renton, for longer than he felt comfortable.

He rolled off his bunk, taking a moment to massage his aching neck. Then padded over to the table and inspected the meager fare on offer. Mostly it was emergency-style rations, the type found in shelters and evacuation pods. Long-life, low-taste. Still, it was food, and even if it was not very appetizing, he thought it best to get some form of nutrition into him. He sat down at the table and looked up at the guard, who seemed to be fixated on arranging a bowl of small, slightly wizened apples. Again she looked at him directly, holding his stare. Then her eyes flicked down to the fruit. *She's trying to communicate something,* he realized. He kept his face blank, trying not to reveal any reaction.

"How's our captain, you can't keep us in the dark like this," Matteo shouted over from his bunk.

The guards walked back out in silence.

"Bastards!" he shouted after them.

Renton picked up a small stunted apple from the top of the

pile and saw something that was definitely not organic nestled below. It was a tiny earpiece. He reached over again, selecting another equally substandard apple, palming the earpiece as he did. He tried his best to make it look like he was simply selecting a better option. Yet his heart was pounding and he felt he would start sweating at any moment. He pocketed the earpiece as casually as he could and concentrated on eating his meal.

He looked over to see the others staring at him from their bunks, like a pack of domesticated dogs waiting for their master to give them the go ahead to eat. He took a sip of water from a bottle and raised it up to them. "Are you waiting to see if I die first?"

"How do you know they're not trying to poison us?" Matteo raised himself up and came over.

"Seriously, if they wanted us dead there would be simpler ways to do it," he jerked his head at a vacant seat. "Sit, get something into you, keep the strength up."

Matteo picked up a protein cube, took a bite, and then gave an expression that said, *I've tasted worse*. He sat down and started eating. Yuna and Alice soon followed suit.

"I don't understand why you don't get angry, Renton," said Matteo as he took a bite from one of the apples.

Renton just shrugged. "Would it help?"

"Give it a rest, Matteo," said Yuna. "Renton's right. No point in wasting energy on ranting."

"It makes me feel better," he took another bite.

After that, they ate mostly in silence. Renton was first to leave the table, saying he was going to take another rest.

"Might as well," said Matteo. "Damn all else to do around here."

He climbed back onto his bunk, lay down, and pulled the blanket up over his head. He took out the tiny earpiece and fitted it into his right ear. Instantly, a recorded message started playing. He recognized the voice; it was his aunt.

CHAPTER 24

TIME TO GET OUT OF DODGE

W hat his aunt revealed in the message truly shocked Renton. It had taken all of his willpower just to stay calm and not jump up from the bunk. He learned about the impending Kessler Syndrome. In a few days, they would be cut off, with no hope of returning to Earth for a very long time. It blew his mind. He couldn't possibly have imagined that anything like this would ever happen in his lifetime. Yet here it was, happening right now. But his heart skipped a beat when she told him about the plan to get them out. There was someone on the inside willing to help. The only thing he could not quite understand was the reference to the old Antarctic explorer. *Remember Shackleton and the voyage to South Georgia Island.* What did this mean? Was it a portent of things to come?

He knew the story, of course, it was legendary. The lunar south pole, the most populous area on the Moon, was named after him: Shackleton Crater. He was an Anglo-Irish Antarctic explorer that lived around the beginning of the twentieth century. But his legendary status was not gained by spectacular discoveries, like that of Howard Carter and the tomb of the Pharaoh Tutankhamen. No, his was earned though an epic tale of survival against all odds.

An ill-fated expedition set sail for the Antarctic only to find itself trapped in a thick ice floe. The ship had to be abandoned, and for several weeks the crew, now camped out on the floe, watched helplessly as their ship was slowly crushed by the accumulating ice. They remained there for several months hoping the ice floe would take them closer to land, but when this failed to happen, Ernest Shackleton made the decision to get his men into the few remaining lifeboats and try and make it to the nearest island. After five harrowing days at sea, they finally made it to an inhospitable and uninhabited rocky patch called Elephant Island. Yet, there would be no hope of rescue as the island was far off the shipping routes. Shackleton realized that if he and his men were to survive, someone would have to try and sail all the way to the nearest whaling station on South Georgia Island, over seven-hundred nautical miles away, across some on the worst seas on the planet, in nothing but a patched up wooden lifeboat. This was the epic journey that he and five other men embarked on, on April 24, 1916.

For fifteen days and nights, they battled stormy seas, freezing temperatures, hunger, and exhaustion, all the time in fear that their flimsy lifeboat would capsize. But against all odds, by a combination of skill, determination, and luck, on

May 8, the cliffs of South Georgia came into view. Yet, they couldn't land as the winds had picked up again and soon reached hurricane-force. All that day and into the night, they clung on and rode the storm further out at sea. Finally, early the next morning, the exhausted men managed to land on the southern shore.

But they were not done yet. Between them and the whaling station lay over fifty kilometers of extremely dangerous mountain terrain. With nothing more than a short length of rope, a single carpenters ax, and screws pushed through their boots to aid climbing the icy slopes, Shackleton and two others set off on the treacherous journey.

Thirty-six grueling hours later, the three men stumbled into the whaling station much to the shock of the men working there. They could not believe this ragged man was the famous Shackleton. Everyone had assumed that the expedition that had set sail almost two years earlier had been shipwrecked, with all lives lost.

Renton knew this story, in fact anyone who had been to Shackleton Crater probably knew it since there was a section in the museum there dedicated to this story. *But what had it got to do with him?* he wondered. In the end, his aunt's message was short and to the point, mostly. He was about to take the earpiece out when another message started. Another woman, younger, very calm, and precise.

Listen very carefully, I will only say this once. SINO are planning to keep you here indefinitely as they think you might have information on FISA infrastructure that could be useful. After that they will kill you. I can get you out, but it won't be easy. You must do exactly as I say, when I say it, no discussion. Late tonight the door to your quarters will automatically unlatch, be ready to leave when it does. Cameras will be disabled. Go left, and head down the long corridor. I will meet you there. I will identify myself as Spider.

The camera in the small area just in front of your sanitary area has already been disabled. You can communicate with the others at that spot, do it one at a time, do it very quietly, don't do anything to raise suspicions. Listen for the door to unlatch tonight. Be ready to go when it does.

The message ended. Renton waited a while just in case there might be something else, but there wasn't. He took the earpiece out and tried to assimilate all that he had heard. His initial thought was who to share this with first. Matteo could potentially flip out and blow the whole thing. Alice? But he wasn't quite sure of her state of mind. Yuna, then.

He pulled back the covers and raised himself up to sit on the edge of the bunk. Yuna was still sitting at the table, sipping on a bottle of water, lost in thought. He wondered how he was going to get her to follow him to the sanitary area. Maybe a note, but he had nothing to write with, and if they spotted him passing a note then that could possibly be game over. Maybe Alice would be better after all. He could be closer to her without a potential drama.

She was sitting on the edge of her bunk, staring at the floor, her long hair hanging down around her face. He closed his hand around the earpiece and went over to her and sat down beside her, she leaned a little into him. He reached out and held her hand, pressing the earpiece up against her palm. She looked down, but before she could say anything, he said in a whisper, "Stay cool, act normal, someone's smuggled in a message for us."

Alice kept her cool, she squeezed his hand. He leaned in again. "Please don't take this the wrong way, but you need to follow me to the toilet."

This got a reaction. She glanced at him and raised her eyebrows. He pressed the earpiece into her palm again, reminding her of what this was about, then slowly rose from the bunk, still holding her hand. She followed.

Renton pointed at the ceiling and mouthed, *no camera here.* He took the earpiece and placed it in her ear and whispered, *listen.* He watched her expressions change as she listened to the messages. First it was wide-eyed, then open-mouthed, then a hand went to her mouth, followed by another. And all the time her eyes flicked between staring into the distance as she concentrated, then back to him as if to seek confirmation of the enormity of what she was hearing. When the recording finished, she just looked at him and mouthed *oh-my-god.* But she stayed cool, even though she was shaking a little.

"You have to get Yuna to listen to this," he whispered.

Alice took out the earpiece and nodded.

"Do it here," he jerked a thumb at the ceiling. "No camera."

She nodded again and they opened the door and walked out. Yuna fixed her gaze on them. He wasn't sure, but he thought he caught the hint of a smile on her face. Later that afternoon, that smile had disappeared as she exited the sanitary area with Alice. She looked at him and gave a slight, conspiratorial nod of her head.

Matteo had been oblivious to all this coming and going,

having been stretched out on his bunk for most of the time. But when he finally rose to use the toilet, Renton was waiting for him when he came out. As Matteo listened, Renton warned him several times, *do not freak out.*

He didn't. In fact, quite the opposite. He was cool and calm. "Looks like it's time to get the hell out of Dodge," he whispered.

CHAPTER 25
DESPERATE PEOPLE

Renton couldn't sleep, not that he tried. He, like the rest of the crew, simply lay in their bunks pretending to sleep while waiting anxiously for the sound of the door latch releasing. It felt like the longest night of his life, hours went by and nothing happened. On several occasions, he was tempted to get up and check the door, but he resisted, as did the others.

When it came, he almost didn't believe he'd heard it. It was unmistakable, a solid thump as the magnetic door bolts retracted. He sat up in his bunk and glanced over at the others who were also beginning to move. He stood, slipped his feet into the prison-issue slippers, and padded over to the door. The only light in the room came from the dull red glow of a row of LEDs in the air filtration unit. Not much to work with, but enough. He felt the touch of someone on his shoulder, it was Matteo. Behind him he could just make out the shapes of Alice and Yuna. He tried the door, it moved. He turned back and gave the thumbs up.

Outside, the corridor was equally dark, illuminated only by dim indicator lights on the various systems that were randomly dotted along its length. His heart rate rose, his senses on high-alert. He kept low, touching the wall with his hand as he slowly made his way into the darkness. Every so often, he would reach back to feel for Matteo, making sure they were keeping close together. The corridor seemed endless and Renton began to wonder if this Spider person was going to show up; maybe he had gotten the instructions wrong? Then suddenly, up ahead, he saw the blinking of a white light. It flashed a few times then stopped. This prompted him to move quicker. A hand reached out from the darkness to grab him. He turned to see a figure, dressed all in black. She raised a finger to her lips then pointed behind her along another corridor. She moved off; they all followed.

She brought them to a set of steel stairs, indicating to tread lightly as they began to ascend. This opened out into an area full of industrial equipment, machines for the mining and transportation of ore. It looked to be both a storage area and workshop, but so dark it was impossible to get a sense of its size. Yet it must have been big as large machines would loom out of the darkness as they moved. Finally, they came to an airlock, where light flooded out as the doors cracked open. They entered and for the first time, Renton could get a good look at this agent who was helping them.

It was the same person who had brought the food on the

second day. She was diminutive with a face that was a mix of many races, hard to pinpoint any one in particular. A person that could fit in anywhere; probably why she had chosen this profession, or perhaps this profession had chosen her. In every other aspect, she was unremarkable.

"Thanks... for helping us get out of here," Renton whispered.

She cast him a quick glance and nodded. "We'll be entering a pressurized rover parking bay. Stay calm, do exactly as I say."

Renton nodded back. The others said nothing, all were equally compliant.

The airlock door opened into a wide, dimly lit bay with several rovers lined up side-by-side. As they exited the airlock, three figures stepped out from the shadows all with the Xiang Zu insignia on the breast pocket of their jumpsuits. Renton froze, assuming they had been rumbled.

But Spider remained calm. "Everything ready?"

He realized then that these guys must be part of the escape operation.

"Yes, all good, rover's ready, EVA suits inside."

"Good," Spider turned to the crew. "Let's go."

But before they could take a step, one of them stepped out in front of Spider. "Slight change of plan. We're coming with you."

"That's not the deal, Haitao. You're getting well paid for this."

"Money's not worth a shit to us if we're stuck up here forever." One of the others stepped in behind his colleague, backing him up.

Renton stepped to the right, putting some space between him and the fight that looked like it might break out any second.

"We've heard the reports coming out from the Xilinex Corporation. They say we'll be isolated up here for decades. You told us it was only a year."

"Yeah, you've been bullshitting us, Price."

Price, thought Renton. *So that's what they called her here.*

"It's Xilinex that have been bullshitting you."

"It's not just them, Price. We've got reports of a mass evacuation happening. We're going with you or no one goes anywhere."

"Fine," Spider gave a conciliatory gesture with her hands. "But you better have enough suits because I ain't leaving without these people."

"We do."

"Okay, then. Let's go."

They all began to move off to the rover, when Yuna spoke. "What about Mackenzie. We can't leave her behind."

Spider spun around, and for a moment, Renton thought she was going to do some harm to Yuna. He stepped in front of her. Spider's face contorted with frustration.

"Your captain is strapped to a bed in ICU with more tubes coming out of her than a cryogenic cooling unit. She ain't going anywhere. If we tried to bring her, we would just end up killing her. Now if everyone is finished whinging, can we just get fucking going?"

"We're going," Renton said, as he gently pushed Yuna forward.

They clambered into the rover, a standard industrial unit, short on comfort, long on practicality. One of the Xiang Zu people headed for the cockpit and took the controls. The rest of them got suited up into heavy-duty mining suits, built for tough conditions.

Renton picked up a helmet, ready to attach it.

"You're not going to need that yet," said Spider. "It will be a few hours before we get to where we're going. Just leave it in the locker."

Renton put in back in its nook and then went to check on the others.

He tapped Matteo on the shoulder. "You good?"

Matteo smiled. "Trying not to shit myself."

"Just hang in there. We'll soon be home-free."

"Can't help thinking about the captain," said Yuna. "It's bad we're leaving her behind."

"I know, but we don't have much choice," said Renton. "I can imagine what she would say about it too. Call us a bunch of bloody wimps, or some such."

Yuna gave a faint smile. "Yeah, probably."

Renton looked around to check on Alice but she was already suited up and running through the diagnostics routine. He gave her the thumbs up and worked his way up into the cockpit. Spider had taken over the controls so the Xiang Zu guy could get his EVA suit on. Renton wedged himself in the seat beside her. They had already left the base and were rumbling across the lunar surface. It was pitch black outside. "Night has come," he said.

"Fourteen days of darkness. Not that we're going to be around for it," Spider glanced over at him. "Assuming your aunt comes through with that shuttle."

"She will," he gave her a considered look. "Why do you need her anyway? Aren't you Space Division or something?"

"Keep it down, will you?" she jerked her head behind her. "Don't want to upset the locals. They're still trying to figure that out."

"So why do you need Selene for the ship?" he kept his voice low.

"Because, SD are planning to keep me here. I'm more useful to them on the inside. But the way I see it is I've done my duty. So, I needed a way out, and you gave me the perfect opportunity."

"So we're just a way for you to get your ass off this rock?"

"That's about it. And lucky for you, or you'd be stuck here too."

Something on the cockpit readouts caught her attention. "Damnit. Haitao, get in here, now!"

Haitao, the leader of the Xiang Xu crew, came into the cockpit, now fully suited.

"What?"

Spider pointed at a screen. "We got company. You were supposed to make sure this didn't happen."

"It's not possible. I tagged this trip as a routine maintenance call out. They wouldn't suspect anything for hours. Not until we didn't return."

Renton studied the terrain map etched on to the cockpit

screen. It rendered the surrounding area in thin lines of elevation each one calculated from a universally agreed datum, since there was no sea-level on the Moon. They were traveling through a mostly flat surface along a well-worn transport route. Behind them, on the map, a marker blinked. He tapped on it to drill down to the associated data set.

"Their speed is constant, they're keeping their distance," he looked at Spider. "They're not chasing us, they're following us."

The SD agent thought about this for a moment, then turned back to Haitao. "Who else did you tell?"

He raised his hands. "Woah, no one."

"Don't bullshit me."

Haitao shook his head. "Look, I had to get a few others involved. It was very tricky setting all this up."

"Well that's just great. Don't tell me the entire Xiang Zu work force is beating a trail behind us. You'd better find a way to ditch them."

By now Renton had taken control of the navigation console. "Do they know where the rendezvous is?"

"No. That I kept to myself," she gave Haitao a cold look.

"We can hack our rover's tracking beacon, take it offline, go dark and head off-road. We can navigate using the topographical display," he pointed at the screen.

"You know how to do that?" Spider looked a little skeptical.

"We're engineers, it's what we do." He turned around and shouted back into the cabin. "Alice? Going to need your hacking skills up here."

"I can't navigate with the tracking beacon off," Spider looked genuinely concerned.

"I can," Yuna stepped into the cockpit.

Spider considered her for a moment, clearly not convinced that she should just cede control of the rover over to the people she was supposed to be rescuing.

"Spider, unless you have a better way of losing that tail then you need to let Yuna take the helm. Trust me, she's the best there is," Renton caught Yuna's eye. "Honestly, we wouldn't even be here if it wasn't for her getting that broken ship down to the surface, with no engine power. We would all be just a great big ball of space dust."

Spider conceded and stood up from the pilot seat. "Okay. I need to get into an EVA suit anyway."

Yuna took the seat, strapped herself in, and then looked back at Haitao, who was still hovering over them with a mix of concern and confusion etched on his face. "You'd better get back in there and buckle up, we're in for a bumpy ride."

He nodded. "I hope to hell you guys know what you're doing." And went back to sit with his crew.

Renton was still riding shotgun, so Alice took the middle seat in the cockpit and began delving into the navigation system. She tapped a few icons and instantly the layout changed to common English. "My kanji is rusty. Don't want to go pressing the wrong button."

The navigation screen shifted to the horizontal and the local topography of the Sea of Tranquility was rendered in simple 3D, to better visualize the undulating landscape. Alice gestured, and the projection zoomed out showing a wider view of the region. They could see the marker for the other SINO rover not far behind them.

"That's us," Alice pointed at a small blinking dot. "Once we kill the beacon, that goes."

"As long as you can keep us centered on that map then I can get us across to the other side." Yuna seemed to be warming to the task; at last she had something to keep her mind off the fate of the captain. She pointed at the image. "All this area around here is called Couchy, all SINO. We'll head west until we get to the Couchy I Rille, a long trench. We follow that northwest until it flattens out. Then we head west into Tranquility proper, heading for the emergency shelter on the southeastern edge of Sinas Crater. We should pass within a few kilometers of Moon Base Delta. Better get settled in, it's going to take a while."

"Got it." Alice moved over to a different interface and got busy searching the rover's schematics for the physical location of the tracking beacon. She pointed at a section of a wiring diagram. "Looks like it's located in the roof at the rear. You can access from a panel inside the airlock."

Renton rose from his seat. "Okay, leave it to me." He went back into the main cabin. "Matteo, have a look around for some tools, we've got a job to do."

"What are we doing? Making this bucket go faster?" He undid his seat harness and started rooting around, opening lockers and hatches.

"In there," said Haitao. "You'll find a set of tools in there," he pointed to a large floor locker near the cargo hold.

Renton and Matteo gathered up what they needed and moved to the rear of the rover and entered the airlock.

"I don't trust those guys. They're desperate people, and

desperate people do desperate things," said Matteo as he undid the retaining screws for the overhead panel.

"Yeah, me too. We need to keep a close eye on them. A few weapons might help." Renton held up a rivet gun used for quick repair of metal hulls and shielding. It used high-energy electromagnets to imbed metal spikes. In many respects, it was similar to a railgun—a Gauss weapon, with a very short range. But it was small and compact.

"Any more of those?" Matteo asked.

"We can have a look once we get this beacon disconnected."

They worked away, finding their rhythm, and it felt to Renton that he was back to normality, back to doing the job he was trained to do. And for a few precious moments, the trauma of the past few days receded into the background.

"That should be it," Matteo declared as he unplugged the electrical connections on the tracking beacon.

"Let's go check. Here, you hang on to this," Renton handed him the rivet gun.

Back in the cockpit, Yuna had switched off all the rover's exterior and interior lights. A ghostly gray, low-light, head-up display now projected onto the interior windshield showing the landscape ahead. Renton glanced over at the 3D navigation screen, which Alice was studying intently. The luminescent lines of the topography reflected across her face.

"We're off-grid. Good work," she offered him a smile and a momentary glimpse of her former self.

"This is going to take a few hours," said Yuna. "But once we pass into FISA territory Spider says we can contact FISA, maybe even your aunt, let them know we're okay and on our way. You should try to get some rest while you can."

"What about you?"

"We're okay here for a while. Alice said she'd take over once we're out on the plains."

"Okay, but let me know as soon as we make radio contact." He went back to the main cabin, strapped himself in opposite Matteo, and dozed off.

CHAPTER 26
THIS IS HOW IT STARTS

D r. Han Sundar's job as an analyst at MASTERM had ingrained in him an acute awareness of the thin thread by which the current technological civilization hung. Like any species that relied on a limited range of resources, if anything were to disrupt that supply, then its days would be numbered. Consider the fate of the panda, a specialized herbivore known as a folivore—one that eats only leaves. But not just any old leaf, exclusively bamboo shoots. Not a great plan if that food supply is threatened. Now the panda exists solely through human intervention. Fortunately for the species, it looks very cute.

The bamboo shoots that human civilization relied on were data communications, and that relied on the satellite constellations—the Datasphere. Yes, there was still an old legacy system of copper and fiber, but this was expensive and satellites were cheap. So, over time, most communications had migrated to the constellations, and without those, everything would grind to a halt. It was with this understanding of the precariousness of the Datasphere, and hence human civilization, that prompted Han to start making preparations some years back, just in case. He didn't make a big deal of it and kept it to himself. Yet over time, he built his contingency plan brick by quiet brick.

He had considered learning some survivalist skills as this seemed, on paper at least, to make a lot of sense—learn how to hunt and forage. But in truth he knew he would be useless at it. He was a data analyst, a numbers guy, and so stuck to what he knew. He began by building simulations of how a disruption to the Datasphere might pan out in practice. It was clear from the outset that food shortages would become a major issue very early on as the distribution networks broke down, possibly in as little as two weeks. After that, people in the cities would start to migrate out into the countryside and into the forests in search of food, to hunt and forage. But with potentially millions of people pouring into the hinterlands, all with the same basic plan, it would soon get very crowded and very dangerous, very quickly.

This survival equation also assumed that nature could replenish its stocks as fast as humans could consume it, and Han only needed to remember the fate of the Passenger Pigeon to know that this was never going to happen. Back when the first Europeans started migrating across the North American continent, there were estimated to be a population of around five billion of these birds. Unfortunately for the pigeon, it was both nutritious and easy to hunt. Some reports said that all you needed to do was fire a shotgun in the air and you would have dinner. Over the span of a few decades they were hunted to extinction. The last wild Passenger Pigeon was reported to have been shot in 1901.

In the end, Han decided his best plan was to hunker down and wait it out. It was one of the reasons he had held on to the observatory and over time began to enhance it. He rebuilt the wall that surrounded the property, upgraded the energy system with additional solar and storage, and began to build up a stock of long-life foods—mostly the type used in space as these were produced to the highest standards. Yet, as he and Sheneese turned off the main highway and headed up into the mountains, the worry in his mind was, would it be enough?

Their first stop-off was at a big box store they knew just outside the small town of Jackson's Creek. It was where they normally loaded up on supplies when they were heading up for weekends. Han knew it well, so as he drove the car into the parking lot, he was already drawing a mental map of where everything they needed was located inside the store. They would get in and get out as efficiently as possible.

He had never seen it so busy. While people were not quite panicking just yet, they were certainly sensing a change in the wind. He considered leaving and trying somewhere else, but in the end decided to just get this task over and done with. There were no guarantees that any of the other stores would be less busy.

They grabbed two large shopping carts and pushed in through the front doors only to be greeted by several large, handwritten signs reading: *Network Down, NFC only. Apologies for the inconvenience.* NFC meaning Near Field Communications, essentially money stored on a personal area network. This could be transferred simply by presenting your phone, tablet, or watch to the interface on the checkout. But if you had to connect with a remote bank for the transfer, you were out of luck. Back fifty years ago, this would have read; *no cards, cash only.* For anyone who didn't have the foresight to download money onto their personal area network, they were screwed. Already several arguments were in progress at the checkouts as irate customers vented their frustrations at the staff.

"We'd better make this quick," said Han as he began pushing his cart deeper into the store.

"Agreed, looks like it could get ugly," said Sheneese as she eyed the tension building at the checkouts.

A lot of the aisles were already looking depleted, mostly dry goods: rice, pasta, pulses, items with a long shelf-life. But they wasted no time deliberating on what to stock up on as Han had already made a list. They had planned to split up to get it done quicker, but there was a tense, almost frantic, atmosphere building in the store so they thought it best to stick together. It slowed them down a little but felt a lot safer.

By the time they got to the checkouts, there were several long queues. It didn't help that at least one-in-three people didn't bother to read the signs on the way in, leading to prolonged arguments and escalating tensions. But eventually they reached the checkout and started scanning as fast as they possibly could.

On the checkout next to them, an older man accompanied

by what looked like his two sons were about to move off with four carts piled high with goods when he heard the assistant say, "Sorry sir, NFC only," she pointed to one of the signs.

"What do you mean? That's bullshit."

"Sorry sir, network's down."

"Well, I ain't leaving here without my goods. So you'd better just deal with it."

Two security guards moved closer. One spoke. "Sorry, sir, you can leave your goods over here. We'll keep an eye on them until you come back with a way to pay."

He squared off with the security guard and gestured at him with an angry finger. "I've been comin' here for twenty years, must have spent a half million. So me and my boys are taking this stuff with us now. I'll drop back later and pay; you know I'm good for it."

"Sorry, sir, store policy, you must pay now."

Han realized that he and Sheneese had slowed down, becoming distracted by this drama playing out just a few meters from them. He exchanged a glance with his wife, who could also sense trouble ahead. They sped up again.

It happened in an instant. The man whipped out a handgun, held it steady with both hands, and pointed at the head of the guard. He called to his sons, "Start moving those carts!"

The guard stepped back and raised his hands in an act of appeasement. "Just lower the gun, sir. No one needs to get hurt."

Han finished the scan, dumped the last of their purchases into the carts, and pressed his wrist to the payment terminal. It pinged an acceptance. "Let's get going," he gestured at the doors and they started moving. Behind him, he could hear the standoff play out.

"Exactly, so you and your buddy just step aside." There was a momentary silence as everyone at the checkouts froze. Except for Han and Sheneese who were already at the exit. Two loud gunshots rang out, followed by screams, followed by a stampede as people ran for cover.

Han wasn't sure what happened as he and Sheneese were out the door and pushing their carts as fast as he could over the rough asphalt. He looked behind him to see the older man and his two sons pushing their own carts. It must have not worked out so good for the security guards. Behind them was a mass of people also pushing carts full of goods that he assumed hadn't been paid for. It was a free-for-all; the looting had begun.

They piled everything into the car and made a hasty exit out of the parking lot. As he drove Sheneese looked behind them to witness what was going on. "My god, that was intense."

Han gave a solemn nod of his head. "Yeah, this is how it starts."

CHAPTER 27
HITCHHIKERS

R enton juddered awake with a nudge from Alice. "Renton?"

He opened his eyes and lifted his head, rubbing his neck as he did. "Eh?"

"We're across the border. Spider's made contact with FISA, they want to talk to you."

"Oh, okay." As he rose, he glanced around the cabin to see Matteo, Haitao, and the other two Xiang Zu workers all dozing. Someone was snoring, probably Matteo.

He moved into the cockpit, where Spider was talking on comms, a hand cupped over one ear. He could only hear her side of the conversation. She stood up when she saw him.

"Yeah. He's here now. Putting you on," she pointed at a headset hanging from the ceiling of the cockpit. He grabbed it and slotted it over his head.

"Hello?"

"Renton?"

"Yes."

"Oh, thank god. You've no idea how good it is to hear your voice." It was his aunt. "You got out?"

"Yeah, just crossed the border, traveling across Tranquility."

"The shuttle's waiting, a crew out of Central, colleagues of your captain, I believe."

"We had to leave Mackenzie behind."

"So I heard. Listen, things are getting... problematic up here so don't hang around. Get off the surface as quickly as possible."

"You don't have to worry about that."

"Take care, Renton. See you back on Earth."

"Thanks for getting us out."

"You're not out yet. Thank me next time we meet."

The connection closed. Renton pulled off the headset and hung it back in its cradle.

Alice gestured at the 3D navigation map. "We've got good news and bad news. The guys who were following us have slowed and fallen back. Bad news is we have two more rovers heading out of the SINO base."

"More people trying to get out?" Renton asked.

"No," answered Spider. "These are operatives, military. Either they're chasing down the first rover, or chasing us down, or possibly both."

Renton studied the markers on the map. They all seemed quite a distance away.

"The thing is," Spider continued. "They're not stupid, they'll know we're crossing the border into Tranquility, and probably have a good guess as to where we might be heading."

"The emergency shelter?"

She nodded.

"We've still got time on our side," Yuna pointed to an area on the map. "We're here, around an hour ahead. So long as they don't send a shuttle out, we should be off this rock long before they catch up."

"You think they'll cross the border?"

"For sure." Spider seemed very certain of this. "Word from my Space Division overlords is that everyone's tooling up for a turf war. By everyone, I mean the major powers, including some of the corporates. Borders don't really matter anymore; soon it will be a free-for-all."

"Why are they staying?" Renton asked, more as a question to himself. "Don't they know they'll be stuck here?"

"The prospect of complete control over the entire Moon is just too much for them to resist. Maybe they think the debris cloud will be cleaned up in a year or two, or maybe they think —or have been told to think—that it's just a load of crap spewed out by FISA. Who knows? Either way, some are staying and ready to battle it out for control."

Renton shook his head. "They'll be fighting over nothing. What good are the resources if you can't get them back to Earth."

"Ah, but you're not thinking the long game. The way SINO sees it is that at some point in the future, and that could be a year, a decade, or maybe even a century, the debris cloud will be cleared and travel can resume. If they have total control up here, and with an Earth starved of resources for so long, they will have enormous leverage over the entire world."

Renton laughed, "Ha, that's ridiculous, you can't possibly be serious?" But as he looked at Spider, he could see that she was being completely serious.

"Well that's just messed up," said Yuna.

"Yep," Spider nodded. "That's why I want the get the hell out of here. Court-martial or not."

"Court-martial?" Yuna gave her an incredulous look.

"Oh, you didn't know?" Spider sat back and put her feet up on the dashboard. "Well, when I managed to make contact with FISA, they informed me that Space Division were not happy about what I was doing. Not one bit. You see they're sending a shipload of hard asses on a one-way ticket to look after our interests up here. But the thing is, those guys signed up for it, they know what they're getting themselves into. Yet Space Division just assumed I'd continue doing what I do, snooping on SINO. They didn't even give me an option. Well screw that. I sure as hell didn't sign up to die on this godforsaken rock," she turned back and stared out at the impenetrable darkness through the windshield. "Anyway, it's a court-martial for me when I get back."

"Better than staying here," said Alice.

"Damn right, girl."

Alice gave a long sigh. "I'm going to head back inside and try and get some rest." She unstrapped her seat harness and made her way to the interior cabin.

Renton took her seat and looked over at Yuna. "Want me to take over, so you can get some rest as well?"

She shook her head. "No, I'm good. I'm going to see this through."

"Okay."

They sat there for a long time in silence as the rover rumbled across Tranquility. There was not much to see outside except the canopy of stars above them and the vague silhouette of the lunar horizon. Eventually, Renton dozed off again.

He came around after he sensed a change in the rover's moment; they were slowing down.

"Nearly there," said Yuna. Just over this ridge and we should see it."

Renton sat up, peering into the blackness. Behind him, Alice came into the cockpit. "Good sleep?" he asked.

"A little," she replied. "Matteo's still zonked."

"That's because he spent all his time in that SINO place just ranting."

"There," Yuna pointed ahead, as the rover crested the ridge.

They were looking across a wide, flat plain and around four-hundred meters away sat the FISA rescue shuttle, bathed in a pool of hazy illumination from its exterior lights. A few hundred meters further on again, they could just make out the pulsing red beacon of the emergency shelter. The cockpit comms crackled into life. Spider flicked a switch so all of them could hear.

"Glad you made it. You had us worried, we've been waiting for a while."

"Glad to be here," said Spider. "And thanks for waiting. We'll bring the rover up close and walk from there."

"What sort of EVA suits do you have? We're a bit tight on room in this bird."

"It a mix of mining and general, and there's eight of us."

There was a long pause from the shuttle pilot, and the crew began exchanging a few anxious glances.

"Eh... we only have room for five, that's what they told us we'd be picking up."

"Can you do a second run or send another shuttle?"

"Let me run that by Central. But don't worry, we'll sort something out. You'd better decide on the first five, the others can wait in the emergency shelter."

"Okay. It is what it is." Spider ended the comms and looked from one to the other. Nothing was spoken but they all had the exact same thought. It was time to ditch the Xiang Zu hitchhikers.

Had Spider kept the comms private maybe things might have worked out differently. But she didn't, preferring instead to let everybody hear the conversation. This included Haitao and his crew, who were now wide awake and had heard every word the shuttle pilot had uttered. Renton was first to react when they heard the kerfuffle breaking out in the rover cabin. He rushed to the open cockpit door only to be met with a heavy boot to the abdomen, resulting in him flying back over Alice and both ending up sprawling in a tangled mess.

In the doorway, Haitao stood brandishing a rapid-fire gauss weapon. Behind him, back in the cabin, Renton could see that Matteo had another pistol jammed into his neck, preventing him from taking any action. The rivet gun that Renton had given him was now in the hands of the third Xiang Zu hitchhiker.

"I think we'll be taking that shuttle first," Haitao kept the pistol trained on Spider, correctly assuming that she would be the main threat.

"Screw you, that's our ride," she spat back.

"Too bad, you'll just have to wait for the next one." He took aim and fired around a dozen shots into the cockpit electronics. Everyone dove for cover as sparks flew in all directions. The rover's systems shorted out, the power died, and the rover ground to a halt just as Haitao backed out of the doorway and slammed it shut.

Renton was up on his feet and launched himself at the door only to bounce off it again with a groan, clutching his shoulder. His suit was tough but the door was not giving way that easily. "Crap, they've jammed it."

Smoke began to fill the cockpit from a small fire that licked into existence on the central dashboard. Yuna grabbed a fire extinguisher and blasted the flickering flames before they had a chance to grow. It was then that Renton noticed Spider plucking two steel barbs out of her right shoulder.

"You're hit." Alice picked herself up off the floor and tried to help Spider out of the upper portion of her EVA suit so she could staunch the blood flowing from the wounds.

"We have to warn the shuttle crew," Renton examined the comms panel but it was dead. "Damnit. No power, we need to get out of here," he rushed the door again and experienced exactly the same result.

"Look," Yuna shouted. "They're outside."

Through the rover windshield, four suited figures moved across the lunar surface toward the small shuttle, their path illuminated by their helmet lights.

"They've taken Matteo with them," Alice grabbed Renton's arm forcing him to look around at the scene outside.

He could see Matteo being shoved along by one of the crew who had a gun shoved into his back.

"They're using him to talk to the shuttle crew," said Yuna. She had managed to put the fire out but was still holding the extinguisher. Renton grabbed it from her and started to bash at the door hinges. "We need to get out and stop this."

The door began to give and Renton ran at it again, this time with better luck as the door finally separated from the frame and ended up crashing into the interior cabin along with Renton.

"The helmets, they've taken them." Renton saw the rack empty and began searching around frantically in the vain hope that they might be hidden somewhere. But they were gone, probably dumped outside, and without an EVA suit helmet there was no possible way to exit the rover, unless through an umbilical airlock connection.

Alice was helping Spider bandage up her bloodied shoulder, sitting her down in the cabin, and pulling out a first aid kit. Yuna still stared wide-eyed out the windshield as Haitao and his crew propelled their captive toward the waiting shuttle.

"We have to try and restore power, Yuna." Renton needed to get her focused on something they could do to get themselves out of this situation. Because now that the lunar night had arrived, the temperature outside would be a very chilly minus 130 degrees centigrade. And trapped in a rover without power, they would freeze to death long before they ran out of air to breathe.

"They're opening the airlock door!" Yuna shouted. "Look. Those bastards, they're letting them onboard."

Renton could see the green light blink on above the airlock door on the small craft as it began to open. One of the Xiang Zu crew was getting ready to step inside—probably Haitao. Renton needed to do something. But like Yuna, he found himself spellbound by the drama playing out before him. He was watching his ride home slipping away, one step at a time. The second Xiang Zu crew member had now entered the airlock, keeping a gun fixed on Matteo, who seemed to be protesting. In the next moment, Matteo went tumbling across the surface kicking up a cloud of dust as he hit the ground.

"They've shot him... shot Matteo!" Yuna screamed.

Alice and Spider came rushing into the cockpit, just in time to see the last Xiang Zu guy step into the airlock.

"Shit, shit, shit," Renton slammed his fists down on the already wrecked dashboard. "We gotta do something."

But Yuna grabbed his arm. "They're taking off, look."

The shuttle rose slowly until it was a few meters off the surface, almost completely obscured by the dust cloud that the engines kicked up. It spun around and began to ascend. But something seemed wrong. It started to weave this way and that like the pilot was fighting for control of the craft. Then its nose tilted up suddenly, until it was almost vertical. It began to drift backward, faster, and faster. The four of them watched dumbstruck as their last hope of getting home hit the lunar surface and exploded in a great ball of exploding energy.

CHAPTER 28
CHANGE OF PLAN

The four occupants of the dead rover stood mute in the cockpit watching the dust cloud billowing out from the site of the crashed shuttle. It was gone, along with everyone in it, all dead, presumably. Renton, like the others, was frozen by the sheer tragedy of it, not believing what their eyes were telling them. He was finally jolted into action when he sensed some movement in his peripheral vision, over in the direction of his fallen comrade Matteo—he was moving.

"Matteo, he's still alive," he pointed.

All eyes shifted away from the crash site and on to the figure that was trying to gather himself up off the lunar surface and stand.

"He's okay, he's okay," Alice voiced out loud what everyone else was thinking.

But he was not okay, he seemed disorientated, stumbled,

and fell a few times. Yet, his intention was clear, to try and make it back to the rover.

"Alice, help me get the power back on." Renton was finally spurred into action. "Otherwise Matteo won't be able to cycle through the airlock."

Alice surveyed the wreckage of the cockpit dashboard. "We'll need to isolate as many subsystems as we can first."

"I'll go check the state of the battery pack, hopefully we're just dealing with a tripped breaker, rather than anything more serious." He headed out of the cockpit to the rear of the rover and began removing a floor panel that should give him access to the battery control circuitry. Alice shooed Yuna and Spider out of her way, stripped out of her EVA suit, crawled under the dashboard, and began disconnecting the rover's subsystems.

"Looks clean back here, no signs of shorting," he stood up, took Alice's lead, and unburdened himself of the heavy EVA suit. He then popped his head in through the broken cockpit doorway. "How are you getting on?"

"Nearly there, just a few more things to disconnect."

Yuna and Spider were watching Matteo's progress. He had covered half the distance but was struggling, seemingly getting weaker. The shots from the gauss pistol had not only injured him but punched a few holes in his suit, which would be working hard to maintain internal pressure, using up copious quantities of air in the process.

"Okay, I think that's most of the heavy loads disconnected from the main power bus," Alice began extracting herself from under the dashboard.

"I'll flip the breaker and..." he gave them all a hopeful look. "Fingers crossed nothing explodes."

"You'd better hurry," Yuna cautioned. "I don't think Matteo's going to last much longer out there."

Renton rushed back to the rear of the rover, reached down, and cranked the primary power breaker. For a split second, nothing happened, then he heard the hum of the life-support system kick in, and he began to breathe easier. He returned to the cockpit to see Alice back down under the dash again. "Connecting the airlock system now," she announced.

Renton looked back down the rover cabin and saw the airlock status light flick on. "Working," he replied. "Let's leave it at that and not push our luck until we get Matteo inside."

Alice crawled back out and all eyes were now on Matteo's progress; he had almost reached the rover, close enough to see the four of them gesticulating through the windshield and pointing to the rear airlock. No doubt most of what they were trying to impart—loss of power, no helmets, etcetera—was completely lost on him. But hopefully he got the gist, that they were trapped inside and were depending on him to make it back. It seemed to translate as Matteo's gait visibly changed— he dug deep and kept moving. They all moved out of the cockpit and gathered around the airlock door at the very rear of the rover and waited, listening for the telltale sound of the outer door activating. No one spoke, communicating with each other only with anxious glances. It seemed to take forever, and Renton began to fear that Matteo had collapsed somewhere outside, maybe only meters from the outer door. But then they heard the grind of the motors.

"Outer door opening," Yuna called out as she monitored progress on the airlock control panel. There was a rocking movement in the rover as Matteo stepped in, then there was a jolt; possibly he had fallen to the floor.

"Outer door closing," Yuna continued. "Decontamination... pressurizing... forty percent... sixty percent."

At this they all moved back a little, as if to give their stricken colleague more breathing space. The airlock status light turned green and immediately Renton wrenched the inner door open. Matteo was slumped on the floor, his abdomen caked in frozen blood, his face pale and gaunt.

Renton reached down and unclipped his helmet. "Quick, let's get him out of this suit."

"Bastards," Matteo's voice was labored.

"Just take it easy, we'll get you sorted."

They moved him into the central cabin and began to remove the EVA suit. "Sorry, they jumped me while I was sleeping," he said, after they'd got the top half of the suit off.

"It's okay, Matteo. Just take it easy," Yuna surveyed the wounds. Two barbs poked out from his abdomen.

Alice spread out the first aid kit. "Believe me, Matteo, I've never been more glad to see you than now. If you hadn't made it back here, well we'd all be dead."

"They shot me," he looked down at this bloodied torso.

"Hey, for what it's worth, they shot me too," Spider gestured to her bandaged shoulder.

After ten or so minutes, they had extracted the barbs and got Matteo bandaged up. He seemed to have revived a little and he looked slightly better. Renton slumped down on one of the cabin seats and his mind started thinking about their options.

Matteo drank down some water. "By the way, your suit helmets are all dumped outside," he gestured with a thumb. "Just beside the airlock."

"I'll go get them," offered Yuna, since she was the only one still in a full EVA suit. She picked up Matteo's helmet, snapped it on, and headed for the airlock.

"We need to get to that emergency shelter. There'll be supplies there and hopefully a working comms unit. We can try and raise FISA and see what the plan is now."

"There is no plan," Spider slumped down on one side of Matteo, nursing her shoulder. "That was it," she jerked a thumb in the direction of the crashed shuttle and winced with a sting of pain. "Did you see what they sent us? It was barely bigger than a personal transport. That means everything is being utilized; commandeered most likely. Everyone is getting the hell out of here; everyone is panicking."

"That's not true," Alice shook her head. "They won't leave us here, they'll send another shuttle, won't they?" she looked over at Renton for confirmation.

"I know they'll try." It was the best he could offer.

The inner airlock door opened again and Yuna stepped out carrying several helmets that she dumped on the floor.

"Thanks, Yuna," said Renton as he went to pick one up and inspect it for damage.

"How do you suppose we get there, seeing as how the rover is busted and my EVA suit is all out of resources," asked Matteo. "I barely made it back here."

"We go, you stay behind," Renton smiled at him.

"What! You're leaving me here?"

"Just for a while, I'll come back with a spare suit. Then I'll carry you back to the shelter if I have to."

Matteo nodded and smiled. "That would work."

"Spider, how's your suit?"

"A few holes, but nothing some duct tape won't handle. It'll get me there."

"Okay, well I suppose we should get going. Those two SINO rovers are still out there somewhere and I'm sure that crash lit up every scanner in the neighborhood. They'll be heading here soon, that's for sure."

CHAPTER 29
SPACE DIVISION

A Space Division dreadnaught class Starliner, with over a hundred souls on board, accelerated up through the thick Earth atmosphere over Vandenberg on the west coast of the North American continent, on a direct flightpath to the Moon.

Staff Sergeant Alex Doukas currently felt like he was being hammered into his seat as the G forces required to break free of Earth's gravity well bore down on him and the rest of his company. He looked over at Sánchez in the row opposite him, who was gritting his teeth and screwing up his face as they all rode the dragon—their phrase for the intense hell-ride that was lift-off. Beside them, Burton had his eyes closed and looked as if he was sleeping, catching some zees before the real action began. Then again, he could be passed out, it was hard to tell with Burton.

Well, this is it, he thought. *Time to earn the pay.*

He knew what he was getting himself into, he knew the score, they all did. Space Division weren't the type of operation that would mess with your head; they gave it to you straight. Anyone going on this mission would not be coming back for a very long time—because there would be no way to come back. Estimates ranged from two years to forever, assuming he didn't get perforated by a gauss weapon in the meantime. So, volunteers only, and he'd stuck his hand up.

They all had their reasons. Some were doing it out of a wild sense of adventure, a new frontier to be experienced. Others did it for the money—they were the ones convincing themselves that they would be back on Earth in a few years so they could spend it all.

But Alex Doukas wasn't doing it for either of these reasons, nor was he doing it out of a sense of duty. No, he was going on this one-way mission because he knew what was about to happen back on Earth. Some of the others knew it too, just as soon as SD had explained the mission to them. But SD talked more about what was going on in cislunar space, not what was about to go down back on terra firma.

If what they were saying was true, and he had no reason to doubt it, then every data satellite in orbit was heading for total annihilation—the world about to go dark, very dark. Already, there were riots after the payment systems stopped working and some people tried to get their money out in old-fashioned cash, not realizing it had been abandoned as a legitimate form of payment some thirty years earlier. Panic buying had begun and security had been beefed up in a lot of places. But the one that was sending everyone over the edge was the reports of the Datasphere going dark in many regions. Where it did work, it only just crawled along. Of course that got a whole bunch of people riled up who thought it was just the government shutting it down, trying to hide the true story. If it was like that now, then what would it be like in a few weeks, months, years? It didn't take a geopolitical analyst to work it out. Things were going to get real bad.

So he had volunteered. He had done it for his family. Sure he lied and told them it was only for a year. But he knew they would be safe from the apocalypse that was about to hit. Space Division looked after its own. His family now had a nice place right inside the base. It was well protected, well stocked, and nothing, barring a missile strike, could get to them. On the outside of that base perimeter, there was going to be a shitshow once the food started running out, as it surely would.

Some of his buddies thought it wouldn't get that bad, but they just didn't get it. With the main data networks breaking down, how was food distribution supposed to work? It was a completely automated system of stock management. Sure, food would still exist in the big distribution warehouses, but there would be no way of ordering it, and things would become chaotic very quickly. The supermarkets would run out in two weeks, sooner if the panic buying really kicked in. Then what? People would have to fend for themselves, and that was the scary part, he knew what that meant. It wouldn't be a sudden outbreak of neighborliness, sharing and caring. No, it would be taking what was needed by whatever means possible in order to survive.

The G forces acting on his body finally eased off and he was beginning to feel lighter. They would soon be passing through LEO, where all the communications constellations were parked —the danger zone. He gripped the armrests and hoped for the best.

Unbeknownst to Alex Doukas, around three hours earlier, in an orbital shell some 550 kilometers above Earth's surface, satellite BX284-57 of the Starlight constellation was busy doing what it had been designed to do. That was, until a small aluminum hex bolt—itself a product of a previous collision— slammed into it at seven meters per second, shattering BX284-57 into a thousand pieces, give or take. One of these pieces happened to be the satellite's tiny silicon carbide mirror used for laser communication, a material almost as hard as diamond. Almost immediately, a ground-based radar array utilized by MASTERM began tracking this new micro-debris cloud and feeding the angular data into the organization's central computer. But by now, the sheer volume of new information already flooding in had overwhelmed the analytics engine and new data began to be buffered, waiting its turn in the processing queue.

And so, the tiny silicon carbide mirror went unnoticed until it slammed into the crew section of the Space Division Starliner. It blew a hole in the port side, which expanded rapidly as the internal atmosphere rushed out, ripping the hull apart. The mirror itself disintegrated into a hundred tiny shards that kept going, ripping through the company of men and women within. The hull began to disintegrate like a cracked egg spewing its contents out into the void, in a cataclysmic cloud of swirling entrails, venting gasses, and tumbling bodies.

For Alex, one minute he was laughing at some joke that Sánchez was telling him, next he was floating out in the blackness of space. The remains of the ship now just an ever-expanding ball of wreckage. It took his brain a few moments to make sense of his new situation. Something hit the spacecraft, or something exploded internally. He must have been knocked unconscious by the impact. His EVA suit had sensed the drop in atmospheric pressure and automatically snapped his visor shut and pressurized. He had been flung out of the disintegrating ship along with everything else.

Instinctively he called for his squad to report—nothing. He tried again—still nothing. He tapped the suit's thruster controls and halted his outward momentum. Then slowly started moving back toward the epicenter of the disintegrating ship. Bodies, and body parts, floated all around him. It was only then that the full horror of the disaster began to sink in.

He drifted through the detritus, checking the status of his fallen comrades, calling out on comms, hoping that some others had survived. After an hour of searching, checking, and calling out, he came to the stark realization that he was probably the only one of the hundred souls on board still alive. But that would only be for as long as his oxygen lasted, a few hours at best. At least his family would be safe, that's all that mattered in the end.

Some hours later, after he had accepted that he would die out here, floating in space, his comms crackled into life. It was a rescue ship dispatched from the Space Division orbital base station, broadcasting a call to survivors.

Twenty minutes later, with his oxygen tank only moments from empty, he was picked up. Two hours after that, he was on board the SD orbital. Two days later, he would be back with a very surprised and happy family at the base in Vandenberg, one of only two that would survive. He would also notice that the security around the perimeter had quadrupled in his absence.

CHAPTER 30
NEW REALITY

S elene paced the room, back and forth, back and forth. Waiting for news of Renton and the crew of the FISA maintenance ship. They should have been picked up by now, but her efforts to contact Jean over in Central were met with connection problems. One of the FISA techs was working on it. The entire FISA contingent on the Axial Luxor had all gathered together in the FISA sector. This had been designated as an assembly point where they would be organized into groups, then dispatched down to the central docking hub where two FISA spaceships were waiting to take them back to Earth.

The mood was somber, with a heavy cloud of foreboding hanging over everyone. The news of the destruction of the Space Division ship while traveling through LEO had shocked not just the FISA people, but everyone in lunar space. This catastrophe, while horrific in its toll on human life, had the effect of bringing the threat of isolation into sharp focus.

Whatever doubts anyone had about the veracity of the forecasts of a Kessler Syndrome occurring, it was now all very real. From now on, a journey back to Earth would be a lottery, with the odds of not making it rapidly increasing the longer people waited.

The hotel was already shutting down, as staff were being evacuated on shuttles over to the main orbital spaceport. Much of it was being taken offline with only the basic systems remaining, those that governed life support and facilitated the evacuation. The areas around the elevators for accessing the dock were crowded with people, fights were breaking out, and there had been reports of several injuries from crushing and general violence.

"Selene, can you please stop that pacing, you're just driving yourself nuts," Dyson gave her a sympathetic smile.

She stopped and gave a sigh. "I can't help it. I need to be doing something, and it helps me think."

"There is nothing you can do at the moment," he shook his head.

"Attention everybody," Dale, the FISA liaison officer, stood up on a table and addressed the crowd. "We've secured the B5 dock access elevator," he waved a hand in the general direction. "That's the closest one to this sector. Will all people in the first group start making their way there now. And please keep calm, let's do this in a civilized manner, and we'll get it done quicker." He stepped down from the table as people started to gather up their belongings and file out the door.

The sector began to empty as around half of the FISA staff drifted away. Those that remained included some of the senior

FISA directorate, who had chosen to be in the second group as a show of solidarity and hopefully lessen the chances of organization breakdown with those having to wait it out for the second ship. Alan E. Dyson was not one of them.

"Selene?" the tech called over from the comms console he had set up in the boardroom. "Got a connection."

Selene went over and sat down beside the tech, just as the head and shoulders of Jean from Central materialized on the screen. From his body language, Selene instantly expected the worst. He took a deep breath before talking, never a good sign.

"The situation has gotten complicated," he started.

"What the hell does that mean?" Selene replied, keeping her voice down.

"The shuttle we sent crashed. Not sure what exactly happened."

Selene's mouth opened in shock.

Jean raised a hand. "Don't panic, Renton and the crew weren't on board, they're okay. And I have them on another comms connection from the emergency shelter where they're holed up," he glanced over at another screen off camera. "Putting them through now."

An image of the beleaguered crew of the FISA maintenance ship materialized on a section of the screen. Renton and another woman were sitting down, with two others standing behind them, all facing the camera. They looked gaunt and haggard, one looked injured as she had a large bandage covering one shoulder.

"Renton, what happened? Are you okay?"

"Long story. We got highjacked. They took the shuttle. Don't know what went on, but it crashed and exploded," he jerked a thumb over his shoulder. "We're holed up in the emergency shelter. Matteo and Spider here have both been shot up. They're okay though."

"So what's the plan?" the woman with the bandaged shoulder, sitting beside Renton, now spoke. "I'm the one who got them out, the Space Division agent you were dealing with."

"Spider?" asked Selene.

"Yeah. And tell me you're sending another shuttle?"

"Eh... that might be a problem," Jean answered, running a hand through his thinning hair. "Everything we've got is being utilized to evacuate people from the main population centers up to the spaceports. And you're way over in Tranquility."

"Well just get someone to take a detour," said Renton.

"It's not that simple. The Space Division disaster has people spooked, most of the crews are operating on their own, nobody's taking orders, least of all from me." Jean suddenly seemed to get distracted, looking away from the camera at someone else who was talking to him. He waved a dismissive hand at them. "Yeah, yeah, I'm coming," he looked back and shook his head.

"What Space Division disaster?" asked Spider.

"You don't know?" Jean looked wide-eyed at her.

"A company of SD military were on their way from Earth," Selene began spelling it out for them. "The ship was struck just inside LEO, completely destroyed, over a hundred dead, only two survivors."

"Jesus," Spider shook her head in disbelief.

"So you see..." continued Jean. "That's got everybody

running wild up here. I can't get anybody to do anything that isn't about saving their own asses."

"What about the shuttles at the space ports?" asked Renton. "There's gotta be one free?"

"Sure," said Jean. "But you won't get anyone to pilot it, not down to Tranquility."

"So, we're stuck here, that is what you're saying?" said Renton.

"Look, even if I could get you a shuttle and find a crew, by the time you got back to one of the spaceports there might be no places left. And even if there were, there is no guarantee you'd get back to Earth in one piece." Jean looked away again. "Yeah, I'm coming. Goddamnit."

He looked back at the camera, shaking his head. "I'm sorry, guys, I truly am, but there's nothing more I can do. I gotta go or I'll..." his sentence trailed off. "Well, you know." And with that the comms connection closed, leaving Selene staring dumfounded at an equally dumfounded crew.

"They're not going to leave us here, they just can't." One of the other crew members started getting very emotional. Another of the crew wrapped her arm around her and pulled her in tight. Selene could hear the sobbing.

"So that's it. We're screwed," said Renton, more as a statement than a question.

Selene slowly placed her hands on the table, looked down and sighed. "Look, I'm not going to sugarcoat this, but Jean's right, it's everybody for themselves—at least, that's what it's turning into. Except, not everyone's leaving. SINO are digging in."

"So I noticed," said Spider. "They seem to think that it's just FISA propaganda, although not all. Some are not that gullible, like the ones that highjacked us."

"There's also Xilinex," Selene continued.

"The mining corporation?" asked Renton.

"Yes, we think around half have left but they've been bringing up mercenaries. For what purpose, we can only speculate."

"Who else?" asked Spider.

"Some much smaller groups, but most people who can are leaving."

"Well, that's just great," Renton shook his head. "What do we do now? This shelter will only keep us alive for a week or more. And we also have SINO hunting us down. There's a number of rovers heading our way as we speak."

"There is one option," Selene glanced around the room, hoping no one was paying too much attention to her.

"Yeah, what's that?"

"Head for Moon Base Delta. It's a massive facility, with power, life support, water, food production. You could survive there..." Selene hesitated, "... indefinitely."

The crew took a moment to come to terms with what was she was suggesting—that they give up all hope of returning to Earth and instead focus on simply surviving.

"Isn't that mothballed, out of commission?" Renton finally asked.

"Yes, but still maintained. It can be reactivated at any time. You just need the access codes. There are multiple sets. Some I have in my possession, which will give you access to the areas used by FISA maintenance crews. The others, I need to get for you. Those will allow you to enter the FISA sector and ultimately reactivate the entire facility by rebooting the AI core. This will give you complete control and lock all other agencies out of the system. No one else can get in, unless by force."

"You're not seriously thinking of doing this?" An older crew member now shuffled into view. He was bare-chested with a bloodied bandage wrapped around his torso. He directed his question to Renton and Spider.

"Unless you want to spend the rest of your days in a SINO hell-hole, then we don't really have much option," Renton replied.

"Assuming they don't kill us first," Spider added.

"I'll send you what I have now. Once you're inside the maintenance facility, I'll contact you with the reboot codes."

Renton studied his aunt for a moment, then nodded. "Okay. We'll figure it out. Just don't let us down."

The connection terminated.

CHAPTER 31
TRAVERSING TRANQUILITY

Renton stared at the blank comms screen in the emergency shelter for a moment, trying to come to terms with the clusterfuck that was unfolding. Behind him, he could hear Alice trying to console Yuna, who was losing it. That came as a surprise to him. If he had to pick a person in the group that he thought would buckle under the strain, he would have picked Matteo, not the steely flight officer. He felt a hand on his shoulder and Spider came around and sat on the comms bench in front of him.

"If we're doing this, then we need to get our shit together," she nodded over at Alice and Yuna.

Renton spun the seat around. "Yuna, how far is it to the base?"

Yuna shook her head, then took a breath. "Around six kilometers due north."

"Could you navigate us there if we walk?"

Renton tried to push Yuna's brain into operating in her comfort zone, that of a flight officer. She rubbed her face and sat up a little. "Once I have a cardinal point, yes. This area is mostly flat so we should see the base beacons a few kilometers out."

"I thought all you guys were engineers? Can't you just fix the rover?" asked Spider.

Matteo actually laughed, and then regretted. "Ha, stop, you're killing me," he clutched his abdomen.

"What's so funny, it's a simple question," Spider looked confused.

"Yes, we could," said Renton. "Given enough time and spare parts, but we don't have either of those," he looked at Spider with a smile. "And what's funny is that it's an inside joke between us. Every client asks the same question. *You're an engineer, can't you just fix it.*" Matteo laughed again.

Even Spider took the joke at her expense. "Okay so we walk. If it's six klicks then that'll take us an hour, give or take. Matteo, think you can handle that?"

"Yeah, I can manage that. Just don't make me laugh again."

Renton stood up. "Okay, if we're all agreed then we'd better start gathering up whatever resources we can from here."

As the initial shock of their impending isolation on Luna started to recede, the new threat of being recaptured by SINO began to spur the crew into action, and they began to cannibalize the shelter for everything useful.

These emergency shelters were a mixed bag, having been cobbled together from much older facilities from a previous era of lunar development. This one was possibly part of an old base used to accommodate workers building Moon Base Delta. But rather than abandoning the facility, it was handed over to a newly formed, multinational organization created as a rescue service. This came about as a consequence of the numerous deaths of workers that found themselves in trouble because of equipment failure. Something needed to be done and so the emergency service was born, and soon agencies began donating end-of-life facilities that could be retrofitted as shelters.

This one was bigger than most, having been an accommodation module that housed around fifty workers. It had been built into a natural undulation and covered with a thick sintered regolith dome. Power was an old-school solar that also charged an energy storage unit during the long lunar daytime cycle—equivalent to approximately fourteen Earth days. This provided power during the equally long lunar night. There were also two Radioisotope Thermoelectric Generators. These converted heat from the natural radioactive decay of plutonium. Very old technology, but it was trouble free and could be relied on to operate for years without maintenance— of primary importance for a shelter that needed to operate at any given time.

The crew scavenged a workable EVA suit for Matteo along with supplies of oxygen, water, and food. Some of which they piled onto a makeshift sled so they could haul it behind them. Once they were all ready to depart, Renton brought up a map of the area on the main screen at the comms station. Yuna sat beside him and pointed out the main features as the others all stood behind looking and listening to what their flight officer was saying.

"This is us here," she pointed to a marker on the map. Then zoomed out. "And up here is Moon Base Delta, 6.3 kilometers, straight line. Further north is Sinas Crater, and this is a satellite crater, Sinas K. Over to the right, the terrain is fairly flat, but on this side there's a long ridge, if we keep it to our right, we will be out of sight of any rovers coming down from the end of the Couchy I Rille."

No one spoke for a moment as all contemplated the map. Finally, Spider said, "If SINO are coming down that way, they'll pass Moon Base Delta. We'll need to consider that they might be checking the base out when we arrive."

"Yeah, well, that's something we'll just have to deal with when we get there," said Alice, as she snapped on her helmet.

They all gathered outside and took a moment to do a comms check, as well as making sure that everyone's suit was working. Yuna then cast her gaze around the barren, desolate landscape before pointing ahead. "This way. Let's go."

Walking on the Moon, even though its gravity is only one-sixth of Earth's, is not a simple task. Much of what humans have physically evolved to do on Earth has to be unlearned. The process is more of a hopping, bouncing motion, which takes time to get familiar with—resulting in much falling over before any proficiency can be built up. But the advantage of this ungainly gait is that a lot of ground can be covered very quickly, much more so than what can be achieved back on the home planet.

After a borderline comedic start, where members of the crew with the least experience spent most of the time picking themselves back up from the ground, they began to find a rhythm, bounding across the dusty terrain with purpose. Yuna took the lead, with Renton taking up the rear and pulling the sled of supplies behind him on a long tether. A tricky operation as he needed to synchronize the rhythm of his forward momentum with that of the load he was pulling. Nevertheless, they made good progress; better than expected. Yet they had to stop several times, partly to let Renton catch up, and partly for Yuna to check the map on her wrist-mounted console. This linked to the FISA geo-positioning satellite system in lunar orbit. Unlike the nav-sats orbiting Earth, these, along with most of the cislunar satellite infrastructure, had been protected from the worst effects of the solar storm by the Earth eclipse.

Yuna pointed at a rise in the terrain. "If we head for that ridge over there, we should be able to see the beacons at the edge of the base. Not too far now," she added, and moved off.

A few moments later, she stood atop the ridge scanning the terrain beyond. "There! I see them," she called back to them over the comms, waving an arm toward the north.

Renton was last to mount the ridge and could feel the same sense of relief at finding the beacons as the rest of the crew. He imagined it was not unlike a sailor of old, seeing the flash of a familiar lighthouse in the distance. The beacons were faint and hazy—probably around two kilometers away, almost on the lunar horizon. Any further and they would be obscured by the curvature of the Moon. They wasted no time and moved off again down the far side of the ridge with a renewed vigor now that their destination was in sight.

After another fifteen minutes of pushing hard, they had reached the flat plain that marked the outskirts of the base. They could see it now, its domes silhouetted against the canopy of stars, illuminated briefly in a red glow from the flashing beacons. They stopped to take a breather; Matteo was clearly struggling and slowing down noticeably. "How are you holding up?" Renton asked and he laid a hand on his colleague's shoulder.

"Just... give me... a minute... to catch my breath," he bent over, resting a hand on his knee and the other holding his abdomen.

"Take as long as you need," Renton replied. "We're nearly there."

The others also took a moment to recuperate. Alice and Yuna sat down, but Spider stood and scanned the area all around.

"Renton?" she called.

"Yeah, what is it?"

She pointed over to the east. "Do you see lights over there? White lights?"

Renton strained to see anything in the distance other than darkness. He moved his gaze along the undulating horizon and saw a quick flash of white light. "Yes, I see it. You think it's SINO?"

"Can't be anything else," she replied, her focus still fixed on the spot far off in the distance. By now the light seemed to have risen from a dip in the terrain and was now steady and moving in their direction.

"Better move. We don't want to get caught out in the open," said Renton as he turned around to find that the others were all back on their feet, having also seen the rover lights.

They moved as fast as they could, even Matteo seemed to have found another gear. Each time Renton chanced a glance to his right, the rover lights seemed to be closing in on them, and there was not just one but two rovers.

Up ahead, the massive central dome of Moon Base Delta loomed out of the darkness, its outline dotted by a scattering of small pulsating beacons. Closer to the ground, a single green light indicated the southern airlock of the FISA sector. They pushed harder. Renton's legs ached, as muscles that hadn't seen much use in months were now being called upon to keep propelling him forward. Alice began lagging behind and he dropped back to keep her motivated. "Nearly there... just up ahead... keep moving."

She kept moving. Over to his right, the outline of the rovers could now be seen, and no doubt they would have spotted the five figures bounding toward the southern airlock entrance. They sped up, bouncing violently as they negotiated the undulating lunar surface.

"Renton, hurry!" Spider's voice burst out of his comms. He looked around but couldn't see her as she had already disappeared down the ramp leading to the maintenance crew airlock entrance. He ditched the sled of supplies; it was slowing him down. He dug deep, his body now fueled more by adrenaline than simple will. The others were also rushing down the ramp, some falling and tumbling. Spider was waving him on, urging him to hurry, as none of them could gain access without the codes he had stored in his wrist console. He tripped and tumbled down the last half of the ramp.

Yuna and Spider helped him up. Matteo had collapsed, he could see him breathing heavily through the helmet visor, his face screwed up in pain. Alice, too, was sprawled on the ground, slowly trying to get herself reoriented.

"Please tell me those codes are gonna work," Spider's anxious face glared out from behind her visor.

Renton didn't reply, already the superstructure above was being illuminated by the searchlight of the fast-advancing rovers. He pressed a hand to the airlock door control panel to open the dust cover, it rose up to reveal an illuminated control interface. He detached his wrist console and held it up against the screen allowing it to communicate over near-field.

The ramp was now flooded with light. He looked up to see a rover skid to a halt at the ramp entrance. Fortunately, it was too narrow to get down. The interface screen confirmed the code. ACCESS GRANTED appeared in big green letters, and the outer airlock doors began to separate.

Spider and Yuna grabbed Matteo by a collar strap and were dragging him through the opening doors. Renton helped Alice up and the two of them pushed in behind. Yuna slammed the button to close the airlock. As Renton turned to face out the now closing outer doors, several figures were already emptying out of the rover and moving down the ramp. One hefted a gauss weapon and started firing, just as the outer doors finally shut.

For a brief moment, Renton checked himself to see if he had been hit. But the shots were wildly off the mark.

The airlock cycled through its decontamination and repressurizing routine as Renton still kept one eye on the outer doors, expecting at any moment for them to open again. But they didn't. A green light pulsed overhead as the inner doors opened and the crew began to slowly open visors, unclip helmets, and drag themselves out into the old FISA maintenance crew area of Moon Base Delta.

"Can they open that airlock and get in this way?" Spider said, as she unclipped her helmet.

"I don't think so. This is on the FISA side of the base, and they don't have the codes," Renton replied as he checked on Matteo, who was sitting on the floor with his back to the wall trying to catch his breath. His face was beaded in sweat. "I'll be fine... just give me... a minute."

"We'd better get you checked out. There should be a medbay here somewhere."

Matteo just nodded. "In a minute."

"What now?" Alice had moved further into the maintenance area, looking around, taking stock of the supplies and equipment. Even though the base was officially off-limits to all agencies and put into sleep-mode, it still needed periodic maintenance to keep the minimum of systems ticking along. An agreement had been reached where small maintenance areas could be accessed by each of the participating agencies. This was the FISA area, but there were others all around the base, one of which SINO could access. From there, they could theoretically enter the main facility and ultimately get to this sector. But that would take some time.

The crew began to move around and explore the space. As they did, lights and systems began to flicker into life. It was an area a little bigger than the shelter they had just vacated, a circular domed structure, around twenty meters across. They found a rest area, with beds, hygiene, and a galley. Renton and Yuna brought Matteo over to a bunk and helped him out of his EVA suit. The bandages around his abdomen were a bloodied mess.

"I'll see if I can find the first-aid kit and get this sorted. We need to stop the blood loss." Yuna began searching around.

"Hang in there, buddy, we'll get you sorted soon," Renton tried to assure him.

Matteo gave a weak smile and nodded.

"Hey, guys, come check this out," Alice called out from somewhere at the back of the facility.

Renton patted Matteo on the shoulder. "You take it easy." Then went off to find Alice.

She was standing in front of a massive industrial airlock door. "That must be the way into the base."

Renton moved over to investigate the interface, wiping a layer of dust off it. He unclipped the unit from his wrist and presented it to the interface.

It beeped. ACCESS DENIED. "Crap, these codes don't work." He tried again, same result.

"Your aunt did say there were multiple different code sets, and she would send them to us once we got here," Spider came up beside them.

Renton sighed. "We'd better make contact, then. No time to waste."

They returned to the main work area to find Yuna standing beside a holo-table that had just sprung to life. A 3D schematic of the entire base blossoming out from its surface. "This place is huge, I never realized it was so big," Yuna began to zoom in and move the map around.

Renton cast his gaze around the semicircular operations area surrounding the holo-table. There were multiple screens and workstations, one of which Spider was now studying.

"I think this is comms," she said to Renton as he came over. "I presume FISA or Space Division get some form of alert when this maintenance facility is activated."

"Yeah, that's how it works. They should already know that we've made it this far. And hopefully Selene has the codes that give us access to the base proper."

"And keep the enemy out," added Spider.

"Yeah. All we have to do now is wait."

Alice gestured at a workstation interface and a wall-mounted screen flickered to life showing a camera feed from outside the maintenance sector. Two SINO rovers were parked up with several people milling around on the surface, all with gauss weapons clipped to the front of their EVA suits.

"What do they want with us? This just doesn't make any sense," said Renton. "If the negotiations have collapsed then surely they don't need us as bargaining chips?"

"It's because they're bastards!" Matteo shouted over from where he was supposed to be resting.

"You need to understand their mindset," said Spider. "On

the one hand, we've insulted them by escaping, they won't like that. But on the other, I suspect they might want you for your specialist knowledge of FISA infrastructure. Seeing as how you are a technical crew."

"I suppose," conceded Renton. "But then again how far are they willing to take that? Will they follow us in there?" he pointed off to the big airlock door at the back.

"I suspect we'll soon find out," said Alice.

Renton slumped down on a seat. "Nothing we can do except wait and hope that my aunt comes good with those access codes."

CHAPTER 32
GOTTA GO

Selene tried to raise Dyson on her personal comms. He had gone down with the first group to the central dock and she had to catch him before he boarded the flight back to Earth if she were to have any hope of extracting the reboot codes for Moon Base Delta.

No connection. It could be that the hotel's internal network was down or that Dyson had simply decided to go dark. Either way, Selene now had no other option but to physically chase after him. She hurried out of the boardroom, past shouts of protest from the other FISA staff still waiting patiently for their turn to head for the dock.

"Sorry, emergency," she called back as she ran to the elevators that provided access to the central dock. This was a much more complex system than the main hotel elevators as they had to move from an almost one gee environment to zero gee.

She arrived to find crowds of people all trying to cram into them. Several hotel security staff had been posted at the entrance and given the thankless task of keeping order. She scanned the crowd hoping to spot Dyson. But she saw none of the first group of FISA staff, so he must have made it down to the dock.

Damnit, she thought. *I'm never going to get through this crowd.* Yet she had to try. She made a beeline for the most senior looking of the security guards.

"I need to get down to the dock. I need to contact Alan Dyson, Head of FISA, it's a matter of the utmost urgency," she flashed her FISA Directorate ID.

The security guard gave it only a cursory glance, then much to Selene's relief, he nodded. "Okay, you can take the maintenance elevator," he stood aside and gestured at a small insignificant looking door with a sign reading: *WARNING! Authorized Personnel Only.*

"Be advised," the guard continued. "It's basic so make sure you are firmly secured when you get in." He opened the door to the elevator, revealing a small compartment with only enough room for four people who each had to be strapped in for the ride. Selene slotted herself into a wall harness and hit the button for the dock. The door closed and the elevator pod began ascending toward the central dock at breakneck speed. She almost threw up. Soon though, she felt the weight lifting from her body as the pod moved into zero gee. The door opened, and she was greeted by another group of security guards. They seemed to have been informed of her imminent arrival. One floated in and helped her out of the harness.

"You know where the FISA ships are docked?" she asked, a little breathlessly.

The guard pointed off down a long corridor. "That way, Gate Five. But be aware, it's pretty packed down there."

"Thanks," she gripped a hand hold and tried to get her zero-gee brain into motion.

Around the inner walls of the corridor were three lines of moving rails, where people could grab on to and be brought all the way to the dock. The center of the corridor also had rails but these were reserved for baggage handling. Selene reached out for a passing grab handle and began moving toward the departure gates. A few moments later, she detached herself and transferred to the access corridor that would bring her up to the docking area for the FISA ships. This access corridor ended in an open space; a waiting area crisscrossed with rails so that people had something to hold on to in zero-gee. Wide open spaces were never allowed in the design of such an environment because it was theoretically possible for someone to find themselves stranded midair, flapping around and unable to move. So even though the area was designed to accommodate over two hundred people, no handrails were ever more than two meters apart.

The area was crowded with the first batch of FISA staff clinging on to the rails like sleeping bats in a cave. She spotted Dyson over near the airlock entrance and made her way over to him.

"Alan," she announced her presence, a little out of breath.

"Selene, what the heck are you doing here?" he looked genuinely shocked to see her.

"I need the reboot codes for Moon Base Delta," she came straight out with it, no point in wasting time with niceties.

Dyson gave an exasperated sigh, seemingly disappointed in what he was hearing from her. "I thought we've been over all this, Selene."

"The rescue shuttle crashed. Renton and the crew are trapped down on the lunar surface. There's no way out for them, no way home."

His eyes widened. "You're joking me? What happened?"

"What happened doesn't matter. All that matters now is how they're going to survive. At the moment, they're heading for Moon Base Delta. SINO are chasing them down. And with that Space Division ship destroyed then there's nothing to stop SINO trying to take control of that base. It will be lost to us— forever. Renton is now our only chance to secure it."

Dyson was silent for a moment then leaned in and spoke in a low voice, "There have been reports of a company of mercenaries docking at the Xilinex orbital. It looks like they're also staying up here," he sighed.

"They could also make a play for Moon Base Delta," Selene replied. "We know that puffed-up puppet Pompodur has had his eye on it for a long time."

Dyson nodded. "It's a distinct possibility."

"And here we are, running away, Alan. No FISA, no Space Division, and most of the other agencies are going or have already gone. We will lose it for sure..." she paused for a beat. "But forget all that, Alan. Do this for me, and for Renton. I can't fail him again. I can't leave him and his colleagues to die a slow death on Luna. This will give them a fighting chance."

An announcement came over the public address for boarding. The crowd start to shift and move. Dyson glanced around at the passengers for a moment, then gestured at his wrist to activate his comms unit. He spent a moment interrogating the information on screen. "You know, as head of the agency, I've been responsible for carrying around these codes for so long that it's almost a relief to be rid of them." He turned his unit to Selene, indicating he wanted to do a data transfer. She reached into a pocket, pulled her comms unit out, and held it close to his. An icon flashed to show data transfer progress.

"There you go. Please don't make me regret this, Selene."

"Thank you, Alan. Thank you."

"Just a word of warning before you go. There's a strong possibility that knowledge of a reboot sequence for Moon Base Delta exists out in the open. By that I mean, it's possible that others are aware that we have such a backdoor. If they discover that you or Renton are in possession of such codes, then your lives will be in even more danger."

"Understood. Thanks for the heads-up. Anyway, safe flight home, Alan," she nodded towards the airlock door that had just opened for boarding.

"Good luck to Renton. I really hope he makes it," he gripped her hand. "Stay safe. And make sure you're on that next flight," he glanced around the waiting area. "Things are getting a little crazy down here." They broke apart as he moved off toward the airlock and was swallowed up in the throng of boarding passengers.

Dyson was right, things were getting crazier by the minute. People were desperately wanting to get on a ship as soon as possible and tensions were running high. She passed several scuffles on her way back to the maintenance elevator and could see the security staff were doing their best to keep more fights from breaking out. But for Selene, her opportunity to get out would have to wait. First, she needed to get back to the FISA boardroom, the only place she knew that had working comms.

By the time she arrived, the last of the FISA people were being evacuated, wedging themselves into the elevators.

"Selene, what are you doing back here? You need to get going," one of the FISA security staff called out to her.

"Just one more thing to do, then I'll head back down to the dock."

"You'd better hurry. I hear it's getting busy down there. You don't want to be left stranded."

Selene ran into the boardroom, sat down at the comm console, and began finding a route to the FISA maintenance facility at Moon Base Delta. She entered her credentials and the FISA logo on the screen disassembled in an elegant animation to present her with a stylized network diagram of all the official facilities that existed, both on the surface and in cislunar space. She gestured at the FISA node, then drilled down to the maintenance facility at Moon Base Delta.

"Selene, what the hell are you doing? You need to go, now!" The same security staff member she had met in the corridor had obviously been given the task of doing one last sweep for stragglers.

"Just go, don't wait for me. I'll be down in a minute."

He gave her a hesitant look, presumably considering if hanging around waiting for this person was worth the risk. In the end he replied, "Your choice," and left.

On the console screen Selene could see that the maintenance facility had been activated some time ago. She breathed a little easier, then gestured at the icon to instigate a connection. A moment later, a visual feed of Renton and the crew gathered around a workstation came into view.

"Renton," Selene's voice did not hide her joy at seeing his face. "You made it."

"Yeah," he glanced off to the side, looking at another screen. "But we have company. SINO are outside, I think they're trying to hack their way in. Tell me you have the codes?"

"Yes. I'm sending you two sets of data. One contains the access codes for the FISA sector of Moon Base Delta. Once you enter, you will be creating an international incident, but I think we're well past worrying about that now. The second is a reboot routine for the AI. You'll have to make your way down to level six in the central core of the base. Download the code I'm sending you onto the primary interface and run it. It will take a while to execute, but when it's complete, you will have total control over the entire facility. No one else can get in, they'll be locked out."

Renton nodded, "Okay, I see that coming through now." He glanced over at Alice and pointed at something on his screen.

"Download it on to a handheld comms unit, and for God's sake, don't let it get into the wrong hands."

"Do the other agencies not have similar reboot codes?" asked Spider.

"Not that we know of. To be honest, I wasn't completely sure if this actually existed, mostly it was just speculation and rumor. It was put there as a backdoor, just in case."

"Does anyone else know we have these?" asked Renton.

"I'm not sure," Selene gave an apologetic shrug.

"Crap," Yuna pointed at something on a screen. "They're inside the airlock."

"Gotta go," Renton moved away from the camera. In the background, the others started gathering up their stuff. Two of them helped the injured Matteo to his feet.

"Thanks for this, thanks for everything," Renton said as he turned to go.

Selene couldn't fight back the emotion; a tear escaped and channeled its way down her cheek. "I should have done more, I just..." her voice trailed off.

"You did more than you had to, Selene, taking in a broken soul all those years ago and mending it. It's up to me now. Goodbye, and good luck."

The comms link terminated, plunging Selene into a void of silence. She hung her head for a moment, then wiped her face and began making her way back to the elevators.

CHAPTER 33
INTELLIGENCE

Pompodur Rossen Adarok stood and watched the armada of ships slowly leaving lunar space, all heading for Earth. He had transferred to the Xilinex orbital, a state-of-the-art space station with a large rotating torus providing approximately 0.5 artificial gravity—a level that Pompodur found to be just perfect. While it was nowhere near as luxurious as the Axial Luxor, it was a far cry from the depredations experienced at the Xilinex facilities on the lunar surface. And, now that the corporation had given him the top job, this station would be his new home for the foreseeable future.

How long would that future be? he wondered as he stood in the sleek expansive boardroom gazing out through the huge faux window that ran along the entirety of one wall. It used a high-definition display to simulate the actual view but adjusted for rotation. If this were a real window, the exterior vista would be rotating at a speed that most people found disconcerting.

To his right, most of the view was taken up by a quadrant of the Moon, and from it could be seen the arc of ships launching off the surface, with incandescent trails reaching ever upward. There were hundreds of them, most probably old escape craft carefully maintained for years just in case of an emergency. Well, here it was.

Directly in front of him, almost at the limit of his vision, he could see the twinkling daisy-chain of lights that was the Axial Luxor Hotel. He had departed from there some time ago, in what was relative calm and made his way, along with the rest of his retinue, to the Xilinex orbital. He wondered what was happening at the hotel now; had panic set in yet?

To his left he could see the engine burn of a multitude of ships, some mere dots of light, no bigger than a twinkling star. Others, much closer, streaked across his field of view, leaving a blue plasma trail in their wake, all heading for the small blue marble that was Earth.

How many would make it? So many leaving—no, they're not leaving, they're fleeing, he thought. And with each ship that pointed its bow toward Earth and powered up its engines, his new job was being made easier. The facilities and bases were being cleared out, abandoned, ready for the taking. Just SINO stood in his way, yet they were proving very resilient to his propaganda campaign. Few, if any, had left. They would be a formidable nut to crack, considering they had exactly the same plan as Xilinex—total dominion over all lunar resources.

Still, it seemed FISA and their dependencies had collapsed.

Their military wing having suffered a catastrophic disaster, leaving them totally demoralized. Fortunately, the two ships of mercenaries that Xilinex had sent had arrived unscathed, and any moment now the new Xilinex Corporation Lunar Board would meet with the mercenary commander and discuss the takeover.

He turned around and put his back to the viewing wall. The boardroom itself was grand in size, taking up a significant portion of the station's torus. Yet it was almost completely empty of furnishing or adornment, spartan and utilitarian. The only thing in the room was a large circular holo-table with seating for twenty people. But they wouldn't be needing that many today—or any day from now on.

Of the thousands of Xilinex people that currently lived and worked on the Moon, over forty percent had elected to leave. However, the number of people on the executive council choosing to leave was more like seventy percent. Only three now remained, excluding Pompodur. Anton Levrosky and Ossian Corbell he knew reasonably well, both technocrats, wedded to the company. He had always assumed that they had no life worth living back on Earth, and this seemed to have been the case. Marcus Coldiron, on the other hand, surprised him. Like Pompodur, he was a man driven by ambition, but where they differed was that Marcus expected it to be handed to him on a plate. He wasn't prepared to do the work, and Pompodur hadn't known him to take a risk on anything of any merit. Yet here he was, throwing the dice like the rest of them.

No doubt these three were all wondering how the heck Pompodur got selected as the new President. *Let them wonder,* he thought. It didn't matter now; he had been given this position and he was damn well going to keep it.

The doors at the far end of the room opened and in strode General Kurt Wagner, the mercenary commander, with two others by his side. Pompodur sidled over and offered his hand. "You are very welcome, General." His grip was as Pompodur expected, firm, confident, and efficient. Pompodur gestured at the holo-table. "Shall we begin, then?"

As they took their seats, he could see that his colleagues were cautious of this unfamiliar addition to their little cabal. Military personnel were not something they had any experience with, unlike Pompodur. Perhaps this was another reason for his sudden appointment to the top job.

"How well do you know our operations up here?" Pompodur asked as he gestured at the holo-table to bring up a 3D image of Luna.

"We've been thoroughly briefed on all Xilinex operations and facilities."

"Well, I should bloody well hope so for all our sakes," said Marcus, a little too sarcastically for the General's liking.

He let it go and continued.

"We've been given a number of strategic objectives, but our operational options will be determined by whatever intelligence we can gather on SINO intentions and the current situation on the ground."

"The current situation is that SINO intend to do the same thing as us. I thought that would be blindingly obvious to a military strategist," Marcus continued to poke at Wagner, whose eyes narrowed and lips tightened. Pompodur could see that the General was probably itching to punch Marcus in the face. Time to cool things down a bit.

"They're not to be underestimated, General Wagner. They view things ideologically, always a dangerous foe. They see their ways as superior to the vacuous pursuit of profit by the corporations, and the decadent mores of the agencies: FISA, INDOCON, and the others. My guess is they regard this as their time—the whole of the Moon is theirs for the taking—a natural outcome of their superior hierarchical structure."

"That all sounds a bit... dramatic, even for you, Pompodur," said Anton.

Pompodur ignored this. Instead, he looked at this new General, then swept an arm around to gesture at his colleagues. "While my fellow board members here have concerned themselves with the technicalities and practicalities of operating an extensive mining and exploration corporation, I've spent my time dealing with the dark arts of politics and information manipulation," he gave a wry smile. "And so I've had a lot of dealings with SINO in this regard. Recently, I've been trying to broker a deal with them, and believe me when I tell you that they are medieval in their worldview. All my efforts to sow doubt and panic in their lower ranks have had very little outward effect. Most of them still remain, and those that managed to evacuate do so under the threat of hefty prison sentences when they return to Earth."

"You sound like you almost admire them," said Ossian.

"Perhaps I do, but only insofar as I like a challenge. But enough of this. How do you see it, General?"

Wagner gestured at the holo-table and proceeded to

manipulate the 3D holograph of the lunar surface. "This is our latest intelligence on levels of evacuation and abandonment." The map zoomed in on zones of current control, population centers, infrastructure, and so on, all highlighted with markers indicating estimates on abandonment and level of strategic importance.

"FISA are all but gone. Space Division has already been decimated and can now be disregarded as a threat."

"Again, this is all blindingly obvious, General," Marcus interjected, with more than a hint of arrogance in his voice. "Surely your intelligence has more to offer than this?"

Pompodur was about to tell Marcus to put a sock in it but Wagner was quicker to respond.

"Tell me, Mr. Coldiron. What exactly do you do up here?" he sat back and waited for a reply.

Marcus was clearly not used to anyone questioning him in such a manner and seemed genuinely flustered by it.

"I'm an Executive Director of the Xilinex Mining Consortium, one of the richest corporate entities in history," he sneered at the General. "Or does your *intelligence* not stretch that far?"

Wagner remained passive, then brought up an internal Xilinex dossier on Marcus Coldiron. It hovered over the holo-table. "Interesting you should mention that. It says here, and I'll just give you the short version, that you are a useless imbecile that Xilinex have been trying to get rid of for a very long time."

Marcus jumped up from his seat. "This is an outrage. You don't get to speak to me like that."

"It also says that you are dispensable." And before

Pompodur's synapses had even time to process this last statement, Wagner whipped a gauss pistol out from nowhere and put a short metal spike into Marcus Coldiron's skull—via his eye socket.

He went flying back across the empty floor of the boardroom, finally coming to rest, flat on his back, some five meters away. A long streak of blood marked his passage.

"Fuck!" Pompodur jumped back from the table, as did the other directors, and stared at the lifeless form of the director.

"You shot him!" Anton exclaimed, stating the obvious.

"That's right, I did. But I think you'll find we'll get along much better without him." Wagner disappeared his pistol back into a slit in his tunic. Pompodur looked over at his colleagues, trying to gauge their reaction after the initial shock had passed. They both looked back at him, clearly assessing his reaction as well.

"You didn't need to kill him," said Ossian finally.

"Oh, but I think I did. He would have just held us back," Wagner gestured with a hand back at the strategic map on the holo-table. "Now, can we get back to how we're going to achieve this mission. That is, unless there are any more questions about my *intelligence*?"

Pompodur considered the situation, as no doubt were his fellow directors. On the one hand, it could be said that this... sociopath... had just killed an innocent civilian in cold blood. Yet, on the other, it could be argued that, within a split second, he had stamped his authority on the mission by eliminating his enemy and demonstrating that he wasn't screwing around. He had a job to do and by god he was going to get it done.

Pompodur grinned, internally. He liked this guy's style. He opened his hands in an expansive gesture. "I'm all ears," he said as he sat down again.

Anton hesitated for a beat, before coming to the same conclusion and also sat down. That left Ossian, who was still contemplating Coldiron's body lying on the floor. "What about him?" he asked matter-of-factly.

"What about him?" replied Wagner with a shrug.

Ossian looked from Wagner to Pompodur, nodded, and he too sat down at the table.

Pompodur held an open palm out to Wagner with a smile. "Please, continue."

CHAPTER 34
ACCESS GRANTED

I t was clear that SINO were not going to let it go. They had worked to hack the outer airlock door to the FISA maintenance area that Renton and the crew had been holed up in, while they waited for Selene to come good on the codes. And not a moment too soon as SINO had breached the outer airlock door. Renton could see them on the camera feed readying their weapons as the outer doors opened. They'd be on top of them in minutes.

"Come on, we gotta run," Spider shouted back at him as she shepherded the others toward the massive access door at the rear of the maintenance facility.

Renton eyed the download indicator on his handheld comms unit as it inched its way to completion, then snatched it off the data interface and ran to the rear of the facility. The others were frantically constructing a makeshift barricade from storage containers. Not that it would hold anyone back but might slow them down a little. He ran to the door interface, wiped the dust from the screen, offered up the access code—and held his breath.

This door was a much more formidable looking structure than the airlock into the maintenance facility. Crafted from titanium and built to withstand pretty much everything except maybe a direct asteroid strike. The maintenance facility they were evacuating was a much more recent structure, added on at a later date by a lesser engineering god. The interface illuminated, and Renton exhaled. After over a decade of disuse, it had awoken to his call. Something heavy clanged inside the door's machinery followed by the sounds of great motors grinding and whirring as the long-closed entranceway broke its seal and swung open.

From the far side of the hasty barricade, Renton could also hear the sounds of another door, the inner airlock of the facility was being breached and SINO were coming through. The crew pushed and dragged themselves inside the massive airlock, into what seemed like a dark cavern. Renton swept the walls with a flashlight until he found the control panel. Thankfully it was rudimentary, a simple open and close button option. He hit the close, just as they heard SINO barging their way through the barricade. The door began to swing closed again, the crack of light streaming through from the maintenance facility growing narrower, like the crescent of a waning Moon.

A SINO operative appeared on the other side and Spider unleashed a barrage of steel barbs at them from her gauss pistol. *Phitt... phitt... phitt.* The sound echoed in the darkness, or maybe it was return fire. Too hard to tell since the door had closed. They were safe, for the moment at least.

"Everyone okay?" Renton called out as the airlock lights flickered and buzzed, protesting their long disuse. They cast an eerie green hue around the interior, which was large enough to fit a rover, and then some.

"Spider?" Yuna's voice held a note of alarm in it.

Renton spun back around to see Spider slumped on the floor, her head to one side. He dropped down beside her and saw the three dull metal barbs, protruding from her chest, neck, and forehead.

Yuna stifled a shriek.

Spider was dead.

"No, no, Spider, no." Alice dropped down beside them, shaking her head, trying to hold back the sobs.

They sat for a moment, all gathered around their dead friend, each lost in their own thoughts and remembrances.

"She just wanted to go home," said Matteo, his voice deep with emotion.

"We all just want to go home," Renton whispered, like he was vocalizing an inner thought. "But home is where we cannot go."

He stood up as the massive airlock completed its cycle and the inner door began to open revealing a dark and vaguely alien tunnel. Lights began to flick on, one at a time, off into the distance. After a moment, he reached down and gently lifted Spider's body up into his arms, then turned to stare down the long dim tunnel.

"This is home now," he said, again almost to himself, and began walking forward.

CHAPTER 35
SURVIVE SOME MORE

Not a single person could be seen or heard as Selene made her way down to the lobby of the Axial Luxor. Everyone was now down at the dock, guest, and staff alike, either boarding flights or waiting to board. She hurried.

Oddly, she began to wonder what would happen to this orbital after everyone had been evacuated. How long would the systems keep functioning? How long before the power failed on this abandoned hulk and it came crashing down to the lunar surface? And how many other orbitals just like it would do the same? *That would be spectacular*, she thought.

The elevator lobby for the dock was also eerily quiet, not like the last time she came this way. It invoked a strange feeling in her, a feeling that everyone had already left, that she was all alone in this vast luxurious space-station. Nothing more than a ghost within the machine.

Not so. The doors of the elevator opened onto the dock

concourse with an explosion of chaotic scenes. People yelling, screaming, pushing, and shoving. A heaving mass of panicked travelers all fighting for seats on the last ships leaving. It was like the last moments of a twenty-second-century Titanic, or how Selene imagined it to be.

Phitt... phitt...

She heard the telltale sounds of a gauss weapon spitting out barbs, more screams, and a body of a young man wearing the hotel staff uniform floated into view. It took her a moment to realize he was dead. The situation was out of control. How was she going to get through this chaos to where the last FISA ship was docked? She pushed herself out from the confines of the elevator and toward the throng of people. She had only gone a few meters when she spotted her assistant, Nicci, who looked distraught. Blood dripped down her face, her clothes were ripped and torn. She clutched onto a handrail like a stranded sailor clutches a life raft. A young man tended to her along with a much older man who also had blood oozing from a gash on his neck.

"Nicci, what happened?" Selene flew over grabbing the same handrail as her assistant to break her momentum.

"Selene, oh god, it's crazy. They're fighting, killing each other down there." Tears ran down her face, mixing with the blood.

"Some assholes jumped the guards," the young man explained as he applied a makeshift bandage to the older man's neck. "Then started shooting. Everyone scattered in panic."

"Bastards," added the older man just as a new wave of screams echoed up from further along the concourse. This was followed by a violent shudder as if the station had been hit by something big.

The young man looked at Selene. "Not good."

"No," she replied, sensing that this situation was only going from bad to worse. "Quick, let's get back into the elevator."

Nicci's eyes widened. "But... but what about..."

"Our flight home?" said Selene, as she looked down along the concourse to see a mass of panicked people heading their way. "I think we can kiss that goodbye."

She prized Nicci's grip from the handrail and shepherded her into the still open elevator doors. The two men followed close behind. The station shuddered again with the sound of an explosion and down along the concourse, they could see bodies being pushed along by a blast wave.

"Shit." The young man hit the button to close the doors and start the elevator moving before it could reach them. They felt the elevator pod rock and shake as it was buffeted by the blast wave expanding up into the elevator shaft. The lights flickered and alert klaxons blared out as Selene clung on to a handhold and prayed that they would make it back to the outer ring.

The shaking stopped, the lights stabilized, and the doors finally opened spitting them all back out into the hotel lobby.

"Decompression alert. Something's damaged the dock," the older man said as he slumped down on the floor pressing the bloodied bandage to his neck.

"How do you know?" asked Selene.

"I'm one of the floor managers."

"Is it bad?"

He gave a shrug. "Pretty bad for those who are dead, I'd say."

"Depends on how much damage," said the young man. "That sector will be automatically sealed off," he pressed an ear to the elevator door. "I don't hear the klaxons anymore. Could be that it's contained," he looked back at the others. "Deejay Bale," he jerked a thumb at his chest.

"Selene Mene. This is Nicci Anderson," she gestured at her assistant, who was beginning to shake, probably from shock.

They turned to the hotel manager. "Jeff Bodega," he replied with a sardonic smile and a limp salute. "Well, that got messed up pretty quick," he added.

Selene took a moment to pull herself together, as the implications of the situation began to sink in. She was not going home, that was clear. Not now, not ever... probably. She put a hand out against the wall to steady herself, she was feeling sick. Was it shock, or was it simply the thought of being stranded here?

"You okay?" she heard the young man ask.

"Yeah, fine, just give me a second." She rubbed her face with her hand and tried to get a grip. It would do no good to fall apart now. She turned around to check on Nicci, who looked a mess. "We'd better get you to the medbay," she eventually said. "Any of you guys know where that is?"

Jeff gathered himself up from the floor, still holding his neck. "Come on, I'll show you. Heading that way myself."

"But what about the ship? We need to get back down to the ship," Nicci was reluctant to move.

Selene gave her a matronly look. "There's no way to do that now, Nicci. That blast probably took out the dock."

The stark realization of their predicament began to dawn on her assistant. She began to shake again, this time not from shock but from sobbing. Selene gently took her elbow and nudged her forward.

"I need to find out what damage has been done," said Deejay as he followed along, seemingly unfazed by their situation.

"How are you going to do that?" asked Selene.

"The central operations deck. It's where the medbay is. Where the entire station is managed from. I can check on the damage and see if there are people still down there."

"Maybe the ship's still okay?" Nicci's face brightened.

Deejay shrugged. "Probably not."

Selene caught his eye, giving him a stern look.

"Eh... but it is possible," he added, getting Selene's meaning.

They took a staff elevator to a level just below the outer ring of the station's torus. This entire level was known simply as Operations. It was the beating heart of the great hotel, where all the staff lived, where the stores were kept, and where every aspect of the Axial Luxor could be monitored. Jeff brought them to an enormous and well-equipped medbay. It was the size of a small hospital and, when it had the staff, could accommodate all but the most sophisticated of surgical operations. This was not surprising seeing as how medical treatment would otherwise be many thousands of kilometers away—and such things mattered to the clientele of this hotel.

He brought them into one of the general clinics and began to pull open drawers, finding what he needed immediately.

"You've some medical training?" Selene asked.

"Aye, all floor managers do. Me more than most. Spent a bit of time in the army," he looked over at her as she ushered Nicci to a bench. "Just don't ask me to do any organ transplants," he winked.

"I'm going to Sys-Ops, see what the hell is going on," said Deejay.

"Sys-Ops?" asked Selene, as she pulled Nicci's hand away from her injured head. At first glance, it didn't look too bad.

"Systems Operations Room, where we monitor everything."

"Maybe you should go with him," Jeff gestured with his head again. "I can handle this."

Selene gave a glance at Nicci who seemed a bit calmer now.

"I'll be okay," Nicci said, then nodded with a faint smile.

Access to Sys-Ops required a lot of locked doors to be opened. Fortunately, Deejay had the required access level. Selene suspected there might be a bit more to this guy than met the eye. It was a wide circular area with a central holo-table horseshoed by rows of workstations, each one designated to a different subsystem within the orbital. Most of the opposite wall was a vast display—currently showing a lot of flashing red. She assumed this was not good.

"Okay, let's see." Deejay made a beeline for one particular workstation and began to interface with it. The screens flicked with schematics and scrolling data. "Hmmm," he said, several times. Then gestured to bring up a camera feed on the wall monitor. It showed an image from somewhere along the main dock. Clear space could be seen where an outer hull should be.

"Looks like a ship collision. See that one floating out there?" he zoomed in on the image.

"My god, what the hell happened to cause that?"

"Who knows. The good news is that sector is now sealed, so no danger to the station."

"Any survivors down there?"

Deejay flicked around different camera feeds until he came to an undamaged sector. It looked to have around a hundred or so people milling around, still alive.

"Survivors," he said matter-of-factly. "But it looks like they're trapped down there. Power's out for the elevators. I think I can fix that."

"Wait, hold up. Don't do anything just yet," Selene put a hand on his shoulder.

"What? But we have to get them out of there."

"Yes, yes, of course. But we don't want another stampede. Do you have a public address system?"

"Yeah, it's over there."

"I'll talk to them first, try and calm things down and see if they can get themselves organized."

He brought her over to a workstation and showed her how to broadcast. Selene took a deep breath and began.

"Listen up." Immediately she could see the reaction on the crowd down below, mostly it was one of relief. "We're working to get you out of there. We'll have the elevators back in action shortly. However, these only take twenty people at a time, so if you all rush in when the doors open, it will just stall again. So please organize yourselves into groups, injured first and anyone with medical training. We'll have you out of there very soon." She switched off the mic and watched as the crowd began to look around at each other. Soon the natural leaders began to emerge and organize the others into groups.

"Is this visual data being recorded?" she asked Deejay.

"Yes, everything is saved. Why?"

"See those people doing the organizing down there? We're going to need them if we're to survive."

Deejay looked at the screen, seeing it through different eyes. "I reckon you're right about that. Considering we're stranded here, no functioning ships, no way back to Earth."

"Look on the bright side. At least we picked a vast luxury hotel for our desert island. We can probably survive here for quite a long time."

"And then what?"

"Then we find another way—and try and survive some more."

CHAPTER 36
DECISION MADE

Chen Gongbo opened his helmet visor and looked at the airlock entrance door to the FISA sector of Moon Base Delta that was now firmly shut. On the ground beside it lay one of his men, Li Doping, a good man. Several barbs from a gauss pistol protruded from his EVA suit and one protruded from his now shattered visor. That was the one that killed him. The escaped FISA captives, and the Space Division spy, were now on the far side of that door, the first people to do so in over a decade. Yesterday, this would have triggered an almighty international incident, a clear breach of treaties, almost a reason for war. But today? Well, today it meant almost nothing. Just some desperate souls trying to survive—like the rest of the people that had remained on this godforsaken dust-filled rock.

"Can we hack this?" he turned to one of his techs and pointed at the access interface.

The tech shook his head. "Unlikely. It's not like the other

one," he jerked a thumb at the airlock to the maintenance area, the one they had just come through. "That was easy. This one here is old; much more complex." The tech then sensed that this might not be the answer Chen Gongbo wanted to hear, so he revised it. "Eh, we could try, would take a long time though."

Chen waved a hand. "No need. Carry on."

"Yes, sir," the tech nodded, and went back to hacking the comms station.

Chen would have to let it go. There was nothing much to be gained by wasting resources chasing down these people. What technical details they knew about FISA infrastructure was probably no more than SINO knew already. And SINO now had a more significant problem to deal with. Word had just come through that a company of Xilinex mercenaries had just arrived from Earth. This was bad news; they were tooling up for a fight for the spoils. Things could get nasty very soon.

"Sir?" the tech called over from the comms station. "You might want to listen to this."

Chen walked back to the where the tech had been working away trying to discover if any communication had gone on while the escaped crew were holed up in here.

"This interaction took place around fifteen minutes ago," said the tech as he played back a section. It was communication between the crew and Selene Mene, and what he heard her say changed everything. She had just given the FISA maintenance crew the one thing that SINO had assumed didn't exist, reboot codes for the AI core in Moon Base Delta. He listened to it twice just to make sure.

"Can we access the data transfer?" he asked the tech.

"No sir, no records. This is just an audio log."

Chen nodded. "Okay, good work."

If what he had heard was true, and he had no reason to doubt it, then there was absolutely no way he could let them go through with reactivating that AI. To do so would be to deny Moon Base Delta to SINO, and every other agency that had been involved with it, not that he cared about them. There was no question about what he had to do now. He would have to follow them in and put a stop to it. Better yet, acquire those codes for SINO.

He turned back to his tech. "You sure there's no way to hack that door?" he gestured back at the massive airlock.

The tech grimaced. "Eh, maybe, given enough time. But if they've physically locked it from the inside then," he shook his head, "we're out of luck."

It didn't matter since Chen still had other options. He turned around to his men who were busy removing Li Doping's body. "Listen up. I want everybody back in the rovers. We're heading for the Northern Gate. We're going to enter through the SINO sector of Moon Base Delta and find these people."

CHAPTER 37

MOON BASE DELTA

W ay back when the Moon was still a raging torrent of volcanic activity, great rivers of lava had flowed across its surface. Over time, the outer layers of these flows had cooled and solidified leaving an inner core still hot enough for the molten lava to exist in long meandering rivers called lava tubes. As the Moon's birth pangs began to settle down, the lava retreated leaving a spider's web of empty subterranean passages. In some instances, where the roofs of these hollowed-out passages were close to the surface, they had simply caved in, leaving an open pit.

It was inside one of these pits that the central core of Moon Base Delta had been built. A vast multilevel lunar metropolis that extended out from this central core along intertwining lava tubes for several kilometers in all directions. At its peak, it housed almost five-thousand people all working and living in harmony until the great pendulum of human civilization swung back again toward conflict and fracture. Now it accommodated just four lost souls, wandering through its great tunnels in search of sanctuary.

"This place gives me the creeps," said Yuna as she looked around the strange organic structure of the tunnel interior. "It feels... alien."

They had been walking through the tunnel for some time; there seemed no end to it. Renton's arms were beginning to ache. He really should put Spider's body down and take a rest. But he was hoping to get inside the central core of the base before he did.

"It is weird," Matteo agreed. "Like a giant wormhole."

"Ancient lava tube, coated with sintered regolith," said Renton. "The entire base is built into a vast labyrinth of these tubes that stretch for several kilometers in every direction, or so they say."

"You seem to know a lot about this place, Renton," said Alice.

"Yeah, like I said, my aunt was involved in it. Not quite sure what she did, but it got me interested."

"What happened here?" Alice continued. "Seems like a colossal waste of resources just to abandon this place."

"I'm not really sure," he looked around at the walls. "I heard stories when I was young all about Moon Base Delta. But I don't how much is true and how much is just myth."

"What sort of stories?" Yuna was curious to know more.

"Hold up," Matteo gripped his abdomen again. "I think I need to rest for a bit."

"Sure," Renton wasn't objecting. He placed Spider's body carefully down on the tunnel floor and they all sat down for a brief rest.

"How much further?" asked Yuna.

Renton consulted the screen on his wrist. "Not far, another half kilometer to the entrance for the FISA sector of the central core. Then we'll be properly inside the base."

"Tell us, what stories did you hear about this place?" Alice was also curious.

Renton took a moment, looking around at the strange tunnel he had now found himself in. "This place was built a good while before the war began back on Earth, just at the tail end of a long period of peace and cooperation. It was supposed to be a kind of model of how we would colonize the solar system in the spirit of human cooperation."

"I could have told them that wouldn't work," said Matteo.

"It was managed by a centralized AI, which governed every system, including the population."

"The population?" Yuna looked skeptical.

"That's what I was told," Renton gave a shrug. "The AI tracked and managed each colonist's health, productivity, general well-being, and so on."

"Sounds like a surveillance state," Yuna frowned.

"Or a techno-utopia," countered Matteo. "Until the AI became self-aware. And we all know how that ends."

"What did happen?" asked Alice. "How did it all end?"

"The war started back on Earth and the society here began to fracture along national allegiances. The story goes that the AI then tried to compensate for the imbalance but had no models for dealing with this scenario."

"And then the naughty AI killed all the nice humans in the colony," said Matteo, as if he were telling the end of a fairytale to a group of young children.

"The solution was to deactivate the AI and split the base up into several individual sectors across agencies lines. But without the AI, the base became difficult and very expensive to operate. Consider that at this time there were a lot of other population centers springing up on Luna. Eventually they decided to just put it on life support and shut the rest of it down."

"This may seem like a stupid question," said Yuna. "But do you think it is wise to go rebooting this thing?"

"I don't see we have a choice," said Renton. "Moon Base Delta is a vast and highly complex system. We're going to need that AI to run most of it. Otherwise it would take us an eternity to figure it all out."

"And lock down all the other access gates," Alice added. "Don't forget that SINO still have their own way in here."

Yuna stood up. "Then I suppose if we're going to do this, we'd better get going."

"Matteo, you rested enough?" Renton asked as he too stood up.

"Yeah, let's get going."

Renton picked up Spider's body again and began walking.

The tunnel eventually terminated with another massive airlock similar to the one at the maintenance facility. They spent the next few minutes walking through this airlock until it finally opened out into a cavernous garage area full of old surface vehicles in various states of disrepair. Above them, a few ceiling lights flickered on revealing the skeletons of ancient gantries and walkways. The dim light also afforded them a view of the side walls that seemed to house old workshops and storerooms.

"Wow, would you just look at this place," Matteo turned a full three-sixty trying to take it all in. "It's massive."

They stood for a moment just looking around at this ghostly boneyard.

"So, where to?" asked Alice.

Renton walked across to a long empty workbench and gently lowered Spider's body down.

"I'll leave Spider here for a while. We should be safe enough now. We can come back later when we find a suitable place to lay her to rest properly." He then studied the map on his wrist unit, the others gathered around.

"We're here," he said as he pointed to an area at the edge of the base. "All this here is the FISA sector," he circled his fingers around a section of the map. "We need to get to this central area here. There's a medbay, and a control center. We can figure out how to get to the AI core from there."

"I hate to be the first to mention this but what about food and water. All we've got is what we've brought with us and that's not going to last more than a day or two."

"How do ten-year-old rations taste?" Alice gave a smile.

Renton looked over at Matteo who was sitting on the floor. His face was pale, his breathing labored. "You don't look so good, buddy."

The engineer gave a faint smile, "Just... run out of steam, I think."

"We need to keep going, try and get to the main FISA operations area."

Matteo waved a hand, "In a minute."

"We don't have much time. SINO also have access to this base through the Northern Gate. If they decide to follow us, then we've got even more problems." Renton bent down and lifted Matteo into his arms to carry him. Matteo didn't protest. "Lucky we're on the Moon and not Earth, or I wouldn't be able to lift you like this."

Matteo gave another faint smile. "Doesn't mean we're dating."

They moved through the cavernous garage area, with Yuna and Alice taking the lead.

"Hey, would you look at that," Alice stopped in front of a row of humanoid industrial robots. Heavy-duty semiautonomous machines around three meters tall used for lifting and moving.

"Atlas XB-25." Alice moved in closer to inspect one of the units. "I used to work on the control software for this model. First job I ever had. I thought they would all be scrapped by now."

"These guys don't look like they've moved in a while," Yuna wiped the dust off an interface surface. "Still powered up though," she glanced down the line of robots. "Strange how this place still has power and life support after all these years."

"They always intended coming back," said Renton. "I presume that's what the maintenance facility was for, to keep everything ticking over."

They continued on. Renton was anxious to get Matteo to somewhere he could rest and check on his wounds. The dash to the maintenance facility had opened them up again and he was still losing blood. They exited the garage and into another tunnel; this one was much smaller and well fabricated with sleek smooth walls. On one side ran a track with a row of transport pods parked up near its entrance. They were open-topped, some with seating, some simply for transporting cargo.

Yuna investigated, wiping dust from the control interface. "I think these might still be working. She tapped a few icons on the screen and a transport map materialized. "Let's try it. Hop in."

They clambered into the pod, Yuna tapped a few more icons and the pod hummed into life. It began to move forward with the painful grinding sound of bearings that had not moved in years. "That sounds horrendous. I hope this thing doesn't explode."

But the grinding soon mellowed as the pod blew off the accumulated grime of a decade of inactivity. It brought them down along the tunnel, lights flickering on as they moved, then it entered an elevator platform and ascended through several levels. They could only glimpse what these levels contained from the illumination provided by the platform. Finally, it spat them out into a wide concourse, a terminus.

Renton consulted the map again as they clambered out of the pod. "We're on the main FISA level. Medbay is nearby, that way," he pointed to the left. "Control room straight ahead." He lifted Matteo once again. "Okay, buddy, nearly there. Then you can rest."

They laid him down on a gurney in a seemingly well-equipped clinic. Alice and Yuna raided the storage lockers looking for supplies to dress Matteo's wounds. Renton helped him out of the bulky EVA suit; he looked gaunt and pale.

"I got this," said Yuna as she came over with a bundle of medical supplies in her arms. "Don't know how much of this is still in date but it's better than nothing," she dropped them onto a trolley. "You go find that AI core."

Renton and Alice left Yuna tending to Matteo and headed for the control room. Lights flicked on as they entered a circular area populated by control systems, workstations, and screens—none of which were active. In the center stood a small holo-table that Renton moved over to and began to examine. He unclipped his wrist unit, which contained the activation codes. "According to Selene, we can reactivate the FISA sector from here." He placed the unit on the interface pad of the holo-table and tapped an icon to transmit the codes.

Almost immediately, the workstations began to flicker into life as long lines of data started scrolling down each screen. The holo-table also booted up and a schematic of the Moon Base Delta facility blossomed out from its surface. Then, status alerts stared flashing as the activation sequence discovered a litany of errors in the operation of long moribund systems. Alice glanced from screen to screen, then up at the primary monitor that was now festooned with data visualization charts, most of which blinked red.

"It's gonna take a lot of time to figure all this out. Lots of system problems. Looks like we'll be busy for a while. I suppose the first thing to look at is water processing, see if that's working. After that we need to think about food processing," she glanced back at a workstation screen. "I recognize this," she pointed at the scrolling lines of code. "It's the control system for all the industrial robots," she looked over at Renton with a smile. "There's a little bit of me in that code. I never thought it would end up here."

Renton's attention turned back to the schematic on the holo-table—a 3D wireframe of all sectors, each color coded and overlaid with its identifier: FISA, SINO, INDOCON, JAXA-KARI, and a number of others, some of which Renton didn't recognize. Perhaps these others no longer operated on Luna.

The only sector with detail was the FISA sector; all the others were just ghosted out, so it would be impossible from this schematic to know how they were structured and organized. He gestured at the table interface and the schematic zoomed in on the FISA sector. "The AI core is down on that level," he pointed to an identifier. "I need to get down there before SINO enters the facility. Assuming they're planning to follow us."

"I suppose we have to work on the basis that they will try." Alice came over and studied the schematic. "It's also possible they're already inside. We've just no way of knowing."

They both looked up to see Yuna entering the control room.

"How's Matteo?" asked Renton.

"As well as can be expected. He needs blood. Failing that, just lots of fluids and rest. But he should be okay," she looked down at the 3D schematic. "You think SINO are already in the facility?"

"I'm working on the assumption that the worst thing that can happen to us, will happen. Since this seems to be our history so far," Alice had a defeated look on her face.

Renton studied the schematic again. "If SINO are going to enter the facility then they'll come in at the Northern Gate, here. Then probably try to enter our sector somewhere along this interface line. Can we track that? Camera feeds, motion detection?"

Alice looked around at some of the workstations. "I'm sure it's possible, but I'll need time to investigate."

"See what you can do. In the meantime, I'd better get going," Renton clipped the comms unit back onto his wrist and began to leave the operations room.

"Has anyone thought about what would happen if the AI is rebooted and SINO are already inside the FISA sector?" Yuna called back to him.

"No, but I'm hoping we'll have some lockdown control, maybe isolate them," Renton gave a shrug. "I suppose we'll find out."

He checked his comms earpiece. "Keep me posted. Try not to let me walk right into them."

"Will try," Alice replied without looking at him. She was already digging into the code on one of the workstations.

"Maybe I should go with you," Yuna began to move.

"No, it only takes one to do this, and who knows what's going to happen if and when that AI is rebooted. No point in more people than necessary risking their asses. Just keep me updated." He turned, left the operations room, and headed for the elevators at the far end of the FISA sector that should take him all the way down to the level that housed the AI core.

CHAPTER 38
CRAZY IS GOOD

Alice watched Renton go, then turned back to survey the sea of system alerts blinking across almost all screens in the operations center. Yuna stood beside her, looking lost. "You think you could figure out the surveillance system?" Alice pointed over at a workstation.

"I can give it a go," Yuna sat down and started investigating. She wasn't a software engineer like Alice, but as a flight officer, she had a natural understating of complex systems and a reasonable proficiency with code.

They worked for a while in silence. Slowly, Alice began to get a better picture of the monumental task that was ahead of them in bringing Moon Base Delta back to life. Yet, for the first time since the massive solar storm, the Carrington Event, she felt like it was just a normal day at work. This is what she did, analyzing system failures, and fixing problems—and for a short while she began to relax and find her rhythm.

She focused her initial investigations on critical systems—power and life support. The FISA sector already had power provided by the main fusion reactor, that was what had kept the facility preserved all these years. But that had operated at a very low level, just enough to keep the interior pressurized, now entirely new areas were coming online placing more demands on the reactor. Keeping the base interior pressurized also had its disadvantages since oxygen is a corrosive gas. Over time, it would partially degrade some of the infrastructure if not continually maintained. Probably why they built the maintenance facility, just to keep things ticking along, but still there were a huge number of power problems in different sectors. Those would have to be tracked and traced by hand. *Plenty of work for Matteo and Renton*, she thought.

But this was not too much of a concern; more worrying was the air quality that seemed to have a very high level of contaminants. So much so that she sent Yuna off to find some face masks in the medbay when she went to check on Matteo. But the air filtration system had ramped up when they activated this sector and she could see the contaminated levels begin to decrease as she worked. So it was a problem that would solve itself without any intervention from her. Same went for water, of which there was plenty. Back in the early days, no one thought it was possible for water to exist on the Moon. That was until India's Chandrayaan-1 impact probe discovered water ice in the basin of the Shackleton Crater at the south pole. But it wasn't until they started to explore these ancient lava pits that they discovered water trapped deep beneath the surface. It's what made this base possible.

The water filtration system had also kicked in so it was another issue that would solve itself over time. She moved on to food production which was nonexistent; a major problem. The base had a number of agri-production areas, but everything in there would be dead, probably nothing left but dried twigs and dust. Maybe there was seed storage somewhere but that was a long-term project, nothing that would solve their immediate lack of supplies. There was also an agri-lab where food could be synthesized—proteins, amino acids, carbohydrates, and many other nutrients and vitamins—but again this had not been active for a decade and Alice simply didn't know enough about the complex chemistry involved to even speculate on how or if this could be booted up back into production. However, they still had some rations, enough for a day or two, and they could go back and raid the maintenance facility, maybe even try and find the supplies they had to dump during their dash from the emergency shelter. All that might last them a few weeks. After that? Well, they would just have to figure something out.

Yet if they were going to have any chance of getting this base self-sustaining then they would need all the help they could get and that meant bringing all the maintenance droids and robots back to life. This was Alice's next system interrogation, something she knew very well, unlike food production. They'd already passed a number of industrial robots in the garage sector on the way here, so she started there. There were six in total, and three powered up immediately on her command. The others glitched out—more work for Renton and Matteo.

As she wove her way through the base's systems, she began to realize that she was only scraping the surface. There were gaps in the command and control along with rough and ready patches into a deeper system. This must be the layer that the AI functioned on. Not surprising since it operated as system control for the entire base. All Alice was dealing with was a data layer that had been grafted on to this, long defunct, AI layer. This must have been appended when the AI was decommissioned and the base split up into separate sectors. As she probed, she wondered what would happen if Renton managed to reboot it.

"Eh, I think we might have a problem?" Yuna's voice suddenly interrupted her train of thought. Alice had become so lost in her own work she almost forgot that Yuna was working beside her.

"Tell me about it," she answered, sounding exasperated. "I'm seeing nothing but problems."

"No, I'm not talking technical. I'm detecting a bulkhead activation on the FISA–SINO sector interface."

Alice looked over at her friend. "Where?"

"I've got some of the internal surveillance systems up and running. I think I can put it on the table," she stood up, moved over to the holo-table, and gestured a few commands. The 3D schematic of the base zoomed in on a sector of the base where the FISA area and SINO areas butted up against each other. "There," Yuna pointed at a flashing marker. "There's a bulkhead door that's just been activated."

"Any visuals?"

"Some," Yuna gestured again, and a series of camera feeds displayed as 2D images over the table. They showed the view at various points along a dim corridor. But there was nothing moving.

"Where's that?" asked Alice as she studied the feed.

"Along this connection route here."

"Crap, they're inside," Alice pointed at the feed. Several armed SINO operatives were moving down along the corridor.

"We need to warn Renton," Alice tapped her earpiece.

"Renton, this is Alice, we've got company. Do you copy?"

No answer.

"Renton, do you hear me. SINO are in our sector."

Still no response.

Yuna, sensing Alice's increasing distress, asked, "What's the problem?"

Alice shook her head. "He's not responding, probably out of range of these comms, too much rock in this place."

"We need to warn him. I'll go," Yuna started to move.

"No wait. We don't know where they're heading and I won't be able to communicate with you either."

"We have to do something; we can't just leave him out there."

"Do we have lockdown control? Can we block them? Corral them in one area?"

Yuna shook her head, "I didn't get that far. Maybe, but I'd need more time to figure that out."

Alice thought for a moment, then gave Yuna a strange, conspiratorial look. "I have an idea," she finally said, in a slow measured tone. "It might sound a bit crazy, but sometimes crazy is good."

"Anything I can do?"

"Yes there is. You do what you do best; pilot," Alice pointed at a workstation. "Grab a seat, I'll show you what I have in mind."

CHAPTER 39
XILINEX

The newly formed board of the Xilinex Corporation's Lunar division gathered around the boardroom holotable for a second time, after a short cooling off period so that the room could be cleaned up and to allow for everyone to acclimatize to the new reality. This time General Wagner outlined the primary strategic objectives in the forthcoming battle for control of Luna—without any unnecessary interruptions.

"You have to understand there's a wider war at stake here, it's not just about the Moon and its resources," he swept a hand across the 3D map that blossomed out from the table's surface. "What happens up here will shift the balance of power back on Earth."

This wasn't news to Pompodur or the others on the board. They all knew what was at stake and what Xilinex back on

Earth wanted from them—and that was to achieve complete control of the supply of Helium-3.

Since the world had transitioned to fusion power many decades ago, it had become dependent on supplies of Helium-3 —an incredibly rare element on Earth, yet abundant in the lunar regolith. Two corporations dominated the supply of this vital resource: Xilinex and Xiang Zu. Xilinex had the lion's share of the resources and market. However, it was Xiang Zu that had the most efficient method of delivering this precious cargo back to Earth, one that had the potential to survive reentry through the debris cloud, something that couldn't be said for the more traditional methods that Xilinex utilized.

The General shifted the map to the location of Mare Crisium—the Sea of Crises—and then zoomed into focus on a sizable Xiang Zu Helium-3 processing facility. Its most prominent architectural feature was a two-kilometer-long partially enclosed rail that ran from inside the main processing structure along a slightly elevated ramp to an abrupt end some one-hundred meters above the surface. This was known as a Mass Accelerator, a gigantic electric rail gun that fired projectiles out into open space at a velocity of over three kilometers per second. But it was not some demonic weapon to protect the Moon from hordes of marauding space invaders. It was a cargo delivery system.

With low gravity and no atmosphere, it took considerably less energy to escape the pull of the Moon than it did for Earth. A simple rail gun could accelerate a cargo projectile out into space and send it on a trajectory that would eventually allow

Earth to pull it into its orbit. From there, small thrusters would adjust its flight path to bring it to a point where it could begin entering Earth's atmosphere. When it had lost most of its momentum, drogue chutes would be deployed pulling out the main parachute, slowing the capsule down to a dusty landing in the Gobi Desert in the northern region of Inner Mongolia. From there it would be collected, the Helium-3 extracted, stored, and ultimately sold to the many global customers that relied on fusion power to supply their nation's industrial energy needs.

It was a delivery system technology that Xilinex did not possess. They relied on standard cargo ships—and that was no longer an option. But with the capture and control of this Mass Accelerator, Xilinex would have total domination over the entire market back on Earth, bringing with it a significant shift in global power.

"This is our primary target," General Wagner stabbed an index finger at the map location. "We need to take it now before SINO have time to realize the threat and reinforce this facility."

"What's our estimation of capsule throughput, given the ever-increasing debris cloud that is now orbiting Earth?" asked Anton, ever being the technocrat.

"Aerospace division estimates a fifteen percent success rate," Ossian consulted the screen on his tablet. "But they are working on more robust designs that can withstand greater impacts, so we're looking at getting that up to thirty percent or more."

"Our secondary objective, after we secure the Mass Accelerator, will be to secure the water resources in Shackleton," Wagner shifted the 3D map again. "If we can achieve this, then we effectively put the remaining population under our control."

"Excellent," exclaimed Pompodur, nodding vigorously. "But we need to act quick before people have a chance to regroup after the evacuation. However…" he paused for effect, making sure all the others were paying attention to him. "There's been another development that I think needs our consideration," he took control of the holo-table and flipped it back to the Sea of Tranquility and Moon Base Delta.

"Not this again," said Wagner with barely concealed annoyance. "We've dismissed this already as a strategic objective."

Pompodur raised a hand. "Bear with me," he turned to the General. "No doubt you are aware of the recent SINO activity around this facility?"

The General nodded, a little reluctantly. "Yes, we've been tracking them for a while. A group of SINO operatives, five possibly six, entered the base at the northern access point. We believe they are effecting the recapture of a FISA maintenance ship crew who have taken refuge in the facility. But this is a sideshow, and not relevant to the execution of our primary strategic priorities."

"Indeed but hear me out. During the talks on the New Lunar Accord, I acquired some information sources, certain staff in the employ of the Axial Luxor. Paid informants; if you will. One of these sources has recently informed me of the possible existence of reboot codes for the AI core in Moon Base Delta."

"Reboot codes?" Wagner's face morphed into a look of

incredulity. "I thought FISA completely decommissioned this AI years ago."

"That's what we were all led to believe. However, the potential existence of reboot codes suggests that FISA were not being fully honest with us."

"What's the deal with these codes?" Anton was becoming noticeably more interested in this new development. "Assuming your source is reliable."

"Moon Base Delta was originally designed to be completely managed by an advanced AI. This was supposedly shutdown when the base was split up into different sectors. These reboot codes are to reactivate that AI," explained Pompodur.

"And that means?" asked Anton.

"Full control over the entire base—all sectors. Everybody else is locked out. No way in unless you nuke the place..." Pompodur paused as the others began to reevaluate this situation. One by one, he could see them all looking back at the 3D map, including Wagner. "My instincts tell me that the FISA crew may already have these codes. Which leads me to believe that SINO must also know of their existence, otherwise why would they go to the bother of chasing them when their recapture is more or less worthless."

The General pursed his lips and studied the map of Moon Base Delta. "So your concern is that SINO could take complete control of this facility and use it as a base of operations going forward?"

"Precisely. You need to consider that Moon Base Delta is potentially a self-sustaining fortress capable of supporting thousands of people. The majority of the structure is underground with limited exterior access points. If a group were to commandeer it then they could survive there indefinitely and it would be next to impossible for us to dislodge them. If the group turns out to be SINO, then that could be problematic for us. At the same time, we can't allow that FISA crew to take control either. They could prove to be a thorn in our side, particularly if more of the stranded population starts to migrate there. We need to eliminate this threat and acquire those codes—if they do exist. Even if they don't, we still need to deal with this problem now, before it escalates." Pompodur stood back and hoped his entreaty would have the desired effect with Wagner.

The General was clearly reconsidering it. "Any thoughts on how we gain access?" he finally asked. "And where these groups might be located if we do get in?"

Pompodur smiled. "Again, the New Lunar Accord talks have proven fruitful. We negotiated access to the base via the JAXA-KARI sector, some time back. We can enter through that sector. As to where they might be located..." he began to manipulate the 3D map, this time zooming in on the base. "The AI core is located on Level Six of the central sector. That's probably a good place to focus on."

"Okay," the general gave an emphatic nod, then turned to one of his lieutenants. "Take a shuttle and a half dozen men and secure that base. Eliminate everyone. Acquire those codes; if they do exist."

"Yes, sir," the lieutenant gave a curt salute.

Pompodur grinned with satisfaction as he watched the lieutenant march out the door. Finally he could see a route to acquiring Moon Base Delta.

CHAPTER 40
AI CORE

Every now and again, Renton would check the map displayed on the comms unit clipped to his wrist to make sure he was heading in the right direction. His first waypoint was a set of elevators that ran almost the complete height of the central core of Moon Base Delta.

As he moved, lights flickered on to illuminate his way, and in some instances gave him glimpses of the areas on either side him, most of which whose function and purpose he could not ascertain. He was currently moving through a wide communal space, akin to a town square. It was too dim to see the periphery but he did pass several ornamental raised gardens, surrounded by public seating. All that remained were the skeletons of long dead trees and shrubs. More lights flickered on along his path and he could now see the wide elevator lobby. He wiped the dust from the call interface and it too flickered into life. The doors to one of the elevators opened with a sharp hiss that made him jump as he was not expecting it. Bright light flooded out from the open doors, and as he entered and turned around, he could see back along the way he had just come. The space seemed even more eerie, like an empty abandoned shopping mall; all that was missing were the shopping trolleys. The doors closed and he began to descend.

He tapped his comm. "Alice, Yuna. Can you hear me?" No response. He tried a few more times and realized that he must be out of range. And for the first time, as far as he could remember, he felt utterly alone. It was as if the entire universe had just ended, everything and everyone he had ever known had gone. Now all that remained was just him and this derelict monument to technological hubris. A high-tech mausoleum for him to live out a slow death. He couldn't bear it, this feeling of utter isolation.

He tapped his comms again. "Alice, Yuna, anyone? Do you hear me?" No response. He tried a few more times, still no response. Panic began to rise in him.

Get a grip. You're just spooked, that's all, he told himself, while taking a few deep breaths. The panic began to subside as the elevator doors opened. *Just get to the AI core. Don't think about anything else,* he thought, as he stepped out into a rectangular lobby. On the opposite side a long glass wall cordoned off what looked like a server room. He walked over and peered through the window. The area was illuminated only by the lobby lights and that of the elevator, but it was enough to make out row upon row of black monolithic server racks, disappearing off into darkness. Renton found the door, opened it, and was instantly assailed by a strange humming sound. *Cooling fans?* he wondered. As he passed between the black monoliths, he was surprised to see some of them still functioning, with tiny lights flickering on their facias.

He came to the end of the row to yet another door, which required him to enter the access codes again to gain access. It opened out into a cavernous circular area, at the center of which should be the AI control interface. It was dimly lit and difficult to get a sense of its size. More squat monoliths sat in rows radiating in towards the center. Around the walls he glimpsed other doors, presumably leading to the other sectors of Moon Base Delta. Here and there were scattered packing crates, industrial robots, and push carts, arranged as if they had been abandoned while in the process of clearing the place out.

He moved towards the center; lights flickered on as he went. At last he came to a low circular holo-table, the largest one he had ever seen. He cautiously moved over to it and as he did, the area above slowly illuminated.

The table was inert, and devoid of any controls, except for one edge where a small flat rectangular area extended out. He examined it, wiping away the dust to reveal a small sign that read *Control Interface*. Below it, in much smaller bracketed lettering, read *Auxiliary*. He contemplated this for a moment. *Auxiliary? There must be more than one way to access the AI,* he thought.

He gestured over the flat screen and it flickered into life with a strange logo of a spinning world that he did not recognize as belonging to any agency he knew. It then split apart and presented two flashing words: *Access Required.*

The moment of truth, he thought, as he unclipped the comms unit from his wrist. He tapped a few icons to expose the access codes and was about to present it to the interface when he heard a commotion coming from behind him.

He swung around to see several SINO operatives rushing into the area. One took aim at him, and before Renton had a chance to react, shot him in the right shoulder. The comms unit flew out of his grip and went skidding across the floor. Renton screamed in agony. The pain was excruciating, spreading up his neck, across his shoulder and down along his arm. He had trouble just keeping upright. He finally opened his eyes, only to see the unit with the reboot codes being picked up off the floor by none other than Chen Gongbo, the SINO operative who had incarcerated them after the crash.

Chen turned the unit over in his hand, examining the device, then slowly walked over to where Renton stood, grabbed him by his uninjured shoulder, and shoved him away from the edge of the holo-table. Another of the SINO operatives then jerked the muzzle of a gauss weapon into his ribs and forced him to move back several meters, motioning for him to sit on the floor. Renton complied, with much pain in the process.

Chen leaned over the interface ready to enter the reboot codes. But, just like when Renton attempted the same action, he too was stopped short by several well-armed military bursting in through the JAXA-KARI door on the opposite side. Renton dove for cover, lying flat on the floor, as a ferocious exchange of fire commenced.

Renton looked around for an escape route as he tried to figure out who the hell these people were. JAXA? Surely not.

Maybe Space Division? They were clearly not on the SINO side so that was good. But were they on his side?

He crawled under the lip of the holo-table toward the base just as a SINO operative collapsed onto the floor beside him clutching at his chest, where two steel barbs protruded. Blood began pooling where he lay.

Phitt... phitt... phitt... the sound of gauss weapons spitting barbs filled the room, coupled with the shouts and screams of those who were hit. Renton inched his way along under the table without further injury and looked back to where most of the SINO operatives had gathered. The one on the floor looked to be dead, unmoving, cold eyes staring up. The others had taken cover behind a stack of crates—which were slowly disintegrating under a barrage of fire. Renton was no expert on gauss weapons but it was becoming clear to him which side had the superior fire power. Whoever these new people were, they came prepared for a battle. But so far, he did not seem to be of any interest to them—yet. This might give him an opportunity to get the hell out of here while these two groups were busy putting holes in each other.

He tried to reorientate himself. He was facing SINO; the other group were southeast of him. He crawled around the base of the circular holo-table to his left, heading to a point opposite the two warring factions, then crawled out from under the table, but still keeping low. He took a look around to try and remember which direction the FISA door was located. But he had become completely disorientated, it all looked the same: server racks, crates, maintenance robots—which way was the door?

A SINO operative slid under the lip of the holo-table a few meters to his right, firing blind over his head in the direction of the other group. Renton stalled for a beat thinking he had come for him, but the operative's focus was on laying down cover fire to allow his comrades to move to better positions.

Renton made a dash for the server racks and slid to a halt between two rows. Here he pushed himself up tight against the metal casing and chanced a look back. The space under the holo-table where he had just vacated was now occupied by a fighter from the other group. On his left shoulder was an insignia that Renton recognized, not from one of the agencies but from the mining corporation, Xilinex.

Mercenaries, thought Renton. *The've hired a private army.*

The SINO operative that had been laying down covering fire took a hit and went sprawling across the floor, clutching his thigh as blood pooled out across the floor. The Xilinex mercenary reloaded his weapon, then looked around and spotted Renton, and immediately took aim and fired. By now Renton was scuttling as fast as he could behind the server rack. The barbs missed him, embedding themselves into the corner of the metal casing instead.

Crap, he thought, *they're shooting at me. What the hell for?* But there was no time to figure out the reason, he just needed to make a run for it. He broke cover, dodging his way around the server racks until there was nothing but empty space in front of him. He was hoping to come out in front of the FISA door but he had become completely disorientated and was instead looking straight at the door for the INDOCON sector, which he could not get through. Fearing that the Xilinex mercenary might be chasing him he began desperately searching for a place to hide. On the right of it were a stack of crates pushed tight against the wall; not much of an escape route. On the left of the door were two of those old industrial robots that he had first seen in the garage. Again, not an option for cover.

He was beginning to think that this might be the end of the line for him when he noticed one of the robots begin to move. At first, he thought he was seeing things, but it was definitely moving. Very slowly at first, like it was stiff from a long period of inactivity. But then it took its first step and began to flex its limbs, extending its arms, and working the massive grippers that were its hands. Renton sat mesmerized by this seemingly random robotic ballet as his brain tried to figure out who, or what, was operating it.

The robot clunked its way across to the other side of the INDOCON door, picked up one of the storage crates like it was nothing, moved a short distance through the rows of server racks, and then flung it in the direction of the SINO operatives. The response came almost instantly as it was hit by a barrage of steel barbs from a multitude of gauss weapons. They clanged and clattered as they hit the machine, but had no discernible effect on it. The robot picked up another crate from the floor and flung it at its attackers. Renton chanced a look around to follow the crate's trajectory. It went sailing through the air in a high arc and landed with the dull thump of a heavy weight, into the bulk of the SINO group. Screams escaped from the mouths of those caught under its fall.

Again, another hail of barbs assailed the robot, which seemed to react as if it were human, turning sideways, raising an arm as if to protect its head. That's when Renton realized that it was being operated remotely by a human, and that human was most probably Alice.

Another crate went sailing through the air. But this time it was from the second robot that had also entered into the fight. This time, the crate was aimed at the Xilinex mercenaries. All of whom avoided being crushed when it landed, as they had more time to calculate its trajectory. Yet they scattered in all directions.

By now, both groups had given up trying to kill each other and were concentrating their fire on the robots—to no affect. The machines were designed for the harsh, unforgiving environment of lunar mining. A small steel barb, regardless of the number, was no more than an irritant to it. Like a mosquito to a human, annoying but not much of a concern.

Another crate sailed into the Xilinex mercenaries this time taking out two of them. The others began retreating back out the door they had entered through, dragging their fallen comrades behind them, having presumably decided it was not a fight they could win. The second robot clumped its way over and gave chase, disappearing through the same door.

The first robot now ploughed into three of the SINO operatives, an arm swinging as it did, swatting them aside. The rest began retreating.

Renton was so taken up by this sudden turn of events that he had not noticed Chen sneaking up behind him, until he felt the muzzle of a gauss weapon jammed into his neck.

"Up!" Chen commanded. "Stand up."

Renton slowly stood. Chen pushed him forward out of his

hiding place, down along the row of server racks, and into full view of the robot that was still scything through the SINO group.

"Enough!" Chen shouted.

There was a sudden pause in the chaos as the robot turned to observe this new development.

"Deactivate that robot now or I will put a large hole in your friend's head," he moved the gauss rifle from Renton's neck and jammed it into the base of his skull. "Now!" Chen commanded.

The robot dropped the crate it was holding and took a few steps over to Chen and Renton. It then reached down and picked up a dead SINO agent by the head, holding the body aloft with its skull wedged between its grippers. Renton could sense a brief pang of uncertainty rippling through Chen's body as the pressure he was exerting with the muzzle of the weapon began to lessen.

"The only way out of here is through me," the robot spoke with a voice Renton recognized.

"Alice," he blurted.

"That's right. And I'm sick and tired of being hunted and harassed by these SINO bastards. So here's the deal, Chen. You drop the weapon and you get to walk out of here alive, with whatever is left of your crew. Otherwise, I will come over there and crush your skull like a peanut." As if to emphasize the point she raised the dead SINO agent a little higher. A squealing sound emanated from the gripper hand as it dialed up the pressure on the dead man's skull, then it exploded in a spray of blood and brains, some of which splattered over Renton.

With a shaky hand, Renton wiped his face. He couldn't believe what he had just witnessed, couldn't believe that Alice could do something so horrific. But it had the desired effect as he sensed the uncertainty emanating from Chen. Presumably the SINO agent was weighing up his options. He could put a hole through Renton's skull, but in that case he may well end up suffering the same fate as the mutilated operative who now sprawled on the ground—minus a head.

Chen lowered his weapon, took a step back, and pushed Renton forward.

"Okay, you've made your point." Chen dropped the weapon and raised a hand. "We're going."

The robot stood mute for a moment before moving aside to let Chen through. But before he had taken more than a few steps, the robot's hand came down to block his way. "The codes, you can give them back... if you don't mind."

Chen looked at the machine, then to Renton, before fishing the comms unit out of a pocket. He examined it for a moment and tossed it to Renton.

"Not going to do you any good now," he gestured over at the AI control interface. "It's all smashed to bits," he gave a laugh and walked towards the SINO door, his crew gathering around him, carrying the dead and injured.

Renton walked over and examined the interface. It was completely shattered, just a broken heap, crushed under one of the crates that the robots were using as projectiles. *Crap,* he shook his head, then regretted it as his shoulder hurt like hell. *There was no easy way to fix this, if at all.*

"Renton," the robot called over to him. "You think you can

make it back to the operations area? We'll need to chaperone these scumbags off the property."

Renton nodded. "Yeah, I think so." He then looked back down at the shattered remains of the AI interface, the way someone does in the vain hope that maybe the damage is not as bad as first thought. He sighed, then headed off to find the FISA door.

CHAPTER 41

DAO

Renton staggered out of the AI core area and started to make his way back. The pain in his shoulder was getting worse. The adrenaline that must have been pumping through his body during the fight was now wearing off. But he kept moving.

As far as he understood things, the two industrial robots operated by Alice and Yuna were escorting the attackers out of the base and presumably securing those access points. Maybe they would just leave the robots in place, jammed up against the door; he wasn't sure how they were planning to do it. But one thing he was sure of was that SINO and Xilinex would be back and next time they would not be so easy to fight off.

With the AI control interface smashed to bits, there was no way now to reboot the system. This would leave them very exposed in just the FISA sector. Having control over the entire base and being able to lockdown all access points would be a much better way to ensure they could repel any future attacks.

The other issue that puzzled Renton was how Chen knew about the reboot codes. Was there a mole in Selene's retinue? Did they intercept comms? He probably would never know, but the fact remained that Chen knew, and even with the AI control interface smashed, the possibility still remained of taking absolute control of Moon Base Delta.

Did Xilinex also know about the codes? *They must,* he thought. *Why would they have attacked?* Judging by the vicious fight back in the AI core area, they were clearly trying to eliminate the SINO squad.

But there was nothing Renton could do about any of this now. It was all he could do just to get back to the medbay, and hopefully get the injury to his shoulder patched up. As he made his way back up the elevator shaft, he thought about how far they had come, and how much they had lost. Becker was dead, Mackenzie was probably dead too. Spider, their new friend and ally, was also dead. Matteo had been shot and now he himself had been injured. Only Alice and Yuna had managed to get through all this relatively unscathed with just minor injuries from the crash. On top of all that, they had failed to get off the lunar surface and hitch a ride back to Earth. They were stuck here for a very long time, and maybe they would never get back to Earth. But even here, in this supposedly state-of-the-art base, their grip on life was looking extremely tenuous. With no way to reboot the AI, all they could do was hang on for a while, until that moment when they would ultimately succumb to some other outside agency that wanted complete dominion over the new reality on Luna.

He made his way through the communal area; he was feeling very weak now. He pushed on past the skeletal gardens, the abandoned canteens, the dusty and derelict public benches. A door opened ahead of him and light streamed in, silhouetting a female figure. It ran toward him.

"Renton, oh god. Here, put your arm over my shoulder, let me help you." Alice grabbed him by his arm and waist and helped propel him forward. A second figure emerged from the doorway—Yuna. Between them, they shepherded him to the medbay.

Renton was pleased to see Matteo standing up. The color had returned to his face and he gestured at a gurney. "Put him over there." The irony for Matteo throughout all his own battles with injury was that he was the crew member with the most medical training. Now, it seemed, he was getting to use it.

"Matteo, glad to see you're still alive."

"Glad to see you're still alive too, my friend. You had us all worried." He dragged an IV drip on a wheeled trolley beside him. Renton followed the line and saw it was attached to Matteo's arm via a non-invasive pressure interface.

"Where did you get that?"

"Ahh, I needed fluids to help with the blood loss. I told Yuna what to look for and she went hunting around. Found a whole stash of them."

"What? You're telling me that's ten years old? Are you sure it's okay?"

"Hey, I'm up and about, aren't I?"

Renton was skeptical.

"Ha, don't worry. We got the sterilizer up and running. I just zapped it a few times. Nothing in there now except H2O and some salts... and maybe a few dead bugs."

"Can we drink that?"

"Yeah, theoretically. Would be a bit salty, but yes," he raised his arm to show the IV line. "Or you could just go hardcore and take the more direct route."

Renton looked up at Alice and Yuna. "Thanks for saving my ass back there."

"No problem," Alice replied with a smile.

"We chased them out of the access points and jammed the doors as best we could," Yuna added. "It will be much harder for them to gain access next time."

"How did you get the robots working?"

"I hacked two of the workstations to act as a control interface. Remember, I worked on these units back in the day, so it was pretty simple to get them functioning."

"Ahhhh..." Renton let out a yelp as Matteo extracted the steel barb still embedded in his shoulder with a forceps. He dropped it into a metal tray with a clang.

Yuna staunched the resulting blood flow with a swab.

"The AI interface... it's smashed to bits," Renton directed this to Matteo.

"So I heard. Doesn't matter, we have a robot army now," he gestured at Alice and Yuna.

"It wasn't just SINO, there was a whole squad of Xilinex mercenaries. They came bursting though the JAXA-KARI gate. I think we might be caught up in a turf war."

"Yeah, when I chased them out, they kept shouting about this not being over and a whole bunch of other crap." Yuna put pressure on the swab as Matteo began applying a bandage.

"But we can still fix the interface and reboot the AI?" Matteo asked in hope rather than certainty.

"Maybe, but how long is that going to take? And I get the feeling we don't have much time, now that word of the existence of these codes is out in the wild."

"We never seem to catch a break, do we?" Alice sat on one of the other gurneys, folding her arms and scowling at the floor.

"That interface panel," Renton looked over at Alice. "It had the word *auxiliary* written in brackets. So, there must be another, maybe a master interface somewhere. You didn't notice anything when you were investigating the systems in the operations center?"

"Yes, I did. There's clearly two control systems. The one controlling the FISA sector looks to be grafted on to an earlier one, presumably the AI system. There's even a lot of old equipment in there that's been deactivated."

Renton sat up from the gurney, rolled his legs over the edge, and stood up. "Show me."

They moved back into the operations center where Alice and Yuna had set up the remote access for the industrial robots. On the main screen, there was a camera feed coming from the two access gates to the base. One showed the SINO gate, with the robot clamped to the locking mechanism. The same arrangement could be seen on the JAXA-KARI gate.

The last time he was in here, he hadn't paid much attention

to the layout. But now that Alice had intimated that all the workstations and monitors were in fact grafted on to a much older system, Renton began to see the evidence of this. The room, by its nature, was dimly lit, better to see the screens and readouts. At first glance, it was easy to ignore the spaces behind all the operational equipment. But as he began to look past this first layer, he could see that the room was much bigger than he had first imagined. In the darkened background were the clear remnants of a much older system. He moved past this first layer, squeezing through a gap between two workstations.

"Any lights back here?" Renton called out behind him.

Moments later, Alice and Yuna squeezed in carrying jerry-rigged flashlights.

"See," Alice moved the light slowly around the area. "All this was the original operations center, and all this equipment must have been part of the base when it was controlled by the AI."

Renton looked up to see that what he thought was a wall monitor was actually suspended from the ceiling. Behind it was an even bigger monitor that curved around a hundred degrees of the rear wall. Below this, spreading out in a semicircle were rows of workstations, all dark, and covered in layers of dust. As he investigated, he could see that some of this control equipment had been cannibalized—screens and interface panels were missing from some units. He glanced down at the floor. "Alice, can you shine that light over here, on the ground?"

Alice redirected the beam.

"Look," Renton pointed. "See that gap? It runs around the

floor in a complete circle. I'll bet it's a retracted holo-table or some sort of control console."

"There must be a power source somewhere." Matteo had also squeezed in though the workstations, shining a light this way and that, illuminating the alcoves and darker recesses. "If we can find that then we might be able to power it up and see what happens."

"If we're going to be chasing wires along power conduits, I'll need to ditch this IV line. Anyway, I feel fine." He removed the feed from his arm, rubbing his skin were the pressure interface had left a dull red rash.

"What are we looking for?" Alice cast her light around.

"I'd say start with finding the power lines for the current setup," said Matteo. "It's quite possible that they were spliced off the original cables."

It took them some time, hunting around, removing panels, searching under false floors, following cables. It didn't help that Matteo became frustrated by fatigue. Renton also found the pain in his shoulder unbearable at times. Still, they pushed through, shuffling along, following the leads, and eventually they found the power junction. Matteo had been correct in his assumption. The new control center had been spliced off the original power cables for the old AI system, which in turn had been isolated by a heavy-duty power breaker. Theoretically, flipping that should power up the old area.

They spent some more time powering down as many of the new systems they thought were safe enough to switch off just in case they had a current overload when they flipped the breaker.

Eventually, Matteo stood ready to pull the handle, which was located in the corridor just outside the operations center. Renton, Alice, and Yuna stood in the doorway, hoping to witness the reactivation of the old AI system, or possibly a complete loss of everything if there was a catastrophic short-circuit.

"Okay, Matteo," Renton called out. "Hit it."

For a moment it seemed as if nothing had happened. Renton wasn't quite sure what to expect, but he thought it would be a little more dramatic. Matteo came up beside them. "Anything?"

"Not sure," answered Alice, as she moved cautiously into the old operations area. The others followed. There was an audible thump of a motor kicking in followed by a whirr.

"Look," Alice pointed. "The floor, it's rising."

They moved themselves to a position where they could witness the circular floor rise up. It was a disc around half a meter thick supported by two telescopic pistons on either side. It rose up over their heads, then came to a clunking halt, locking itself into position. The poles retracted and a second platform ascended out from the floor. A solid circular base then came to a halt around waist high.

"Old-school holo-table," Matteo pointed at the disc overhead. "It uses two projections, above and below, to create the three-dimensional image. Haven't seen one of these in a while."

Renton moved over to inspect the surface of the table. It seemed totally inert, then a small rectangle illuminated with a faint green hue at one edge of the table, with the words *ACCESS*

REQUIRED. They all gathered around and stared at this patch of illumination like it was a message from another dimension.

Renton unclipped the comms unit from his wrist, tapped a few icons to reveal the reboot codes, and then looked at the others for a second or two before presenting the device to the holo-table.

Almost immediately the entire table illuminated with a pulsating light that coalesced to a central point, then blossomed upward and outward into a speckled double-helix shape. It seemed to dance like a flame rising up from the table—flickering, forming, and reforming. The four crew took a step back in unison at this sudden explosion of electronic life. Then long dormant screens began to activate, lines of code rapidly scrolling upward. Renton looked around in amazement. "Something's happening. I think it's working."

A moment later, the huge curved wall monitor flickered into life and began to display a multitude of unfathomable datagrams.

"What's it doing?" Yuna asked as she stepped further back, looking wide-eyed at the wall monitor.

Moon Base Delta central control activating, a disembodied voice sounded out from nowhere. It was discernible as neither male nor female, but yet had a soothing, authoritative resonance.

"It's rebooting, we did it," Matteo punched the air, barely able to contain his excitement. Renton, too, managed to break a smile, the first one in a very long time. It seemed that after all the hardships they had endured, they were finally catching a break.

Renton let out a yelp as Matteo slapped him on the shoulder. "Oh crap, sorry, I forgot."

"I wonder how long it's going to take?" asked Alice.

Time elapsed since last functioning DAO update is approximately 5,465 Earth days. Significant degradation of base infrastructure detected. Complete system analysis underway. Time to completion... unknown.

"I think the answer is, it's going to take a while." Renton got the sense that they might still be a long way from securing the base, if at all, and that their celebrations could be premature.

"What's DAO mean?" Alice threw this out as a general question.

Decentralized Autonomous Organization, the AI answered.

Renton ventured another question, seeing as how this AI had responded so far.

"We need to ensure that no one is able to enter the base; we need to lock it down. Is this possible?"

Define "no one."

"Any person other than the four of us here, or any person that does not have our explicit authorization," Alice was quickest to respond.

Suddenly, a thin ribbon of laser light flickered from the upper portion of the holo-table and ran up along the height of each crew member.

Do not be alarmed. Biochip identification in progress.

The laser stopped as suddenly as it had begun and now a highly detailed 3D schematic of the entire base blossomed out across the holo-table. It may have been old-school tech but the detail and fidelity were exceptional. There was a collective gasp of astonishment from all four of them. Renton barely had time to digest this visual spectacle when the huge curved wall monitor began displaying a panoramic view of the lunar landscape from a perspective high up on the central core. Again, the fidelity was excellent, so much so that he almost felt he was looking through a window.

"Wow, now that's impressive," said Yuna, her eyebrows raised to new heights.

All perimeter access points for Moon Base Delta have been identified.

The 3D schematic blinked with a multitude of markers; a lot more than Renton had realized. This place was big.

Access now denied to all non-registered citizens of Moon Base Delta, as per your request, Renton Hicks.

They all exchanged glances at each other. Smiles began to form on faces, the stress and strain of all the constant running, hiding, and fighting began to give way to restrained relief, then to joy, then to a mass outpouring of emotions as they all laughed, cried, and hugged.

CHAPTER 42
THE BETTER DEAL

Renton inspected the dark-brown cube that Matteo had just presented to him, with equal parts curiosity and distain. He ventured a sniff. It smelled vaguely of mushrooms.

"What is it?" he asked as he picked it up, turning it this way and that.

"That's a good question," answered Alice as she wandered into the operations center and slumped down in one of the seats. She lifted her feet to rest on the edge of the holo-table. She too had a cube in her hand, except that this one had a bite out of it.

"Theoretically, it's food. Freshly printed by the only functioning synthesizer in the lab. Yummy," Matteo rubbed his stomach.

Renton sniffed again and took a tentative bite—he was hungry, so it wasn't a difficult decision to make. It tasted like it smelled—mushrooms. Yet, it was not entirely unpleasant.

"According to our AI overlord," Matteo jerked a thumb at the ceiling. "It contains most of the necessities for human survival."

"Better than nothing, I suppose." Renton finished off the cube. "Anymore?"

Matteo shook his head. "Sorry mate, production is glacially slow. Might have another batch in a day or so."

Food was now their biggest concern. After the AI had secured the perimeter, it had taken almost fourteen hours for it to fully reboot and conclude its analysis of the degraded base infrastructure. It had produced an enormous assessment list but had at least broken this down into infrastructure it could fix with the help of autonomous maintenance droids, infrastructure that need human intervention—meaning the crew would get to work on these— and lastly, infrastructure that was beyond saving. This final list included food production, specifically food growing.

The problem was not so much technical, but that they simply had no stock to kick things off. The agri-sectors could operate fine, with some much-needed maintenance, but they were missing that most basic of all agricultural resources: seeds. There was no stock anywhere to be found in the base. So their only other option was to search every inch of the agricultural sector to try and find any desiccated plants that might have seeds that were still viable. This was going to be a long and arduous process requiring months of work. In the meantime, they still needed to eat.

Matteo, Alice, and Yuna agreed to make the trip back to the maintenance facility and scavenge for any useful resources.

Renton was left behind to mind the fort since his shoulder still hurt and he'd taken to keeping his arm in a sling. Once the team had gathered up everything they could find, Alice and Yuna ventured out onto the surface and retrieved the supplies that Renton had to ditch on their dash from the emergency shelter.

This was now the sum total of their food supplies, enough for around two months. So it was the food synthesizers in the agri-labs that they would be relying on after that. These literally manufactured protein and complex carbohydrates from inert chemical inputs. But it was slow as each machine had to be thoroughly overhauled and sterilized before it could be put into operation. Yet, they were all thankful that at least they were now safe and secure, even if that did mean lean times ahead. Renton felt the aftertaste of the cube he had just finished eating and wondered if this would be something he'd ever get used to.

Yuna had now joined them in the operations center, which had become their main hangout place. Primarily because they were all still working to get a better understanding of the functioning of Moon Base Delta. And secondly, the view was spectacular. They had cleared away most of the more recent workstations and equipment along with the ceiling-mounted screen, so they now had an unobstructed view of the huge curved wall monitor. Mostly, this displayed a slow panoramic view of the lunar surface around the perimeter of the base—the Sea of Tranquility. He could spend all day just looking at it if he didn't have so much maintenance work to do.

They were all sitting in silence watching this display, each lost in their own thoughts, when the AI interrupted. *Incoming comms request from the Axial Luxor Orbital,* it announced. *Do you wish to acknowledge this transmission?*

Renton sat up. "Yes, yes, absolutely, connect us."

A black rectangle overlaid itself on the grand vista displayed on the wall monitor. It flickered and glitched for a second or two before the head and shoulders of Selene Mene materialized. She was seated at a control room of some kind, looking up at the camera. Behind her, several other people could be seen milling around looking busy. Her face took on a surprised look when the connection was established, then morphed to joy.

"Renton, oh my god. Am I glad to see you. I thought you were dead. We've been trying to make contact with the base for days..." she paused and lowered her head, trying to contain her emotion.

"We had some problems getting here. SINO chased us all the way, they just wouldn't give up..." he paused for a moment thinking of how Spider had died. They planned to give her a proper burial in an area they had picked out near the Southern Gate. That would be later today. "The Space Division agent is dead."

"Spider?"

"Yeah. We wouldn't have made it here without her."

"So many people dead," Selene lowered her head a little.

"Becker and probably Mackenzie too, although we're not sure," Yuna totted up their losses.

"Did the codes work? Did you reboot the AI?" Selene finally asked.

Renton nodded. "We did. It took a while though. SINO followed us in. They knew about the codes. So did Xilinex."

Selene looked genuinely stunned. "How the heck did they find out?"

"Well somehow they both knew and started a war over it right inside the base, on the AI core level. Xilinex came through the JAXA-KARI gate just after SINO had entered. Hell of a firefight. I was caught in the middle."

Selene eyes widened. "How... how did you get out of that?"

Renton gave a laugh. "Alice and Yuna set the dogs on them and chased them off the property," he gestured over to where they were sitting. Alice responded by giving him the thumbs up.

Selene shook her head in confusion. "Dogs?"

"Remotely operated industrial robots. Tough units, you don't want to mess with them, at least not when Alice and Yuna are behind the controls."

"You'd better believe it," Yuna added, punching the air.

"So they're gone?"

"Gone, and yes, we managed to reboot the AI. It took almost fourteen hours to run through the sequence. Then there's a host of system failures to deal with even after that. We're working through them, but it's a very long list, I doubt we'll ever finish it. Anyway, that's probably why you couldn't establish a connection."

Selene visibly relaxed. "So Moon Base Delta is secure," she said, almost to herself.

"Why are you still on the orbital?" Renton gestured at the

screen with his good arm. "Why didn't you leave with the others?"

"Things got a little crazy here. Panic set in, there were riots down at the dock, which ended with a ship collision. That whole sector was destroyed in an explosion. A lot of people dead, no ships survived, no way off now. There's around a hundred of us stuck up here, mostly hotel staff, which is fortunate in a way, as they know where everything is and how the orbital operates. There're worse place to be stranded. It's a luxury hotel after all, and we have plenty of food and water to last us for months. So, we're fine for now. But we've got no shuttles, all of them were destroyed. There's no way for us to move from this orbital any time soon," she gave a resigned smile.

"Do you know what's going on out there? How many more people are stranded?" Yuna asked.

"We're working on that," Selene gave a vague gesture at the people behind her. "We set up a taskforce here to try and make contact with any stranded groups still out there. We're hoping to build up a picture of population size, locations, and what resources are available. I'll send you the details, we're sharing that information with everyone we find. From that, we hope to formulate some plan of action to try and stabilize the situation."

"Sounds like you're establishing a government," said Matteo.

"We're a long way from that. At the moment, it's just a clearing house for information. So far we estimate around two-thousand people still in and around Shackleton and Amundsen, another thousand between the outposts and research bases, and around five-hundred on the orbitals. This isn't including SINO or Xilinex, who are already making tentative moves to commandeer stranded assets."

"Wow, that many still here?" said Alice.

"Possibly more, these are just early estimates. Our initial objective is to just let everybody know what's going on, where people are located, and what their needs are. We've still got plenty of resources but most places no longer have the people needed to operate them. The Soylent Corporation's agri-orbital used to produce thirty-five percent of the food for the lunar market. It still exists, but there's only forty-three people left out of over three-hundred. So they want more to move up there to keep some of the production going. Other places have shuttles, but no pilots, and so on."

"We need food supplies, but more importantly we need to kickstart food production here," said Renton.

Selene started taking notes. "We'll add you to the list and put the word out. You may find some people want to migrate to Moon Base Delta; it's safe, secure, and big."

"Other people coming here?" Renton wasn't sure what he thought about that. Too many people arriving could cause untold disruption. He glanced around at the others.

"We'd have to think about that," said Yuna.

"For sure, that would need some careful management," agreed Alice.

"Listen," Selene leaned in towards the camera. "You need food, or a way to produce it. Some other people may have lots of supplies of what you need. People who are looking for a safe place. This is the way it's going to work for a while, until things settle down. Otherwise people are going to needlessly die out there."

This silenced the crew for a moment. Selene was right, if they were going to survive they would need the help of other people.

"What about SINO and Xilinex?" Renton posed the question that everybody had so far seemed reluctant to ask.

"Trouble," was Selene's instant response. She sat back for a moment and thought about it. "It's clear that they both view this disaster as an opportunity to take control over lunar resources, and that's only going to lead to conflict. My biggest fear is everybody else will be caught up in the crossfire."

"Yeah, we've had first-hand experience of that already," said Renton.

"I've no idea how this is all going to pan out," she continued. "And I can't see how they're going to get any of these resources back to Earth. Maybe they've found a way, or think they have, I just don't know."

"So we're heading for a war," said Renton.

"It does look that way."

"Maybe they've worked out how long it will take to clear the debris cloud," Matteo seemed optimistic about this prospect. "Maybe it's just a year or two."

Selene slowly shook her head. "I hate to be the one to break this but I've seen the projections and they do not look good. We're talking... decades, no going back anytime soon, if ever." Selene's attention was then taken up by something happening off camera. Someone was talking to her, but the voice was too muffled to make out the words. She then nodded and gestured at the seat beside her. A second later, a young man sat down and waved at the crew.

They waved back.

"This is Deejay, one of our techs. He's looking for your help on something."

"Sure," replied Renton. "Shoot."

"Hi," he waved again. "Our comms setup here relies on an old Space Division comms satellite in GEO, to link back with Earth. But we could potentially lose it in a few weeks."

Renton and the other crew were silent and this information only served to heighten everyone's sense of impending isolation.

"But Selene here tells me that Moon Base Delta had a point-to-point optical laser link back to FISA Command. Also, you should have an old S-Band capability."

"S-Band," Yuna's tone was one of incredulity. "That's ancient tech. Isn't that what they used way back on the Apollo missions?"

"Yeah," Deejay nodded. "But anything that utilizes a relay satellite isn't going to work anymore. Only direct line of sight transmission."

"We'll look into it," Renton replied. "We've a lot of stuff to fix here first, so no promises when we'll get around to it."

"That's okay," Deejay gave a thumbs up. "Just keep it in mind. It might prove useful going forward."

"How's it all going back down on Earth? Any news?" asked Alice.

"Not good," said Deejay. "Actually, it's chaos. The complete loss of the Datasphere and everything that relies on it—which is most of modern human civilization."

Renton realized that he had never considered what might happen back on Earth since he'd been so taken up with their own survival. "How bad is it really?" he finally ventured, although he wasn't sure he wanted an answer.

Deejay's response was a large intake of breath and a side-eye at Selene. He wasn't sure how much to say. "Eh... multiple failures in core systems that keep the wheels of human society spinning. But the two big problems seem to be food distribution and the slow collapse of the payment system—there's talk of bringing back cash."

"Cash?" Alice put a hand to her mouth in shock.

"Don't they have backup, contingency, older tech like... undersea cables and such?" said Yuna, not quite believing what she was hearing.

"Yeah, sure, but nothing that can accommodate the bandwidth needed, not even close," Deejay shook his head again. "It's a shitshow, make no mistake."

"Look, what happens back on Earth isn't going to change our situation up here." Selene leaned into the camera again, her voice slow and measured. "We need to keep the focus on ourselves and work to build a future here—this is our mission. It's the only way we will survive."

They were all silent for a while before Renton finally spoke. "Can you still contact Space Division?"

"Yes," Deejay nodded. "But it could go anytime."

"Then could you do something for us?"

"Sure, name it."

"Could you find out what the SD agent's real name was. We only knew her as Spider."

"Will do. I'll be talking to them soon. I'll ask."

***

Later that evening, Renton, Alice, Matteo and Yuna all stood around a low mound of lunar rocks that they had built a few hundred meters from the entrance to the Southern Gate of Moon Base Delta. Lying on top of this mound was a modest aluminum plaque, fashioned from the door of a medical locker. It read; *Here lies Diana 'Spider' Rodriguez – Died 2131 – May She Rest in Peace.* Beside it another, simpler pile of rocks had also been assembled. This one had a plaque which read; *For Becker De Havilland, wherever you may be.*

They all stood in silence for a while, each lost in their inner thoughts. For Renton, he wondered how many more mounds they would have to build in the future. One for Makenzie, perhaps? If they ever do find out what happened to her. And how many more after that?

He gazed up into the nighttime sky, at the vast canopy of stars which perforated the darkness, but what caught his eye was the brilliant blue marble perched just above the lunar horizon. He wondered what chaos was happening back on Earth; what would they do now that the communications networks that everyone relied on were disintegrating?

He looked back at his friends, all silent, all deep in contemplation. Then it struck him, maybe getting stranded here on the Moon wasn't so bad after all.

CHAPTER 43
JUST THE BEGINNING

Two quad-rotor surveillance drones circled in a Celtic knot pattern high up above the old mountain-top observatory, scribing graceful arcs in the cold nighttime air. Their low-light camera feeds transmitting back to a set of monitors inside the main building. The twin drones would keep up this pattern until their batteries began to die, then they would return to base to recharge and another two drones would rise up to continue the endless task of monitoring the surrounding area.

Inside the Equatorial room of the old observatory, Han Sundar flicked a glance every so often at the drone feeds, but his focus tonight was on a view of the Moon from his amateur telescope. The old instruments that had existed in the observatory were long gone. Even the old domed roof, that at one point in its past life could open and rotate, had been welded shut for many decades, never to be operated again. Now the industrial metalwork of its interior structure could only be seen from the bedrooms on the upper floor.

Yet what was an observatory without a telescope, and so Han had installed a more modest amateur instrument a few years back in one of the outbuildings. Its roof was now open and the telescope aimed at a brilliant full moon. The image from the telescope was currently displayed on a large monitor in the main living room of the observatory. Han tapped the controls to focus in on Mare Crisium. He was hoping to see the long line of the Mass Accelerator—one of the few manmade objects on the lunar surface that could be picked up by his small telescope.

Sheneese sat over at a long table shoved up against one wall of the room, her back to him with a pair of old wired headphones clamped on her head. She was tuning in to local broadcasts on an old AM radio. It was one that he had found stored away in his parents' attic a long time ago and had saved it from being trashed. Even though it still worked, its usefulness had drastically diminished as these old AM radio stations were almost all gone, supplanted by the Datasphere.

But now that the global communications network was nothing more than an orbiting dust cloud, people had begun to utilize old-fashioned radio waves for information broadcasts. They dusted off ancient tech they found in museums and storerooms, fashioned rudimentary antennae from basic designs, and began broadcasting on AM and shortwave. Some of these new stations were Local Government but most were just citizens relaying information. Most of them had a very limited range except at night when the waves were reflected from the ionosphere. This was the time that Sheneese liked best, as she could get news from further afield.

"Any updates?" Han asked as he came over and offered her a glass of wine from a bottle he had just opened. It was their one luxury. It was something he had stocked up on since, as he argued, it had a very long shelf life.

"The National Guard are spreading out across the city. And the curfew has been extended. It's now from 9PM to 7AM."

"They took their time doing that," Han noted. "I'd say most of the city has been looted by now."

"They also say that they will be opening another food distribution center. Rationed, of course."

Han looked over at her. "When's that happening?"

"Soon, they won't say exactly."

Han considered this. "They probably don't want to announce it until they're actually open. That way they hope to avoid a food riot. If people know in advance, they will gather en mass."

Sheneese sighed. "You have a dim view of human nature, Han."

He shrugged. "I just haven't seen anything yet to give me a better view," he smiled.

She switched off the radio and moved over to look at the image of the Moon on the monitor, glass in hand. "So what are you looking at?"

He pointed to a barely visible pixelated line. "That."

She moved closer, squinted. "What is it?"

"It's humanity's last hope," he said with a little more gravitas than he had intended.

Sheneese looked at him quizzically.

"It's a Mass Accelerator, built to fling capsules out into space on a trajectory for Earth orbit. It's how we get some of the Helium-3 supplies from the Moon," he sat down on the sofa and took a sip of his drink.

"So why is this humanity's last hope?"

Han sighed and gave an expansive gesture. "We're a fusion civilization. That's why."

"Not exclusively," she countered. "I mean there's solar, hydrogen, other technologies. It's not all fusion energy."

He paused for a beat, giving her a concerned look. "I've been running the numbers."

"Uh-oh, that's never a good sign with you," she sat down on the sofa beside him. "And I've a suspicion I'm not going to like the results," she gave him an expectant face.

"You're right, of course, about other technologies. But solar is mostly domestic and mostly legacy. But pretty much all industry and commercial enterprises use fusion energy through the grid. Even the hydrogen used for transport is manufactured using cheap fusion. And, here's the thing, almost every fusion reactor in operation globally uses Helium-3."

"Which comes from the lunar surface," she finished for him.

Han could see from the concerned look on her face she understood where he was going with this. He nodded. "Exactly. And there were only two ways it gets here. One is a standard cargo spaceship, which is not happening again any time soon. The second is via this hunk of lunar infrastructure," he pointed at the line again. "The good-ish news though, is that the capsules it fires might have a chance of making it through the debris cloud."

Sheneese thought about this for a moment. "But it won't be enough, will it?"

He lifted the wine bottle and refilled their glasses. "Maybe in time they might be able to ramp it up."

"You're just saying that to make me feel better, Han. If you've worked the numbers then you know how long it will be before supplies run out."

"All estimates I've seen on Helium-3 stockpiles show depletion in around three months."

Sheneese took a long drink from her glass. "So, all this chaos," she gestured over at the radio, "with food riots, looting, National Guard on the streets. It's all just the beginning, isn't it?"

He nodded, took a very long drink, then reached over to finish the bottle.

TO BE CONTINUED...

Also by Gerald M. Kilby

RESOURCE CONTROL : MOON BASE DELTA 2

In space, all that matters is survival.

Renton and the crew set about getting Moon Base Delta back online. No simple task. Their efforts are further complicated by refugees arriving in from other areas of the Moon as the ongoing conflict for control of resources is making survival for those caught up in the crossfire almost impossible.

Yet without access to basic resources the colonists in the base can only survive for so long. They soon realize that if they are going to have any chance of surviving then they have no option but to fight for it.

COLONY ONE MARS

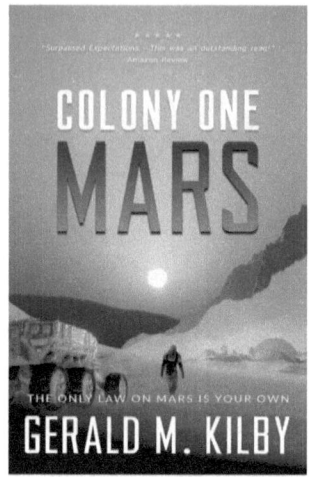

How can a colony on Mars survive when the greatest danger on the planet is humanity itself.

All contact is lost with the first human colony on Mars during a long, intense sandstorm. Satellite imagery of the aftermath shows extensive damage to the facility, and the fifty-four colonists who called it home are presumed dead. Three years later, a new mission sets down on the planet surface to investigate what remains of the derelict site.

ENTANGLEMENT : THE BELT

The discovery of game-changing quantum technology sparks an AI war between Earth's powerful dynasties and the solar system colonies.

A long-lost ship transporting an experimental quantum communications device has just been found in an uncharted region of the asteroid belt. For Commander Scott McNabb, Flight Officer Miranda Lee, and the ragtag survey crew who accidentally stumble upon this lost tech... life is about to become a whole lot more complicated.

ABOUT THE AUTHOR

Gerald M. Kilby grew up on a diet of Isaac Asimov, Arthur C. Clarke, and Frank Herbert, which developed into a taste for Iain M. Banks and everything ever written by Michael Crichton. His novels CHAIN REACTION and BRAIN GAIN are very much in the old-school techno-thriller style while his latest book series: MOON BASE DELTA, COLONY MARS, and THE BELT are all best sellers, topping Amazon charts for Hard Science Fiction and Space Exploration.

He lives in the city of Dublin, Ireland, in the same neighborhood as Bram Stoker and can be sometimes seen tapping away on a laptop in the local cafe with his dog Loki.

You can connect at: geraldmkilby.com